It is indeed a match m...
the marriage between...
the autocratic Damie[n]...
of Victorian Delhi. W...
has been blackmailed...
reckless gambling and that, as far as she is concerned,
the alliance was forged in hell . . .

But once at Shalimar, Damien's paradise kingdom in the hills of Kashmir, Crystal finds it difficult to detest her husband as she should. And in her pride she would rather die than let him know that he attracts her!

By the same author in Masquerade

MISTRESS OF KOH-I-NOOR

MASTER OF SHALIMAR
LYNNE BROOKS

MILLS & BOON LIMITED
London · Sydney · Toronto

*First published in Great Britain 1984
by Mills & Boon Limited, 15–16 Brook's Mews,
London W1A 1DR*

© Lynne Brooks 1984
*Australian copyright 1984
Philippine copyright 1984*

ISBN 0 263 74828 6

The text of this publication or any part thereof may not be reproduced or transmitted in any form or by any means, electronic or mechanical, including photocopying, recording, storage in an information retrieval system, or otherwise, without the written permission of the publisher.

This book is sold subject to the condition that it shall not, by way of trade or otherwise, be lent, resold, hired out or otherwise circulated without the prior consent of the publisher in any form of binding or cover other than that in which it is published and without a similar condition including this condition being imposed on the subsequent purchaser.

Set in 10 on 10½ pt Linotron Times
04-0984-68,000

*Photoset by Rowland Phototypesetting Ltd
Bury St Edmunds, Suffolk
Made and printed in Great Britain by
Cox & Wyman Ltd, Reading*

CHAPTER ONE

'CRYSTAL!' Emma regarded her daughter with dismay. 'What on earth have you been up to, dear? Why, you do look a sight!'

Crystal paused in the course of her headlong flight across the veranda. 'Oh! I didn't see you, Mama, or you, Mrs Hawthorne,' she quickly acknowledged the visitor sitting beside her mother. 'Oh, Mama, it's a boy,' she burst out excitedly. 'Poor Husna has had a bad time of it but it's over now and she's resting. He's quite beautiful, and perfectly healthy. Piebald, just like his father.'

'I'm glad, dear but . . . you really must wash before you sit down to tea!' Wanly, she surveyed her daughter. Over the golden brown face, glowing with excitement, was a flush of pink. Her Titian hair, wild and in total disarray, was adorned by bits of straw from the stable floor and her black skirt was covered in dust. Her hands, which she held aloft, were smeared in blood, of which a few stains had found their way on to a cheek. And, to complete the picture, she was barefoot. Emma Covendale shuddered. It was not, in all fairness to her, a sight to reassure any mother conscious of the demands of respectable British society in the India of 1882, when it was becoming increasingly important for the English to Set an Example.

Not at all put out by her mother's disapproval, indeed quite used to it, Crystal laughed and, with a quick 'Excuse me', disappeared into the house.

Emma Covendale sighed. 'Crystal does get so carried away,' she remarked in faint apology for her daughter's unladylike appearance. 'She's so like my dear Arthur . . . completely mindless of the requirements of propriety.'

Norah Hawthorne chuckled. 'Well, that comes of bringing up your daughter like a son!'

'Oh, I know,' said Mrs Covendale resignedly. 'Arthur—may his soul rest in blessed peace—had such avant-garde notions about India. Crystal would have been much better off going to England with her brother and learning to be a real English lady instead of . . .' She broke off and pursed her lips.

'Oh, fiddlesticks!' retorted Norah Hawthorne comfortably, helping herself to another scone and buttering it rather lavishly. 'Your Crystal is a beautiful, intelligent girl with far more education than most English girls in Delhi. We old fuddy-duddies could do with someone like her to shake us up from time to time!'

Mrs Covendale looked at her best friend witheringly. 'It's all very well for you to talk,' she said enviously. 'Your Sally gives you not a moment of worry, especially now that she's engaged to a nice gentleman like John Bryson. With her sharp tongue and excessive independence, where is my Crystal going to find a nice young English boy to wed?'

'Nonsense, m'dear,' said Mrs Hawthorne amiably, wondering secretly if she could help herself to another scone without upsetting her appetite for dinner. 'What you should be worrying about, Emma dear, is whether she will ever find herself a man who is *interesting* enough for her! I would imagine she would be bored to tears with someone merely *nice*.'

'Yes,' Mrs Covendale sighed, 'I suppose you are right. She does have such extraordinary ideas, quite unlike any that I've heard from other young girls her age. Goodness knows, she could have been married ten times over with a little adjustment here and there. That nice young Alec Waterton, for instance . . .'

Norah Hawthorne decided to risk the scone anyway,

and looked at her friend pityingly. 'Alec Waterton is a young ass,' she said firmly, 'and quite under the thumb of his overbearing mother. I'm glad Crystal sent him packing. Why, he wouldn't last with her for a day! And that goes for all the other young men I've seen in this station, even my Sally's young John. Mind you, I love John like a son and I would rather die than let Sally know my opinion—but he does tend to be dreadfully . . . what is the word I want? . . . passive. Yes, that's it, passive. No spirit at all.'

Emma Covendale sighed again. 'Yes, I know what you mean, dear, but it doesn't make me worry less. Oh, I wish Arthur were alive! He always knew how to handle Crystal. She adored him, you know.'

'Yes, I know,' said Mrs Hawthorne leaning forward and pressing her friend's hand comfortingly. 'Now stop fretting, my dear. Dr Carr is most insistent that no undue anxieties should be allowed to interfere with the healing of your heart. Crystal and Robie are fine children. With his commission in the Army more or less settled, Robie will mature and Crystal will settle down when she's ready, you'll see.'

Mrs Covendale smiled. 'Yes, we are very pleased—and relieved—about Robie's commission. The Commanding Officer has been most kind. Army discipline will be good for him. He's always been such a frail boy—that's why Arthur agreed to send him to England for schooling. He would never have been able to endure the hardship of living in all those archaeological camps of Arthur's.'

'Archaeological camps?' asked Crystal, overhearing the last part of the sentence as she emerged from the room. 'Who's going on an archaeological camping expedition?' Her face was alive with interest. She pulled up a cane chair, sat down and reached for the teapot. Her face, freshly scrubbed, looked more honey-brown than ever. She had brushed her hair into a fluffy topknot and the dusty black skirt had been discarded for a brightly printed one; her blouse was of white starched muslin.

'I was just telling Mrs Hawthorne that Robie would not have been able to endure your papa's digs. After all, they were sorely lacking in comforts, weren't they?'

'Maybe,' said Crystal, sipping her tea thoughtfully. 'But it was a wonderful life, and how I miss Papa and all the fun we used to have!' Her amber eyes clouded wistfully. 'I could live very happily in the wilderness if I had Papa's work to do!'

'Archaeology is a most unladylike profession,' said her mother matter-of-factly. 'There's plenty of work for you to do here at Khyber Kothi, dear.' Turning to Mrs Hawthorne, she added, 'Crystal has been running the entire household since my illness, Norah, and she is doing it exceedingly well. It's such a big house, you see, and there's so much to be done, but Arthur loved this place and so do we.' She sighed. 'We would never be able to call any other place home.'

Crystal grimaced. 'Oh, I don't count *housework* as work at all,' she said warmly. 'I'd much rather be out riding or digging up mountain-sides.'

'Talking about riding,' said her mother, ignoring the remainder of the remark, and frowning, 'couldn't Kadir have delivered the foal himself? After all, it's hardly considered proper for an unmarried girl to attend to such matters!'

'Oh, Mama!' Crystal laughed in affectionate exasperation. 'A birth is a miracle of Nature. What is there to be ashamed of?' With a tactful change of topic, she asked, 'Is Robie not back yet?'

A slight frown again creased Emma Covendale's forehead. 'No, dear. I hope he's not with those frivolous friends of his again . . .' she broke off abruptly as she caught Crystal's warning glance. Robie's occasional flutters at gambling were not something to be discussed even in front of good friends like Norah Hawthorne.

Quickly, to cover the embarrassing slip, Crystal asked brightly, 'I see Sally is not with you today?'

'No,' said Norah Hawthorne. 'Sally is engaged in a losing battle with her *durzee* who, she says, has sewed on one frill too many on her gown. The *durzee*, of course, swears blindly to the contrary. By the time Sally's finished with her trousseau,' she laughed, 'one of them is bound to end up in the lunatic asylum—with me in tow! To say nothing of Mrs Smythe's end of season supper-party tomorrow, for which, of course, a new gown is also being prepared. Surely you are going to it, Crystal?'

Crystal shook her head. 'No, I don't think so. Supper-parties can be so boring—and, after the last occasion, I doubt if Mrs Smythe will welcome me!' She sounded far from perturbed.

'Nonsense!' said Mrs Covendale sharply. 'Of course you must go! Nobody will remember what happened last time, least of all Betty Smythe, who can barely recall what she had for breakfast yesterday! Alec has been round twice to ask if he may escort you. And Robie, of course, will be there.'

Crystal tucked away a disobedient strand of hair that had fallen across her forehead. 'I haven't finished going through Papa's papers,' she said, 'and I do want to complete them as soon as possible. Besides, you know that dancing and such-like don't interest me at all. And I hate making idle talk—I always seem to end up saying the wrong thing. Like last time.' She smiled grimly.

'There will be plenty of interesting young men to talk to,' persisted her mother, 'as long as you do not involve yourself in another political discussion about the Afghan problem. Such matters are best left to the menfolk, dear, now aren't they, Norah?'

'Oh, I'm not so sure,' Mrs Hawthorne chuckled. 'I know I agreed with everything Crystal said at Betty Smythe's!'

'Well, a great many people didn't,' said Mrs Covendale crossly. 'And young men are put off by young girls who talk about politics instead of . . . what young girls should talk about,' she ended lamely.

'You mean babies and servants and who kissed who behind which pillar where and how many times?' asked Crystal, her eyes twinkling. 'Well, I'm not the slightest bit interested in who is busy bedding whom in Delhi these days. It's so infantile!'

Emma Covendale paled at her daughter's outspokeness, picked up her fan and operated it vigorously, while Norah Hawthorne giggled. '*Really*, Crystal, is it necessary to call every spade a spade with quite so blunt a tongue?'

'I'm sorry, Mama,' Crystal replied coolly. 'But you know that that is all women ever talk about at parties.' She laughed suddenly. 'Don't worry,' she said cheerfully. 'I'm quite resigned to my fate as an old maid. If I'm not married by the time I'm twenty-five, in another four years, I shall earn my living teaching Urdu to English children or ask the Archaeological Survey to give a position as a clerk on their exploring tours.' Then, to show that she was only teasing, she leaned over and kissed her mother fondly on the cheek. 'If it pleases you, Mama, then I will go to Mrs Smythe's supper-party. I'll hate it, of course, but . . .' She broke off as Kadir, the general factotum of the family for many years, shuffled on to the veranda steps.

He coughed politely, touched his forehead with his hand in the direction of Mrs Hawthorne, then said in Hindustani, 'Husna is still coughing badly and we are out of cough-balls.'

Immediately Crystal sprang to her feet, and replied in the same language with easy fluency. 'Why didn't you tell me before? Very well, we shall make some more. Now fetch me from the storeroom four ounces of asafoetida, two ounces of nitre, two ounces of raw sugar and take them into the kitchen. The weighing scales are on the top shelf.' Turning to Mrs Hawthorne, she said, 'Please excuse me. I have to go and see to my horse. She's not been very well.' With a quick wave of her hand, she ran nimbly down the steps, followed by Kadir.

For a moment or two there was silence as both women stared after Crystal, one with amusement and the other with anxiety. Then Emma Covendale sighed. 'It's her father's fault,' she said sadly. 'I loved Arthur deeply, as you know, but I do wish he had not been so unconventional! Crystal has taken after him entirely, I regret to say. And people do talk so . . .'

With the best will in the world, this was something even Norah Hawthorne could not deny. Crystal Covendale was, indeed, the subject of much talk in Delhi. Outspoken, spirited, unconventional and as independent in her views as her father had been, she seemed as consistently at loggerheads with genteel British Indian society as genteel British Indian society was with her. The situation perturbed her not one whit; her oft-voiced opinions of the petty prejudices of her compatriots being as strong and forthright as her father's. Arthur Covendale had fallen deeply in love with India when he had first arrived on its shores as a shy young second lieutenant in the British Army, just before the outbreak of the Indian Mutiny in 1857. He had done his duty for his country during those difficult, dangerous, times when every British life was in peril, but he had been disgusted with much that he had seen.

He had lost little time, once the British Parliament had taken the reins of government away from the East India Company, in resigning his commission and associating himself with the work being done by Alexander Cunningham, the first director-general of the newly formed Archaeological Survey of India. A scholar by nature, he had revelled in his new-found interest, exploring the vast, colourful, incredibly diverse subcontinent with unconcealed zest. The explorations into the 'cradles of human civilisation', as he had called them, had fired his daughter's imagination at a very early age. While other English children in India dutifully went through their nursery rhymes and tales of fairy princesses and ogres, Crystal was already stumbling her way through Fa-Hsien's *Travels in India* and the Urdu alphabet. By the time she was eight, she was more than proficient in Hindustani—and in Urdu, the form spoken around Delhi—and knew more about the history and customs of the country than most English women learned in a lifetime.

Much against her mother's wishes, Crystal insisted on staying on in India when the time came for her and her brother Robie to be sent to England—as all English children were—for schooling. Delighted at her interest in the subject closest to his heart, Arthur Covendale agreed readily, over-ruling his wife in the matter. He parted, reluctantly, with his son only because of the boy's continuing ill-health, conceding that the English climate would undoubtedly make him stronger. Taking in hand his daughter's education, Arthur Covendale kept Crystal always with him, even on his long and arduous archaeological tours.

If life at camp was hard, Crystal barely noticed, revelling joyously in the complete freedom from dull routine that it offered. She loved the atmosphere of a camp, the lack of tiresome discipline, the easy camaraderie with the workers, the freedom to roam at will. Her father placed few restrictions on her, allowing her to blossom and grow in her own way, at her own pace. He treated her always as an adult, never forcing his will upon her, encouraging her to form opinions of her own and teaching her how to cherish and value the treasures of this land which he had made his own. While other English girls sheltered themselves fearfully from the sun lest it dull their white complexions, Crystal laughed and played all day among the rolling country of the Himalayan foothills, learning to ride, swim and fish with a proficiency that was the envy of many an English lad. Her complexion, much to her mother's dismay, turned from pale and colourless to a rich, golden brown, healthy and glowing with red roses in her cheeks.

Very often Emma Covendale, unable to savour the

strange nomadic life favoured by her husband and daughter, preferred to remain in Delhi in Khyber Kothi, the house Arthur Covendale had built after he had resigned from the Army, in which they lived now. Father and daughter returned to Delhi every winter when snow blocked the mountain passes and icy winds swept the northern plains. The sojourns in the unfamiliar confines of a town, even for the few brief months of winter, were a cross Arthur Covendale and his daughter bore with fortitude but with impatience and irritation. The silly pretensions and posturings of urban society meant nothing to them except a regrettable waste of time, and they both longed for the happy release that spring would bring to resume once again their gipsy lives among the ruins of old, old, civilisations. Emma Covendale disapproved strongly of her daughter's unconventional upbringing but had long since resigned herself to her husband's stronger will and her daughter's stubbornness in the consolation that the child was knowledgeable beyond her years and could read and write two languages with a confidence many lacked.

By the time Robie returned from England, a well-educated, healthy young man with a good knowledge of accountancy, Crystal was nearly twenty and he a year older. They had not met in the interim. Passages to and from England were expensive and money was scarce. Besides, Arthur Covendale had no desire to waste his time and energy in what he called 'the hedonistic wildernesses of Oxford Street and Piccadilly Circus'. Emma had made one trip to see Robie at school and had stayed in England for six months, but Crystal had never been out of India and showed no signs of having missed anything.

Brother and sister had taken to each other almost immediately, even after such a long separation. Robie had been awed and impressed by his strange, spirited sister, so unlike the young ladies he had encountered at home. And Crystal had been overjoyed at again acquiring a brother who for so long had been just a name at the end of a letter. But, the joys of reunion were soon muted when Arthur succumbed to pneumonia after a bitter spell of autumn weather in the Punjab, where he had been working. It was an illness from which he did not recover.

Her father's death, just under a year ago, had left Crystal utterly shattered. She had lost her dearest, most adored friend, mentor and guide. For months after his death, she wandered around their home, Khyber Kothi, numb with grief, unwilling to accept that he had indeed gone for ever. Neither her mother nor Robie could fill the gap in her life, try as they might. Watching her moping and brooding, Emma Covendale sometimes wondered how she could ever have produced a child who was so alien to her own nature. Why, Emma Covendale often said to herself mournfully, Crystal could almost be an *Indian*! It was not a virtue that would be appreciated by the snobs of the community.

It was very much later that night, long after the paraffin lamps had been lit and the waters of the river Jamuna, upon which stood the town of Delhi, had turned from blue to black and silver, that Crystal finally completed her ministrations in the stables and rose tiredly to return to the house. The thought of tomorrow night's festivity at Mrs Smythe's began to depress her. But she loved her mother deeply even though she knew that she did not understand her child at all. Crystal sighed. If it would make her mother happy, it was not really worth making a fuss about. Perhaps she could go with Robie and avoid having to listen to another proposal from Alec Waterton. The thought of Robie brought a frown to her forehead.

Spying their maidservant, Mahima, laying the table in the dining-room, she asked anxiously, 'Has my brother returned yet?'

Mahima nodded. 'Yes. Robie Baba is in the study. He came in half an hour ago.'

Crystal's brow cleared immediately and she sighed with relief. It was not uncommon, on occasion, for Robie to stay out all night—a cause for great concern to herself and their mother.

The door of the study, at the end of the corridor, opened suddenly. 'Crys? I say, is that you, Crystal?' she heard Robie call out.

'Yes, it is. I'm glad you're back, Robie. We were . . .'

He cut her off brusquely. 'Come in here a moment. I want to talk to you.'

Something in his voice alarmed her. 'Mama . . . ?' she began fearfully.

'No, no,' he said impatiently. 'I've just been to see Mama. She's all right. She's having her legs massaged. No, I . . . there's something I have to tell you.'

'All right,' Crystal called out. 'I'll be with you in a few moments. I want to take out the mosquito-nets from the storeroom. I could hardly sleep last night for the bites.'

Half an hour later, when she entered the study, Crystal stopped dead in her tracks as her eyes fell on her brother's face. It was deathly white. He sat in the chair by the window, unmoving, staring at her without saying a word. In his hand he held a brandy glass.

'Robie!' she cried in alarm. 'What is it? You look so . . . odd. Are you ill?'

She ran to him and put her hand on his forehead. He shook it off impatiently. 'No, I'm not ill, but I wish I were dead.' With a groan, he buried his head in his arms, letting the brandy glass fall to the ground.

Crystal knelt and picked it up, feeling an icy hand clutch at her heart. 'Robie, tell me . . .' she breathed, her face pale.

'I've done something terrible, Crys.' His voice was scarcely above a whisper. He began to shake.

'You've been at the Chowk, haven't you?' It was more a statement than a question. The gaming-house in Chandni Chowk, the famous 'Silver Street' in the heart of Delhi, was a place frequented by notorious gamblers.

Robie and his 'frivolous friends', as Mrs Covendale called them, had been seen there often. Until a few months ago, Robie's flutters had been infrequent and innocuous. But of late he had incurred losses that were beginning to mount alarmingly. Only last month, unknown to their mother, Crystal had been forced to sell a much-loved gold pendant, given to her by her father, to setttle Robie's account at the gaming-house. Repentant, ashamed and humiliated at the ignominy of having his sister bail him out of trouble, Robie had promised fervently never to gamble again. Obviously, the promise had not been kept. Guilt was written all over his pale, stricken face as he sat slumped in the chair.

'How much have you lost?' Crystal asked despairingly, her heart sinking as she awaited his answer.

'Everything,' he whispered dully, 'Everything . . .'

Her eyes dilated with fear, but she could not understand what he meant. 'What do you mean . . . everything?'

And then he told her. For a moment Crystal stared at him in horror, unable to believe the evidence of her ears. 'It can't be true, Robie . . .' Her voice sounded strange and strangled, as her mind went blank with shock. 'It just *can't* . . .'

Khyber Kothi! To throw away their home on the spin of a roulette-wheel, the drop of a playing-card! Oh! It could not be true.

With a groan, Robie laid his head on the table and huge, dry sobs racked his body. For a moment there was no other sound in the room bar that of those terrible, gasping sobs. Crystal could do little except stand and listen in horror. Then a surge of anger flooded her body.

'How could you, Robie, how *could* you? It's not fair . . .' Her voice began to shake. 'It was not yours to gamble away.' Then, as quickly, her anger evaporated. She loved her brother and his misery was more than she could bear. She knelt down beside him and put her arm round his shuddering shoulders. 'Tell me about it, dear,' she said gently, 'Tell me . . .'

He shook his head miserably. 'There's nothing to tell. It just happened. I must have been mad, mad, *mad* . . .'

'You haven't told Mama, have you?' Her heart lurched in alarm.

'No, of course not.' He lifted his head and wiped his eyes with the cuff of his shirt. 'How can I? How *can* I?'

They stared at each other in dismay. Then she laughed shortly. 'A bet such as this cannot be taken seriously by anyone, surely,' she said with far more confidence than she felt. She knew the reputation of the Chandni Chowk gaming-house as a place of ruthless cutthroat professional gamblers. 'Why, taking away a man's hearth and home is nothing short of highway robbery!' Two red spots appeared on her cheeks as her anger returned with renewed force. 'Who is the man you played against?'

Robie shook his head. 'The devil himself, Crys, I swear it! He speaks little, but his eyes . . . they're the devil's own, black like stone and as hard as marble. When he looked at me, I felt I had to obey his command. I didn't want to play against him but, I swear, he *made* me . . . I don't know how, but he *willed* me to play! I kept losing and he kept winning and still I could not stop—until there was nothing left to lose but Khyber Kothi . . . Oh God . . .' he shivered. 'I must have been *insane*.'

Something cold and undecipherable clutched at Crystal's heart. 'What is the name of this . . . this man?'

'What does it matter?' groaned Robie. 'You don't know him. Nobody knows him; he's a stranger to Delhi. Granville. Damien Granville.'

Abruptly, Crystal rose and walked slowly to the window. Damien Granville! It could hardly have been anyone else from the description of the eyes alone—those cold, hateful eyes she herself had gazed into on two occasions in the recent past. It was astonishing how firmly the memory of those two encounters, brief as they were, lingered in her mind.

She had been riding one evening on the banks of the Jamuna, not far from the Red Fort, when the winter winds were still bitingly cold and the trees along the river gaunt and leafless. The peace of the afternoon was suddenly shattered by the most agonising screams one could imagine, accompanied by the sound of dull thuds and hoarse, angry shouts and abuses. Spurring her horse in the direction of the fracas, Crystal found herself heading towards a small village that she knew nestled against the far walls of the Fort. In a clearing among the trees a small crowd had collected, and in the centre of the crowd a demented villager was beating quite mercilessly a young slip of a girl who was screaming in terror. Her clothes, already in rags, now barely covered her nakedness as a rain of lashes descended on to her frail body. Not one man in the crowd dared to intervene, so diabolical was the appearance of the brute meting out the horrendous punishment.

Utterly appalled, and without a second thought, Crystal flung herself off her horse, whip in hand, and fought her way through the crowd to the centre of the clearing and commanded the offender to stop. The man stopped briefly in amazement and stared at her with red, bloodshot eyes, and her nostrils were assailed with a strong stench of cheap country liquor. Swaying on his feet, he hurled a curse in Crystal's direction, too inebriated to know what he was saying, and raised his stick to continue with the exercise. Quick as a flash, as the crowd stood by in petrified suspense, she flicked her whip so that the lash wound round his wrist. As his arm came to an abrupt halt, several men from the crowd rushed forward and grabbed him around the waist, immobilising him completely. For a moment there was plenty of confusion as everybody began to talk at once, and the captured man raved and ranted with enraged frustration, throwing baleful glances in Crystal's direction.

'How dare you beat a defenceless woman?' she called out furiously. 'Have you no shame? If you touch this woman again, I shall inform the police and have you arrested for assault!'

'Leave him to us, *memsahib*,' one of the men gasped. 'He is drunk and not in his senses.' The young girl, gathered hastily into protective female arms, was carried away, casting grateful glances at Crystal and sobbing.

'I come this way quite often,' said Crystal curtly to one of the men. 'If I hear of a repetition of this disgraceful incident, I shall surely fetch the police.'

Face flushed with anger and breathing deeply, she turned to mount her horse and stopped in surprise. Concealed partially by a tree-trunk, with the reins of his horse held lightly in one hand, was an Englishman, observing her with interest. He was dressed in a riding-habit and his head was uncovered. She stared at him, taken aback.

'Who are you?' she asked, put out by the nonchalance of his posture.

He bowed. 'An admirer,' he said. 'It is not every day one comes across such an act of bravery. The man could have attacked you.'

She gave a scornful laugh. 'An admirer from a safe distance, I see! Why did *you* not intervene to stop the poor woman being half-killed by a drunken lout?'

He shrugged. 'I saw no need to, considering how adequate were your own resources. I doubt if I could have done a better job myself. Besides . . .' he smiled thinly, his disconcerting black eyes rife with mockery, 'it is possible she deserved the thrashing.'

Crystal paused in the act of mounting her horse and stared at him aghast. 'You approve of beating a defenceless woman?'

'Certainly. If she had been unfaithful to her husband. Which, I think, was the case in this instance.'

'You do not consider physical punishment an act of

utter barbarity?' She was outraged that an Englishman, in this day and age, could condone such bestiality.

The infuriating smile lingered without making an attempt to reach the eyes. 'Not if it is effective. I doubt if she will dare to betray him again.'

Crystal laughed in shocked disbelief. 'I do not know who you are—nor wish to know!—but I do find your attitudes quite repelling.'

Without waiting for his response, or for his aid in mounting her horse, she jumped lithely into the saddle and galloped away, seething with indignation. What an obnoxious man—whoever he was!

She was soon to find out. The next morning, his card was delivered to her at Khyber Kothi, with a note attached. *Mr Damien Granville*, it read, *begs permission to call on Miss Crystal Covendale, the bravest and most admirable memsahib in Delhi.* She knew immediately who Mr Damien Granville might be, and was much put out by his audacity in daring to address her. She returned the card without bothering to reply. There was something about him that she had disliked on sight, a dislike compounded by this further evidence of his impudence.

'What are we going to do, Crys?' Robie's voice drew her back to reality. There was panic in his tones. 'How can we ever tell Mama?'

'Perhaps we may not need to,' she said with forced confidence. 'Surely . . . surely this man will realise that to expect you to honour such an absurd debt would be cruel . . .' Her voice trailed off.

Robie laughed. 'Damien Granville? Change his mind? If you knew him as I have come to, you would not even envisage such a prospect!' He shook his head. 'Damien Granville has every intention of making me honour the debt. He . . . he warned me when I . . . laid the wager . . .'

'And you ignored his warning?' she asked, appalled.

Robie groaned and hid his face in his arms. 'I told you,

Crys, the man is a devil incarnate. It was as if he was urging me to go on . . . I lost complete control of my senses . . .'

Crystal's heart sank like lead. There was an air of terrible finality in what Robie had said. 'I still cannot believe that he would be serious,' she persisted stubbornly.

'Damien Granville never jests,' Robie said. 'I have . . . played with him before. He seemed to be encouraging me to play! It was as if he had set his mind on Khyber Kothi.'

'He often goes to the gaming-house?'

'Every night! The wager was laid before others. I cannot deny it. And the gaming-house has men, terrible men, to prevent losers from reneging. If it ever came out that I laid a wager and then turned my back on it . . .' He stopped and bit his lip wretchedly. Crystal knew the consequences only too well. He would lose his commission in the Army, receive painful punishment from the gaming-house men—and kill Mama!

There was little more to be said about the matter. For the moment it was only important to keep the dreadful news from Mama. Somehow, they managed to get through supper, making bright chatter, trying to conceal the misery in their hearts. It was not an easy task. They were a close family, brought even closer by the death of a beloved husband and father. There had never been any need for secrets amongst them. Finally, the agonising meal was over and Crystal could retire to her room to arrange her turbulent thoughts. Valiantly, his heart riddled with guilt and shame, Robie sat down to a game of backgammon with his mother.

There was very little sleep for Crystal that night. In between fits of dozing she raged silently against the devil man who had plunged them so heartlessly into catastrophe. She still could not believe that even a man such as Damien Granville would extract so harsh a wager from a mere boy, and expect it to be honoured. The entire idea was monstrous. It was, of course, Robie's fault completely. He was a fool to have allowed himself to become involved with a man as obviously unprincipled as Damien Granville.

Tossing fitfully through the night, fruitlessly chasing sleep, Crystal recalled the second unpleasant encounter she had had with the odious Mr Granville, a mere two weeks after the first by the river. The occasion was one of Mrs Smythe's perpetual supper-parties, or *burra khanas*, as they were called. As usual, conversation among the women centred on such elevating topics as the increasing incidence of mosquitoes, fleas and bed-bugs, servants and their aberrations, the amorous dalliances of those in and out of station, and the ubiquitous rash known as 'prickly heat', a source of great irritation, literally, to the community. In addition, of course, there were the interminable exchanges about 'home' leave.

Bored to tears, Crystal wandered off dolefully in the direction of a group of young Army officers who were in the midst of a heated discussion on the growing fear from the Russians in Central Asia and the increasing vulnerability of the North-West frontier.

'That is why it was so important to mount the second Afghan campaign in 1878,' said one of the officers.

'But the campaign was utterly disastrous!' protested Crystal, joining in the discussion. 'Surely, it served no purpose at all?'

In the lively discussion that followed, her views stood out as the most astute, expressed without fear, causing much astonishment among the officers unused to crossing swords on political issues with a beautiful young girl. The reactions of their hostess, trying desperately to get the dancing started (and not succeeding), were a shade less admiring.

'Young, well-bred English ladies,' Mrs Smythe remarked coldly, 'should not concern themselves with such masculine pursuits as politics.'

'Perhaps,' sneered Stephanie Marsden, envious of all the male attention Crystal was monopolising, 'poor Crystal is not to blame after all, having been brought up without benefit of a good English education at home.'

'Home?' countered Crystal firmly. 'But I *am* home! Indeed, I have never been away from it!'

A young Army captain laughed with a very superior air. 'You mean that you consider *India* to be your *home*?'

'Certainly,' Crystal replied, unconcerned at the scandalised looks she was receiving from Mrs Smythe. 'Perhaps you will, too, when you have been here twenty-one years, like I have.'

'Heaven forbid!' the officer shuddered. 'I could never consider this *barbaric* country as my own!'

An angry glint appeared in Crystal's eyes. 'You perhaps know it well to make so positive a condemnation?'

He laughed derisively. 'I do not need to,' he snorted. 'Six months is long enough to form an accurate opinion.'

'In that case,' said Crystal acidly, 'there really is little point in pursuing this conversation. I see that you are too ignorant even to recognise your own ignorance, let alone to remedy it.'

Before the purple-faced officer could recover from the outspoken retort, she turned away purposefully and made her way to the refreshments table in search of cooling lemonade. Her composure remained unruffled outwardly, but inside she seethed. Her father had taught her to love this country, not blindly but through learning and experience. That others should have neither interest in nor curiosity about it was a fact that never ceased to cause her annoyance.

Standing before the refreshments table, surveying the range of sherbets on it, she was suddenly astonished—and dismayed—to find herself once again face to face with the much disliked Damien Granville. He bowed, and handed her a glass of sherbet, observing with an amused smile the heightened pallor of her face and the angry sparkle in her bright, amber eyes.

'Better and better,' he said blandly. 'There appears to be no end to your accomplishments! I liked the manner in which you demolished that impudent young pup.'

She returned his gaze boldly, and retorted, 'I was not especially concerned with earning your approval.'

He ignored her remark, and his hard black eyes bored into hers. 'Why did you return my card?'

'Because I do not wish you to call on me.'

'Why not?'

For a moment she looked disconcerted, much put out by this unseemly interrogation, then said bluntly, 'I see no reason to cultivate the acquaintance of anyone as . . . as insensitive as you appear to be!'

He laughed, undaunted by her condemnation. 'Because I approve of unfaithful women being thrashed?'

She stared back at him, disgusted. 'No,' she flung out. 'Because I do not like you!'

A look of annoyance flashed across his face and he smiled tightly. 'Very well, then,' he bowed mockingly. 'In that case, I shall have to wait until *you* call on *me*.'

Quite involuntarily she laughed—the suggestion was so absurd. '*I* call on *you*?' she asked witheringly. 'Well, perhaps I shall—the day the sun chooses to rise in the west.'

She made to turn away, enjoying the sight of his angrily flushed face. But before she could move, their hostess rushed up and grabbed his arm. 'Oh, Mr Granville,' she gushed, panting breathlessly with excitement. 'I am *so* glad you could come after all. I had given you up! *Do* come and meet my daughter Charlotte. She has *so* been looking forward to making your acquaintance—as has everyone else in the station.' She cast an uncertain glance in Crystal's direction. 'I see that you have already made the acquaintance of Miss Covendale?' She smiled a little coldly at Crystal.

'Indeed,' said Damien Granville. 'You might even say that we are . . . old friends.'

Betty Smythe looked momentarily alarmed as she fancied Charlotte's prospects with the highly eligible Mr Granville diminishing. Crystal, however, lost no time in setting the record straight. 'No, you might *not*!' she said crossly. 'Mr Granville and I barely know each other.' Indignantly, her head held high, she walked away, followed, infuriatingly, by a soft chuckle. For the remainder of the evening she pointedly stayed as far away from him as she possibly could, nevertheless watching covertly—and with ill-concealed disgust—as the women crowded round him, jostling unashamedly for his attention. That he was an unpleasant, impertinent man she knew already. But she could not help conceding, grudgingly, that there was something about him that drew the eyes and attention. He was tall, broad-shouldered and narrow-waisted, and carried himself with an arrogance that could come only from wealth and the habit to command. His face, narrow and finely featured, was brown as if accustomed to the open, and his strong, square chin seemed to bode little good for those who crossed his path. Across one cheek ran a scar, and he wore his thick black hair longer than most. She noticed that he smiled often, but never with his eyes. In spite of her dislike of him, Crystal was curious. She had never before met an Englishman in India quite like him.

The loud, insistent crowing of their rooster in the back compound brought Crystal back with a jolt to the present. The eastern sky was touched with pink, and already there were muted sounds of activity in the servants' quarters. For a while she lay tiredly in bed, unable to shake off the pall of gloom that Robie's revelation had cast over her last evening. She realised, of course, that it was a matter to which Robie would be unable to attend by himself. Already he was crumbling under the enormity of the disaster he had brought upon them. That he was no match for the diabolical manipulations of Mr Damien Granville, she had no doubt. Which, of course, left only one course of action open to her. Her heart sank as she recognised what it was. She herself would have to seek an interview with the repugnant man. It was a prospect that filled her with apprehension and mortification, especially when she recalled his parting remark to her at Mrs Smythe's—*In that case, I shall have to wait until you call on me!* She had no doubt that the cruel charade at the gaming-house had somehow been arranged for this sole purpose. But to what end, she could not divine. And once again it showed the ruthless lengths to which this man would go in order to realise his whims. It was not a thought that brought Crystal any comfort at all.

Later that morning, with gritted teeth, she sat down at her desk to compose a note to Mr Damien Granville requesting an interview at his convenience.

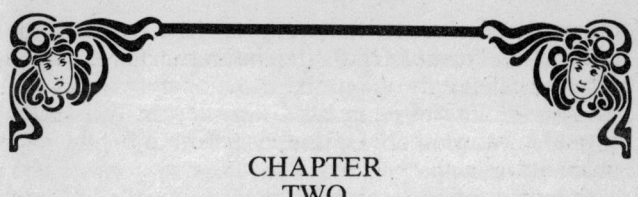

CHAPTER TWO

ALL DAY long Crystal waited for an answer to her note. There was none. Kadir, who had delivered her letter to the address she remembered from his card, had been asked to leave it with a member of Mr Granville's household staff, as the 'Sarkar' himself—the lord and master—was out for the morning. A reply would be sent to Khyber Kothi when he returned. Until six o'clock, when Crystal and Robie were to leave for Mrs Smythe's, with an ever-attendant Alec Waterton, there was only silence from Mr Granville. Crystal ground her teeth in fury. He was obviously determined to keep her in suspense as long as he could. Smouldering in enforced silence, she hated him even more. It would not be politic, she decided, to inform Robie of her decision to confront his tormentor on her own. She had no idea what game Mr Granville might be playing with him; it was best to find out before taking Robie into her confidence.

Completing her toilet half-heartedly for the evening that lay ahead, Crystal wished she had not so readily acceded to her mother's wish in accepting Mrs Smythe's invitation. However, on the other hand, it might prove an invaluable occasion to find out some more about this mysterious stranger who had arrived in Delhi so recently and had succeeded so completely in destroying the even timbre of their lives. She paled at the thought that he might even be there. If he were, she had decided, she would abandon the party and return home forthwith.

Damien Granville was not at Mrs Smythe's. Crystal

breathed a sigh of profound relief as she ascertained the information from her closest friend, Norah Hawthorne's daughter Sally.

'You are interested in Mr Granville?' Sally asked in surprise, knowing how little Crystal cared for the men available in Delhi.

'I am not at all interested in Mr Granville,' Crystal replied indignantly. 'Indeed, I have seldom met a man whom I find so totally unpalatable!'

Sally took silent note of the sudden reddening of her friend's cheeks, but wisely held her peace. She loved Crystal dearly and had no desire to invite her displeasure on an obviously sensitive subject.

Mrs Smythe's present *burra khana*, in honour of some important government official visiting from headquarters in Calcutta, was as dull as all the others but, fortunately, Crystal's outspoken political observations on the last occasion were forgotten and, hopefully, forgiven. She used the evening to make discreet enquiries about Damien Granville. It appeared, however, that no one knew very much about him except that he was a man of considerable wealth, with extensive business and properties in Kashmir. He had had a commission in the Army, but had received an honourable discharge following a severe wound after a skirmish with dacoits in the Punjab. He was a gentleman generally known to be somewhat eccentric, and maintained a lavish and large household up in the Kashmir valley. He ran his estate, they said, like a kingdom, and was known as the 'Sarkar' to his staff.

How Damien Granville had received the scar on his cheek, nobody seemed to be certain, but there was considerable conjecture about it. Some of the guests believed that it was the result of a duel fought over the honour of a lady love; others had heard that it was the proof of some cuckolded husband's fury. But whatever the reason for it might have been, everybody agreed that Damien Granville had a way with women—of whom there had been more than plenty in his life, but none as a wife.

Listening avidly to the gossip, Crystal became more and more disenchanted with the man she would be confronting soon. None of the information promised the prospect of a pleasant interview. That he was also a gambler for extraordinarily high stakes—and an unscrupulous one at that—nobody appeared to be aware of except Robie and herself. Quite understandably! It was hardly likely that Damien Granville would care to reveal such a sordid aspect of his character to respectable and rigidly censorious British society.

It was as she rode home with Robie after the party that a sudden question occurred to her, as they alighted from the carriage in the porch at Khyber Kothi. She frowned. 'You say you staked Khyber Kothi and lost,' she asked, perplexed. 'What did Damien Granville stake?'

'Why, his estate in Kashmir, Shalimar. Didn't I tell you?'

Crystal shook her head and gasped in surprise. 'And if he had lost . . . ?'

Robie gave a short, bitter laugh. 'Damien Granville never loses,' he said briefly. 'Damien Granville is a born winner.'

Nevertheless, Crystal marvelled at the *sang-froid* of a man who would be willing to chance his all on the spin of a wheel—not in a fit of wild insanity, like Robie, but in ruthless cold blood. Inadvertently she shuddered, although the night was warm. Damien Granville would prove to be a formidable adversary!

For two days there was no word. Hanging in suspense, fuming in rage and mortification, Crystal waited, wondering how to proceed next. Then, just as she had decided, reluctantly, that a second letter would have to be sent, Damien Granville's answer arrived. Tearing open the envelope in the privacy of her room, she unfolded the stiff white paper with shaking fingers. It was a curt, formal note containing but one sentence:

Mr Damien Granville will be pleased to receive Miss Covendale at eleven ayem on Friday morning. It was signed by someone called Gulab Singh, designated as private secretary to Mr Granville.

In spite of the deliberate abruptness of the wording and the lack of Mr Granville's own signature, Crystal's heart leapt. Her pulses raced with nervous excitement and her mouth ran dry. It reminded her of the time when she was fourteen, when she had waited with her father for four days to sight a man-eating tiger in the Kumaon, north of Lucknow in the Himalayas. Her father had handed her a gun—in the use of which she was already adept—and had pointed quietly towards the clump of trees where the tiger had been sighted. 'He's yours,' he had said calmly. 'But don't miss on your first shot.' She hadn't. It was the first and last time Crystal had killed an animal, especially in the name of sport. Nevertheless she remembered the terrible excitement that had surged through her body as she had raised the rifle and waited for the tiger's head to appear in her focus.

Now, as she sat staring at the letter inviting her to meet Damien Granville, the same terrible excitement and nervousness engulfed her body. It was almost as if she would be riding into battle again—a battle the outcome of which was as unpredictable as her encounter with the tiger!

There were still two days to Friday, and Crystal had little recollection of how she succeeded in getting through them. Robie was becoming more and more desperate, turning to his stronger, more forceful, sister for succour. His eyes looked hunted and Crystal was fearful lest their mother suspect the nature of their worry.

'You must pull yourself together, Robie,' she said to him severely. 'It would not do for Mama to guess what has happened.'

'But what are we going to *do*, Crys?' Robie cried. 'The manager of the gaming-house has already sent me two reminders of the settlement that has to be made—and the second note was distinctly threatening. I would go and see Granville, except . . . I shudder at the thought of meeting him again. He frightens me!' It was an admission he would not have made to anyone except his sister.

Crystal's heart melted with compassion for her tormented older brother. Quickly, she gave him a comforting hug. 'Don't worry, dear,' she said gently. 'Leave it to me. I will think of some way out.'

With a sigh, Robie hugged her in return, his face brightening immediately. 'What would I do without you, dear sister,' he asked softly. 'As I have always said, you should have been the man of the family. I . . . I am such a . . . failure.'

Crystal rapped him firmly and angrily on the hand. 'Don't you ever dare say that again to me, Robert Covendale, do you hear? You are *not* a failure by any manner of means! What happened was a mere error of judgment which, I am sure, you will never, never make again.'

Robie sighed again and kissed her on the cheek. 'Yes,' he said listlessly. 'Of course you are right.' There was something about the way in which he spoke the words that worried Crystal dreadfully.

Chandni Chowk, the main commercial thoroughfare of Delhi, bustled with frenetic activity, as always, on Friday morning as the Covendales' carriage passed through, driven by Kadir. It was a long street, very wide, with a canal flowing down the centre and trees bordering the sides of the waterway providing cool shade for passers-by. The shops heaved and throbbed with custom, and the many smart open landaus parked on either side of the street signified the great popularity the Chowk's commercial establishments enjoyed with the affluent communities. There was very little that one could not buy in the Chowk, from shawls to sweetmeats, jewels to European-style hats, and fabrics of every description. Other wares were spread out on the pavements, making it difficult to walk.

They passed the Sona Masjid, or Golden Mosque, and the Khooni Durwaza, the 'Bloody Gate' where the cruel Persian king, Nadir Shah, had mounted a horrendous massacre of thousands of innocent people when he sacked Delhi in the mid-eighteenth century.

Crystal had passed through Chandni Chowk a thousand times, and yet it never failed to thrill her. But today, as she sat in the carriage, stiff and unseeing, her thoughts were very definitely elsewhere—at the interview with Damien Granville that lay ahead. It had been difficult to lie to her mother as to the purpose of her outing, as family secrets did not come naturally. Nevertheless, she had had to spin a vague tale about having to order supplies for the storerooms and, possibly, to visit Mr Lawrence, their family solicitor who was helping her with her father's papers.

She had dressed with special care, hating herself for spending time on her toilet, something she had always considered of secondary importance to many other things in life. But she knew that Damien Granville was supposed to have a keen eye for the ladies and, degraded as she felt at the thought, it would be advantageous to look her best. Emma Covendale regarded her daughter with surprise.

'Why, Crystal!' she exclaimed. 'How very charming you look, dear! But . . . all this merely to go shopping?'

'Well, *you* always complain that I don't pay sufficient attention to my appearance,' Crystal said defiantly. 'So I have decided to heed your advice.'

'I see,' said Mrs Covendale slowly, her astonished eyes taking in the smart gown of eau de nil grosgrain, the beautifully arranged coiffure and her daughter's subtle, but very rare, use of cosmetics. 'Well, I am pleased that you have finally decided to make yourself look nice. You really are a very lovely girl, dear, if only you would pay more attention to your toilet.'

The carriage turned off the main road in the direction of the river. The mansion in which Damien Granville had made his home in Delhi was well known; it belonged to an old widowed Begum who preferred to live in Lucknow. She often let her opulent mansion to visitors, but only the very rich could afford her rent. It was not a particularly good looking house; its appearance was confused and cluttered with a dozen styles of architecture ranging from Greek to Persian. But the gardens were lovely, with the flowering trees that bordered the velvet green lawn in full blossom on this warm, fragrant, morning in early spring.

As the carriage rolled slowly up the drive towards the porch, Crystal felt her palms becoming clammy, and there were already unfamiliar flutterings in the innermost recesses of her abdomen. Brought up to face unexpected situations with equanimity, she felt a strange dread of the task ahead. Nevertheless, she knew it would be fatal to allow Damien Granville to see how nervous she really felt. Taking a deep breath, she composed her features into a mask of icy hauteur, and stepped confidently from the carriage.

To greet her at the entrance was a tall young Sikh in scarlet turban and a uniform of starched white drill. By his side hung a sword in a gilt scabbard. As Crystal descended from the coach, he bowed stiffly and clicked his heels in military fashion.

'My name is Gulab Singh, Mr Granville's private secretary. The Sarkar is occupied for a while, and has begged your indulgence for a few moments. He has requested you to wait in his study. Please follow me.' He spoke in excellent Urdu. Obviously he had been informed that Crystal spoke the language well. Curtly she nodded, gave instructions to Kadir to wait for her in the compound, and made to follow the splendidly garbed young Sikh.

The interior of the mansion was as bizarre as the exterior, with many signs of a luxury that was overwhelming. Crystal had a confused impression of lush Persian carpets, brocade draperies and cool marble staircases as they made their way along lengthy corridors and through countless salons, each more elaborate than the other. It was not a house that inspired confidence for one on a mission of some delicacy, and the atmosphere was heavy and oppressive with the smothering fragrance of over-sweet incense and cloying roses.

They arrived eventually at an apartment on the first floor which was obviously Mr Granville's. Waiting for them in a salon, somewhat less opulent than the rest, was a *khidmatgar*, evidently his personal bearer, who ushered her into an adjoining chamber that was furnished like an English office. This was obviously Damien Granville's study, where the interview was to be conducted. Large and airy, the room was very different from the rest of the house, with a huge bow window. To one side was an enormous carved mahogany desk, and the walls were lined with bookcases from floor to ceiling.

'The Sarkar will be here presently,' said the *khidmatgar*, bowing. 'Perhaps *memsahib* would care for some tea?' Of Gulab Singh there was no sign.

Crystal shook her head with a brief smile. 'No, thank you.' The *khidmatgar* bowed and left the room.

Slowly she removed her gloves, took a quick glance at herself in a mirror to see that her coiffure was still neat and tidy, and then strolled over to the window, which looked out on to the river. She was, on the whole, relieved to have a few minutes to herself during which to review the proposition that she intended to place before Damien Granville with the object of settling Robie's horrendous debt. She still could not believe that any man could take the scandalous wager seriously, but then this was a most extraordinary man with strange attitudes in life. There was no knowing how he would choose to consider the situation.

Outside, it was a beautiful day and the sky was deeply

blue with a few fleecy clouds. The river below hummed with human activity as it lapped the walls of the mansion compound. Just beneath the window a group of fishermen were repairing their fishing-nets spread across the muddy bank. On the turgid waters of the Jamuna small rowing-boats went about their daily business, carrying in their shallow holds cargo or passengers clad in brightly-coloured garments. On a series of steps to the left sat a group of *dhobis* beating their piles of clothes against flat stones before washing them. A boat, looking fat and pot-bellied, sailed majestically past, its deck crowded with people bound for the far bank of the river. In the distance, Crystal could see the hazy outlines of the enormous Red Fort, one of the most impressive monuments of Delhi and the stronghold of successive Moghul emperors.

The ormolu clock on the wall of the study chimed the half-hour. Crystal frowned. She had been waiting thirty minutes already and still there was no sign of Damien Granville. She felt a stab of anger at his lack of courtesy, but then realised that the long wait was very possibly deliberate. Her heart sank further. He was determined to make this interview as difficult for her as possible!

Before she could dwell longer on this uncomfortable aspect, the door opened abruptly. 'Forgive me for having kept you waiting, Miss Covendale,' his deep, authoritative voice almost preceded him into the room. 'I was conducting some business which could not be postponed.' Crystal's pulses quickened in renewed nervousness as he walked slowly towards the window and bowed very correctly over her hand. The touch of his hand on hers felt cold and she could not repress a very slight shiver. He noticed it, of course, immediately. A faint smile flickered over his mouth and he raised an inquiring eyebrow. 'Perhaps a cup of coffee to warm you?'

Crystal did not return his smile, withdrawing her hand quickly. 'I was wondering if you had forgotten about the appointment,' she said pointedly, 'since I arrived on the stroke of eleven, as arranged.'

'So I was told,' he said calmly. The door opened and the *khidmatgar* entered, bearing a tall, brass hookah such as Indian aristocrats smoked. Neatly, he arranged the coils of the long cord at the foot of a leather armchair near the window, placing the hookah on a low table beside it. A pleasant scent of tobacco invaded the room.

'Please be seated,' Granville said, indicating briskly a chair. 'Some Turkish coffee, Abdul,' he ordered the *khidmatgar*. 'Miss Covendale is feeling cold.' The sting in his words made Crystal flush as she sank into the chair. Opposite her, Damien Granville arranged himself comfortably in his seat, stretching out his long legs and crossing them at the ankles. Without any sign of discomfiture, he picked up the mouthpiece of the hookah and took a deep breath, making the water-bowl gurgle softly. Crystal's father had sometimes indulged in a hookah smoke when sitting and chatting with the workers on excavation sites, but Crystal had never seen another Englishman do it, although she knew that at one time a great many did.

'No, I had not forgotten about the appointment,' he said suddenly in answer to her earlier question. 'It would be difficult to forget a day on which the sun has risen from the west.' It was said very softly without any expression, but Crystal felt the colour rising in her face and neck. She could hardly expect him to refrain from mention of her rather unfortunate statement at Mrs Smythe's party, bent as he was upon her complete humiliation.

'I would not have sought an appointment,' she said glacially, 'had it not been for . . . er . . . circumstances which have forced me to do so, abhorrent as the prospect is.'

'Oh?' he mocked, lifting an eyebrow slightly. 'And what may these . . . er . . . circumstances be?'

The hypocrite! She did not doubt for a moment that he

was only too aware of the nature of her business. He was merely making certain that her rout was complete. Hating him with every fibre of her body, she swallowed. There was no point in prevaricating further. Every moment spent in the company of this cold-eyed man was anathema. The sooner she came to the point the better.

'I have come about Khyber Kothi,' she said bluntly, her voice cold and brisk. 'I understand from my brother that you *won* it from him in some game of chance last week?' She gave a brief laugh, as though the whole idea were ridiculous.

He observed her coolly. 'That is correct.' He said nothing more, occupying himself with fanning the hot coals in the bowl of the hookah. Obviously he was waiting for her to continue.

Crystal struggled for words, her distaste for the man opposite rising by the minute. There was something about the arrogance of his countenance, the proud bearing of his head held high and erect, that made the bile rise in her throat. She swallowed again. 'Khyber Kothi is our home. Our only home. I cannot believe that you intend to take this wager seriously.'

His head snapped back sharply and his jet black eyes hardened. 'Why not?'

Crystal stared at him aghast. 'You mean that you intend to *claim* your winnings in a wager as monstrous as this?'

'Certainly,' he said as if surprised that the contrary could ever have been considered possible. 'Wins are meant to be claimed, are they not?'

Her face went deathly white. 'Even though the wager was made by a young lad in a fit of total irresponsibility?' She could hardly believe that any man could be so utterly cruel.

'Your brother's age,' he said quite pleasantly, 'has not prevented him from visiting the gaming-house with unfailing regularity, I see! As to his so-called irresponsibility, that is your problem, Miss Covendale, hardly mine!' His voice was completely unconcerned.

'You *forced* him to play . . .' she gasped, struggling to control herself but unable to stop her voice from quivering. 'It was not fair!'

'It was a perfectly fair game,' he said sharply. 'There are more than enough witnesses to testify to that! I warned your brother repeatedly before the wager was laid. He knew even before the game started that I had every intention of claiming my win should the dice fall in my favour. I have no doubt, had they fallen in his favour, he would have claimed my property—and I would have given it with honour. No man who does not have the stomach for losing should have the impudence to place a bet!' He stood up abruptly and walked to the window, gazing out with his back towards her. 'As for forcing your brother to play . . . come now, Miss Covendale, you cannot mean that seriously!' He laughed. He actually laughed!

Abdul entered the room, carrying a large silver tray upon which reposed two tiny porcelain cups of Turkish coffee. He laid the tray upon a low table beside Crystal's chair, bowed, and withdrew. She was hardly aware of his action, her mind running riot with confusing thoughts. Damien Granville bent down, picked up a cup and offered it to her politely, his face once again impassive. Taking the other cup, he again arranged himself and his long legs comfortably in the leather armchair. 'Drink it while it is hot,' he said calmly. 'It never tastes the same when it cools.'

Obediently, with no will-power to resist his command, she sipped. The coffee was superb, sweet and bitter at the same time, its strong flavours loosening her constricted throat. She finished it in two gulps and placed the cup back on the tray. The welcome interruption had given her time to bite back the bitter tears that were stinging her eyelids and to regain something of her disintegrating composure.

'Mr Granville,' she said finally, her voice once again strong and unwavering. 'If you are under the impression that I have come here either to make excuses for my brother or to cast ourselves upon your charity, I must inform you that you are mistaken.'

'Oh? Then why exactly *have* you come?'

'I have come,' she said, ignoring the insulting question, 'to make you an alternative offer.'

The eyebrows shot up higher than before, and a surprised smile flashed across his face. 'Indeed! You intrigue me, Miss Covendale. I can barely suppress my curiosity!'

The sarcasm in his voice stung badly, but she refused to react any more to the tauntings of the reprehensible Mr Granville. Instead, she faced him boldly. 'Since I have no doubt it is the money involved that interests you, perhaps you might consider appointing a surveyor to assess the value of our property. Whatever the worth, we will undertake to pay it to you within a period of one year from now.'

'And where, may I ask, will you get this money from?'

'My father owned a plot of land not far from the Kutub Minar. I understand that the value of the plot has been rising steadily. I intend to sell it to settle your debt—if this is acceptable to you.'

'And if Khyber Kothi is worth more than the land?'

'Then I will raise the balance somehow. I do not think the means should concern you!'

He surveyed her for a moment in silence, then he smiled his slow, infuriating, smile and shook his head. 'Well tried, Miss Covendale! Well tried indeed! It is an admirable scheme, but . . .' he flicked a few spots of ash from the lapel of his jacket, 'I regret that it is unacceptable to me.'

'But why?' cried Crystal. 'I gather that you do not live in Delhi, that you have a home in Kashmir and that Delhi as a town is distasteful to you. Surely it is the money that is of interest to you?'

'You presume too much, Miss Covendale,' he said blandly. 'However unpleasant I may find Delhi, I require a residence in it which is my own. Indeed, my windfall could not have come at a more appropriate time! I dislike living in rented premises.'

'You intend to *live* in our house?' Crystal asked, appalled at the sudden vision of this hateful man residing in their beloved home.

'That is the general idea,' he said equably. 'Khyber Kothi is a delightful residence. I have no doubt it will satisfy my needs admirably.'

He is rubbing salt into my wounds, she cried within herself. He has not a shade of compassion, of common decency, inside him! 'But, surely it is possible to make some compromise so that we are not deprived of a roof above our heads!' she exclaimed, despising the note of pleading that was creeping into her voice. Oh, how she hated degrading herself before this cruel, heartless man! 'My mother is confined to the house with a heart ailment. The shock of leaving Khyber Kothi would surely kill her. At least you would consider waiting a while before proceeding further . . .' Her voice faltered.

He listened to her unmoving, the expression on his face unchanged. 'I am indeed distressed to learn of your circumstances, Miss Covendale,' he said placidly, 'and I am embarrassed that it should fall upon me to deprive you of your home.' His voice hardened. 'But it was an honest game. If you are to become homeless, the blame must be borne not by me but by your brother.' His expression became one of contempt. 'Indeed, it is he who should be here this morning. I find it difficult to have sympathy for those willing to hide behind women's skirts.'

'Robie has no idea that I am here today,' she flung back at him, sick at heart. 'Knowing the kind of man you are, he would have forbidden me to have anything to do with you.' She rose abruptly from the chair, her eyes glazing with anger. 'It was not an honest game,' she said furiously. 'It was nothing short of highway robbery. And you, sir, are not a gentleman. You are a cold-blooded extortionist! Robie was right—you are the devil incarnate. I can imagine no man lower than you!'

The words poured out in a torrent of vehemence, her face scarlet with anger, her amber eyes darting fire. But if she believed her words would either scathe him or provoke a strong reaction, she was wrong. Instead, he threw back his head and laughed. 'By gad!' he exclaimed with genuine amusement. 'A woman with spirit! Considering the pale specimens of English womanhood I have had the misfortune to meet in Delhi, I salute you, Miss Covendale! You may yet be the salvation of the *memsahib* in India!'

Now, she knew, he was taunting her mercilessly. Hot tears stung at her eyelids as, without another word, she rushed blindly towards the door. With one hand on the door-knob, she turned. 'You will *not* succeed in driving us out of our home, Mr Granville,' she hurled back at him. 'I shall fight you with every last breath in my body, rather than have you defile a homestead built with my father's own life-blood!'

'Wait!'

The word, spoken without urgency, still emerged as an order not to be disobeyed. Without intending to, she halted in her tracks, one hand still on the knob. Was there something still left to be said? Had he thought of more ways in which to complete her total degradation?

Slowly, without undue hurry, he unwound himself from the armchair and stood up. 'Sit down!'

She stared at him defiantly, outraged that he should dare to speak to her so. She made no move to comply. 'If there is anything further you wish to say, I prefer to listen to it standing,' she said angrily, but more angry with herself than with him for having made such a complete mess of this interview. From him she had expected nothing better.

'I now have an offer to make to *you*.'

'Oh!' Her eyes widened in astonishment at the completely unexpected statement. Briefly, a painful spark of hope flickered in her breast. Could it be that the man had some vestige of decency after all? Casually, he strolled over towards the desk, leaned back on it and, with arms crossed, faced her across the width of the room.

'There is one condition under which I might be willing to forget your brother's debt of honour.'

Crystal's heart lurched agonisingly. 'Yes?'

'As you are aware,' he said softly, his eyes never leaving her face, 'I live in Kashmir. I do not know if you are at all acquainted with the area, but it is wild and beautiful, endowed by Nature as no other place in the world. I live surrounded by everything that any man's heart can desire—wealth of which I have plenty, a lush, fertile estate that is full of fruitful activity, a home that I have arranged and furnished to my own taste and which supplies my every comfort. I live as I please. I call no man master.' His dark, lean face was live with arrogance and his eyes shone like black coals glowing with latent fire. 'But there is one thing my life lacks. A woman.' His voice dropped as he said the word.

Under the overt scrutiny of his relentless eyes, Crystal's face paled, then blushed with a colour that matched the brilliant curtains at the window. Struck, as if by a thunderbolt, she stood rigid, her eyes forced into lowering themselves in shame. There was no doubt as to the import of his words. She felt numbed with shock. Was there no limit to this man's shamelessness? Did he have no finer feelings, no shades of delicacy at all? Was he under the impression that she was a woman of the streets of Delhi to be had for the asking in exchange for a handful of coins? She found her hands trembling uncontrollably and clenched them in an effort to still them.

'I am not sure, Mr Granville,' she managed to blurt out, her voice strange and shrill, 'that I have understood the trend of this conversation, but if it is what I suspect, I will not even deign to comment upon it. It is . . . outrageous, *unspeakable*! How *dare* you make such an offer to me!' Her nostrils flared, and her tawny eyes were alight with contempt.

He appeared unimpressed by her reaction. 'Just what do you think my offer is?' he asked in amused curiosity.

'That . . . that I should become your mistress in exchange for . . . for the cancellation of my brother's debt, isn't that it?' Crystal had nothing but contempt for women who took refuge in false modesty when confronted with a bald situation. She had always been taught to call a spade a spade.

'My dear Miss Covendale,' he exclaimed in mock horror, his face a model of outraged innocence. 'You surprise me more and more! I find it difficult to believe that a lovely young untouched English rose like you is even aware of such dreadful creatures as mistresses.' His eyes laughed at her openly. He strolled over to where she stood, the thumbs of his hands tucked insolently in the armholes of his jacket. He towered above her, so close that her nostrils were assailed with the aroma of the tobacco he had been smoking. 'No, Miss Covendale. Mistresses I have galore. I doubt if I could accommodate any more without doing serious damage to my health! You will therefore be relieved to know that I do not want you for a mistress.' His eyes again became dark and intent and he dropped his voice so that it was very quiet. 'I want you for a wife.'

For an eternity, it seemed, the words remained suspended between them in space. All power to move appeared to have gone from her limbs. Crystal's eyes, dilated and incredulous, stared into his without flinching. Then, slowly, she sank into a chair, her knees unable to support her. She ran a hand weakly across her forehead. He was proposing *marriage* to her? This . . . this offensive soldier of fortune? This ruthless gambler who thought nothing of defrauding innocent, impulsive young men? The idea was so preposterous that, without intending to, she burst out laughing. Damien Granville stiffened, his eyes narrowed and his face flushed a deep purple. Before she knew it, his hand lashed out and caught her cheek in a stinging slap. She gasped as the laughter died in her throat, and her hand flew up to her face. For a moment they stared at each other silently, he in fury and she in creeping fear.

'No one laughs in the face of Damien Granville,' he said with deadly calm. 'Least of all a woman. You will remember that in future.'

Her cheek hot and still smarting with the force of his palm, Crystal stumbled to her feet somehow and rushed past him to the door. He made no effort to stop her. 'I would not marry you, Damien Granville,' she spat out at him choking with unshed tears, 'if you were the last man on God's good earth. *I detest you!*'

Opening the door, her head held high and her back ramrod straight, she strode through the salon and walked past the *khidmatgar* into the corridor. Her step did not waver until she had reached the downstairs porch, nor did she glance back. As Kadir came up with the carriage, she opened the door herself and sank into the upholstery, her head still erect. It was not until they were half-way down Chandni Chowk that her posture slumped and her face crumbled. As the tears finally came, she buried her face in her hands.

It was the worst experience she had ever had in her life.

By the time she arrived back at Khyber Kothi, the first shock had passed. Crushing a handkerchief against her stinging cheek, she ran up to her room and examined her face in the mirror. The clear imprint of his fingers stood out boldly, even against the honey brown of her skin. Her eyes blazed with fury at the ignominy to which she had been subjected. She felt besmirched by his touch. How dare he, how *dare* he? She threw herself on her bed and again burst into a flood of tears.

Fortunately, her mother was still in the midst of her

afternoon nap. Of Robie there was no sign. Mahima knocked and offered to bring up a belated tiffin, but, pleading a headache, Crystal brushed it aside. Smouldering with frustrated anger she felt that, momentarily, even the fate of Khyber Kothi was secondary to the monstrous humiliation she had received at the hands of this wretched, tyrannical man. She had been a fool to go to him in the first place. She had been a fool to think that Damien Granville had even a single streak of respectability in him. Oh, that she could undo this inglorious morning! He had made her feel like a beggar and a trollop. Marriage to Damien Granville? She would see him in hell first!

Unable to show her face to anyone with the tell-tale marks on it, Crystal continued to plead a headache through the evening. Her mother had moved into a room downstairs following her illness, as Dr Carr had forbidden her to climb stairs. Crystal knew her mother would not therefore surprise her in her room and she determined to stay upstairs until the morning when, she prayed, the shameful marks would no longer be visible. Robie, even if he saw her, would probably not be able to discern what had caused the angry red spots. Lying in bed and seething, Crystal fumed in frustration, unable to think of any suitable manner in which to wreak vengeance on Damien Granville, but damning him with every curse she could think of.

Worried, Mrs Covendale sent up for her supper a bowl of chicken broth and two hot *chappattis*, the flat Indian wheat bread that was a great favourite in the Covendale household. Not wishing to offend or worry her mother further, Crystal ate the frugal meal, shadowed by the gathering darkness in her veranda, while Mahima turned down the bed, arranged the mosquito-net and opened the shutters.

'Is Robie Baba home yet?' Crystal asked.

'Not yet,' said Mahima. 'He told me he would not be eating at home tonight.'

'I see.' Crystal frowned. In her heart flickered a growing fear that he might have returned to the gaming-house to try and recoup his losses. But, surely, not even Robie could be as irresponsible and foolhardy as to consider that possible. Nevertheless, she worried. In the meantime, of course, there was the unsettled matter of Damien Granville's debt! She had, with great bravado, promised to fight him with every breath in her body—but how? With what weapons? Robie would now have to be told of her morning's assignation with Granville—everything except the appalling conversation at the end. Robie would be infuriated at the insults she had received and might be driven to do something foolish to avenge her humiliation at Granville's hands.

Waiting for Robie, Crystal must have dropped off to sleep, for when she awoke again with a start, the house was dark and silent. Her bedside clock showed almost midnight. The lamp in her room burned low and, in the still of the night, she suddenly heard a board creak next door in Robie's bedroom. Quickly she got out of bed and, throwing on a robe, stepped out of her room. There was a faint chink of light showing underneath Robie's door, and she could hear sounds of someone moving about inside. Relieved that he was at last back, without more than a brief knock, she opened the door and went in. Robie was standing near his writing-table with his back to the door. As she entered, he spun around with an oath, his hands behind his back.

She laughed. 'It's only me . . .' Then she broke off, noticing the deathly white pallor of his face and his wide, staring eyes. 'Robie,' she breathed, 'what's the matter? What have you got in your hands?'

'Nothing!' His voice sounded odd and strangled as he turned away from her. 'Go away, Crys,' he whispered. 'Leave me alone.'

A terrible fear clutched at her heart. 'I will not leave you alone until you show me what you have in your hands,' she said sharply, walking up to him. Taking hold of his hand quickly, she wrenched it forward. It was empty, but something fell to the floor with a dull thud. Her eyes shot open as she realised that it was—a pistol! The blood in her veins suddenly turned to ice. 'Robie, no . . . ,' she whispered, terrified. 'You can't, you *mustn't* . . .'

He pushed her off and flung himself on to the bed, face downwards. 'It's the only way, Crys,' he said brokenly, his voice muffled against the bedclothes. 'There is no other way . . . I've ruined everything . . . I don't deserve to live . . .'

She sat down beside him and ran her trembling fingers through his hair, her heart torn with compassion and terrible fear. 'You must not say that, darling, we love you, Mama and I . . . What's happened has happened, we can't change that. But you can't destroy us further by destroying yourself! It would kill Mama . . . and me . . .' Her eyes filled with tears, but she struggled to appear strong and brave.

'It's as if I've already killed Mama,' he said dully. 'What worth is my life now? I've already destroyed both of you.' His face was full of pain and his eyes red with tension and sleeplessness.

'I won't let you do this!' she said, suddenly angry. 'How dare you give up so easily!' We have to at least make a fight for it!'

He managed a weak smile. 'As I've always said, Crys, you should have been a boy. I'm despicable, worthless, a failure in every way . . .'

'You are *not*,' she cried passionately. 'You are a failure only if you *think* you are! I *won't* let you do this to yourself—and us!'

He looked at her quietly. 'You can't stop me, Crys. You know that. I shall do it tomorrow if not today.'

She gazed at him in despair, taking hold of his shoulders and shaking him hard. 'But we can't let Damien Granville win even more than he has, don't you see? You don't have to do this,' she said wildly. 'You don't need to, now. It's all right, Robie, it's going to be all right . . .' She had no idea what she was saying. All she wanted at this moment was to breathe courage into her crumbling brother, set his mind at rest and divert him, even momentarily, from his terrible purpose.

Robie looked at her warily. 'What do you mean, Crys, it's all right?' The sudden spark of desperate hope in his eyes was agony to watch, his faith in her total. At this moment she loved him so much that the thought of losing him was unbearable.

She forced a smile, her lips white and stiff with effort. 'It's going to be all right,' she whispered. 'Nobody is going to take our home away from us.'

'You mean . . .' The shaft of hope in his eyes brightened as he struggled for words. 'You mean . . . Damien Granville has changed his mind?'

She hesitated only fractionally as her eyes became dull and her heart turned into lead. She gave a small nod. 'Damien Granville has changed his mind.' Her voice was barely above a whisper. 'The debt is cancelled.'

Robie stared at her bewildered; then his face lit up with incredulous delight. 'You mean it, Crys? Are you telling me the truth?'

She nodded, unable to trust her voice. *What am I saying? Have I gone quite insane?* 'Yes, I am telling you the truth. But promise me, *promise me* you will not do anything . . . foolish, Robie . . .'

A long, shuddering sigh shook his frame as he put his arms around her and buried his face in her shoulder. 'How did you do it, Crys? Was it difficult?'

'No,' she said, releasing herself and standing up quickly in case he noticed the horror in her eyes. 'It was not difficult . . . he had no intention of enforcing it anyway.'

'Oh, Crys,' he breathed ecstatically. 'I can hardly believe it! It's . . . it's too good to be true!' Too excited to notice the death-mask that had descended upon her face, he cried, 'I swear to you, Crys, on Papa's memory, on Mama's life, on your life, that I will never, never, gamble again. I swear it! But how did it happen, Crys? What did you say to him?'

Numbly, Crystal turned towards the door. 'Go to sleep now, Robie, go to sleep. I'll tell you about it . . . tomorrow.'

Tiredly, chilled to the marrow at what she had just committed herself to, Crystal slowly returned to her room. There was no going back on it now. If she wanted to preserve Robie's life—and Mama's—she would have to marry Damien Granville!

It was as if, in preserving their lives, she had merely rung the knell on her own.

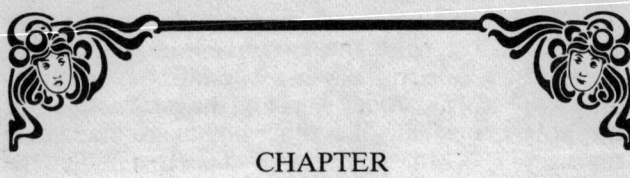

CHAPTER THREE

THE MORNING in early April, a Saturday, dawned crisp and clear, bathing the old city of Delhi in pale gold sunshine. There was still a slight chill in the air but the day held few other memories of the winter that had just passed. The morning was full of promise and the fragrance of spring blossoms was everywhere.

Since very early that morning, even before the rooster crowed, there had been much activity in Khyber Kothi. The servants' quarters and the kitchens hummed with muted excitement as the staff bustled around preparing for the great occasion ahead. Today was indeed a day of supreme auspiciousness, the servants told each other happily, for today their Crystal Baba was to be given in marriage to the finest *sahib* in all of Delhi!

From her veranda upstairs, Crystal watched the excited preparations with blank, expressionless eyes. Tradesmen bearing fruit-baskets and crates of confectionary crowded the compound below as Emma Covendale, comfortably ensconced in a reclining chair, directed operations with the air of a commanding officer on a victory march. Her face was pink and her eyes shone with happiness. It was as though the debilitating illness was happily a thing of the past. Robie had already left to fetch the decorators who would erect the tent in the garden for the evening's reception.

Today is my wedding-day, thought Crystal miserably. I should feel rapturous, overwhelmed with love and happiness. I should want to sing and dance and float on air. But instead, I merely feel . . . dead! In her heart was a dull ache, and her mind, vacant and apathetic, was drained of all thought. The past three weeks had taken a dreadful toll of her. They had been like a continuing nightmare of which today would be the culmination—or maybe the beginning of another nightmare that would remain with her for the rest of her life. By the time the sun went down this evening, she would be the wife of a man she hated. Her vows would bind her to him till the end of her days and he would do with her as he pleased. A shudder passed through her frame and her eyes flooded with bitter, bitter, anguish.

On the morning following Robie's attempt to take his life, Crystal had sent a brief note to Damien Granville. The incoherent commitment she had made to him in front of Robie could not be retracted—except with tragic consequences. The note contained but four words: *I accept your condition*. As she put her name to it, she felt she was signing the warrant of her own death!

Damien Granville lost little time in responding to her capitulation; not with joy, she realised only too well, but in jubilant triumph. The following day a messenger arrived with a letter addressed to Mrs Covendale, seeking an audience. Crystal's mother was surprised—and delighted—at so singular and unexpected an honour. She had already heard a great deal about Damien Granville, known to be a man not only of wealth, but also of some importance, said to have friends in high places. From what Norah Hawthorne had told her, he was also eminently eligible, a fact that filled her with much nervous excitement.

'Do you know, dear, why Mr Granville wishes to see me?' she asked Crystal, studying her face keenly for any indications.

'No,' her daughter replied, her face without expression.

'Perhaps we should ask the cook to make some jam tarts for tea, dear?' she suggested anxiously.

'If you wish,' said Crystal coldly, irritated by the

undue fuss her mother was making over the visit. 'Although I doubt if Mr Granville will have the stomach for more than a quick cup of tea.' He was a man who cared little for social niceties, and the errand which was bringing him to Khyber Kothi this afternoon was, after all, no more than a business arrangement!

But Crystal was wrong. Damien Granville arrived on the stroke of four, not in a riding-habit and on horseback as she had expected, but in a splendid coach and four escorted by liveried coachmen. He was dressed in a deep maroon suit and a white ruffled shirt of the finest Indian silk, and his luxuriant black hair was combed back in an effort to tame the unruly curls. A murmur of awe and admiration went through the staff of Khyber Kothi as he alighted from his carriage, his manner as imperious as ever and his head held arrogantly high.

Crystal's heart sank as she stepped forward to receive him in the porch. He looked as stern and forbidding as ever. He paused for a brief moment to survey her carefully. Deliberately, Crystal had worn her simplest, least impressive dress of printed cotton, much against her mother's wishes. She saw no reason why she should waste time on her toilet when the outcome of the meeting was already known.

Damien Granville bowed, brushed her hand lightly with his lips, retaining her hand securely in his palm. Unable to meet his eyes, annoyed at the warmth in her cheeks, Crystal lowered her lashes so that he might not be able to see the sudden panic in her eyes. How can I bear to spend the rest of my life with him, she cried silently. I shall die, I shall die . . .

'I had not considered,' he said softly, the mere hint of a smile hovering about his mouth, 'that we would meet again so soon.' She looked sharply for any sign of mockery, but there was none. Instead, his face was pleasantly relaxed and his eyes seemed less hard than only a moment ago.

Releasing her hand, which he was still holding, she

said drily, 'Nor I. But then, one cannot always foresee the perverse tricks that fate is about to play on us! My mother awaits you in the drawing-room.' Without giving him a chance to respond, she turned abruptly and led the way into the house. Damien Granville followed with a step that was decidedly buoyant.

What transpired between Damien Granville and her mother, Crystal did not know, nor had she any desire to ascertain. Leaving them together while the conversation still hovered around polite exchanges about the weather, she excused herself and, before either could protest, ran up to her room, where she waited gloomily to be summoned down again. It was just as well that she had succeeded in despatching Robie on an errand before their mother could inform him of Granville's impending visit. Robie would not be back for at least another two hours, which was a relief. It would have been impossible to conceal from him the truth behind the unexpected visit. A mere glance at her face would have been enough to inform him exactly how this bizarre situation had arisen.

Half an hour later, Mahima's knock on her door told Crystal that the moment of reckoning had indeed arrived. Wretchedly, she made her way downstairs, trying valiantly to summon at least a smile. Her mother had sharp eyes, especially where her children were concerned. It would not do for her to suspect that her daughter was anything but ecstatic at the prospect of having Damien Granville for a husband.

In the drawing-room, Damien stood by the window, gazing out into the garden. On the sofa, her face flushed and her hands fidgeting aimlessly, sat Emma Covendale. The remains of the lavish tea on the table before her gave ample proof that there was nothing wrong with Damien Granville's spirits if his appetite was anything to go by!

As Crystal entered the room, he turned and, arms crossed, leaned casually back on the window-ledge. His expression was ruminative and faintly amused. She tried not to glance again in that direction.

Looking extremely flustered, Mrs Covendale beckoned her daughter to a chair beside her. 'I . . . I hardly know what to say, dear! I am . . . quite astounded! Mr Granville has asked for your hand in marriage!'

Crystal said nothing, forcing a smile which she hoped her mother would accept as one of joy. She avoided looking in the direction of the window, knowing she would not be able to tolerate the gleam of triumph that his eyes undoubtedly held. She nodded quickly, her eyes fixed on her hands folded demurely in her lap.

'And . . . what is your opinion in the matter?' her mother asked. 'Are you willing?'

The minimal hesitation went unnoticed by Mrs Covendale. 'Yes.' Crystal's voice was quite steady, the smile never leaving her face.

Her mother looked bewildered. 'But, dear, I was not aware that . . . that you were even acquainted with Mr Granville!'

'I . . . we . . .' The words stuck in her throat, but he stepped in smoothly.

'We have met but briefly,' he explained with an easy laugh. 'But even these brief encounters have been enough,' his eyes twinkled, 'to confirm our . . . er . . . feelings for each other. Would you not say so, Crystal?'

She closed her eyes in an agony of embarrassment and hoped her mother would put her agitation down to modesty. Mutely she nodded, raging inwardly at the mockery he was making of her. Damien Granville was not one to take his triumphs lightly.

'Well, in that case,' Mrs Covendale laughed breathlessly, shaken by his startling revelation, 'you do have my permission, of course, although . . .' she frowned. 'I know so little about you, Mr Granville.'

He came immediately and sat down beside her on the sofa. 'What would you like me to tell you, Mrs

Covendale?' There was a touch of impatience in his voice as if the question constituted an act of lèse-majesté. 'I am perfectly prepared to answer any questions that you may have.'

Deftly, Crystal rose and picked up the teapot. 'I will fetch some fresh tea,' she mumbled, making good her escape again. Outside, she handed the pot to a hovering Mahima and leaned weakly against the wall. Her knees felt unsteady and her head whirled. There was an air of odd unreality about the afternoon, as though she were watching some frightful drama being unfolded on a stage. She paced up and down the veranda, listening to the sudden peals of laughter emanating from the drawing-room. Her mother had not laughed like this since her father died! Obviously Damien Granville was turning on his deadly charm in full, she thought bitterly. It seemed, somehow, like the ultimate betrayal.

'Crystal, dear?' Her mother's summons could not be ignored. Dismally, she went back into the drawing-room. Emma Covendale's face was wreathed in happy smiles. There was no doubt that Damien Granville had succeeded in winning her approval completely.

'Perhaps,' said Mrs Covendale to her daughter, 'you would like to show Mr Granville—Damien—your rose-garden, dear?' Turning to him, she added, 'It is the pride of Crystal's life and very pretty indeed.' Crystal cringed at her mother's transparent device to send them off somewhere so that they could be alone with each other, but she had no choice except to agree with as much grace as she could.

Damien stood up slowly and fixed Crystal with a pleasant smile. 'Nothing would give me greater pleasure,' he said gallantly. He bent over Mrs Covendale's hand. 'We shall meet again shortly,' he said. 'Thank you for a most delightful afternoon and . . . for permission to make your daughter my wife. I am indeed honoured.'

Overwhelmed by his devastating charm, his undeniable good looks and his aristocratic bearing, Mrs

Covendale simpered. She could hardly believe that this most exceptional, most eligible young man, blessed with so much fortune, was soon to be her son-in-law, husband of her difficult, headstrong, daughter. She could barely wait to communicate the news to Norah Hawthorne; indeed to the whole of Delhi. Why, Crystal would be the envy of every young girl in India!

Crystal could hardly blame her mother for her effusive reception of Damien Granville and her immediate approval of his proposition. Certainly he cut a splendid figure such as would warm the heart of any prospective mother-in-law, west or east of Suez. But little did they know, Crystal thought morosely, the terrible, ruthless man who lay underneath this veneer of easy affability! 'The devil incarnate'. Robie had called him. And this was the hypocritical, two-faced man whom fate had chosen as her life-mate!

Down in the solitude of the fragrant rose-bower, Crystal turned to him scornfully. 'You did not waste much time, I see!'

'I never do,' he replied blandly. 'I can see no reason to wait.'

'So, not content with your pound of flesh,' she snapped, 'you want it here and now!'

'Well,' he pondered, fingering his chin lightly, 'perhaps not quite here and now. I wouldn't like to shock your gardeners.'

He laughed and Crystal quickly averted her head to hide the involuntary smile that came to her lips at his outrageous comment. 'There is no need for coarseness,' she contented herself with retorting icily.

He did not answer her charge. Instead, she was startled to feel his hand on her cheek. Like a frightened rabbit, she leapt back, her tawny eyes wide and surprised.

'I am sorry for having struck you,' he said softly. 'But make no mistake—I shall do so again if you ever laugh in my face.' His eyes narrowed ominously.

'I see,' she said bitterly, 'that ours is going to be a charming marriage—a marrriage made not in heaven but in a gaming-house!'

'As good a place as any other,' he said breezily. He put his hand in his pocket and withdrew something from it. 'I think the usual practice is to wear a ring, isn't it?' He slipped on to the third finger of her left hand a gold circlet set with a single diamond the size of a large pea. It was quite exquisite, and Crystal stared at it for a momemt in surprise. The thought of an engagement ring had never even occurred to her. Then she pulled her hand away.

'To prove your ownership?' she asked sarcastically.

'If you wish.' He tilted his head to one side and, momentarily, his eyes mellowed. 'Is the prospect of marriage to me so abhorrent to you?' he asked. He looked almost anxious as he awaited her answer.

She met his look without softening, and the unexpected chink in his armour of steel was too inviting to resist. 'I do not consider an alliance, enforced through blackmail, a marriage,' she said contemptuously.

If she had wanted to wound him, she succeeded admirably. An angry flush stained his rugged cheeks. 'Oh, it will be a marriage all right,' he breathed harshly. 'Make no mistake about that! If you are under the impression that this is to be an arrangement of mere convenience, let me assure you that it will not! I have every intention of exercising my conjugal rights as your lawfully wedded husband.'

Crystal blanched at the fervour of his tone and steadied herself against the fence. For a moment she thought she might faint. Then she felt his arm around her shoulder as he reached out to help her to restore her balance. His face was suddenly alarmingly close, and his adamantine eyes held her gaze with such insistence that she could not look away. She watched with horror as his lips came closer and, swiftly, settled on hers. For an instant she froze—then, flooded with disgust, she lashed out wildly. He laughed against her lips without releasing them, and his arms held her like a vice from which she could not escape. After a moment her body stilled; she seemed deluged with sensations that she could not identify. It was as though her body was no longer her own. Then, just as rapidly, he released her. She staggered back, her senses returning in a flash. She was furious!

'How *dare* you . . . !' The grasp was almost like a sob.

His remorseless eyes mocked her as he leaned nonchalantly against a tree-trunk, enjoying her outrage. 'I dare,' he said coolly, 'because you wear my ring. Or, have you forgotten so soon?'

'You are a . . . monster,' she whispered, her eyes clouding with impending tears. She swallowed hard, determined not to allow him the satisfaction of seeing them fall.

'*And* your husband to be,' he reminded her.

'Under duress!' she cried. 'Or, have *you* forgotten so soon?'

He chuckled. 'Touché! You are a girl of rare spirit, my dear.' His eyes shone with an unusual brilliance. 'I shall enjoy making a woman out of you.' His voice was as soft as a caress.

It was to be an extraordinary courtship. Damien had already announced that he was not in favour of a long engagement. Now that spring had come and the high Himalayan passes were once again clear of snow, he would be returning to Kashmir within the month. It was arranged that the wedding would take place in three weeks' time at St James's Church, where the Covendale family usually worshipped. In the meantime, to satisfy the demands of social convention, they would be seen together in Delhi society to establish their impending relationship in the eyes of their compatriots. The arrangement was made at the insistence of Emma Covendale. Damien himself made it quite clear that, as far as he was concerned, Delhi society could go to hell.

All he wanted was to be away with his bride as soon as possible.

As for Delhi society, it was—frankly—electrified! The bare announcement in the columns of the local English paper was enough to send every mother of a marriageable daughter reaching for her smelling-salts and every marriageable daughter snivelling into her handkerchief.

'It's not fair,' sobbed Charlotte as, thunderstruck, the Smythes considered the announcement over the breakfast-table. 'Damien Granville danced with me thrice and with Crystal not at all! Oh, how could he deceive me so?'

'There is something more to this,' said her mother maliciously, 'and I shall see that it is made public! How can a man like him even consider marrying anyone as . . . as wild and untutored as Crystal?' She snorted angrily.

'Perhaps he likes her,' suggested her husband mildly, peering from behind the pages of a three-month-old issue of the London *Times*. 'After all, Crystal is a lovely filly, however unbridled she may be.'

Betty Smythe threw him a murderous glance as Charlotte burst into renewed tears at her father's tactlessness.

Arriving at Khyber Kothi as soon as they had read the news in the papers, Sally and her mother covered Crystal with kisses. 'I *knew* something was afoot at Mrs Smythe's *burra khana*,' exclaimed Sally happily. 'Why, anyone could see in your eyes that you were madly in love with him!'

'How very clever of everyone,' commented Crystal drily, 'to have discovered my feelings even before I did so myself!'

'I *told* you so!' Norah Hawthorne said complacently. 'All that worry for nothing! I knew Crystal would settle down when she found a man who could match her in wit.' She lowered her voice significantly, 'And such an *attractive* devil as well!'

Emma Covendale accepted all comments in happy

contentment, still unable to believe her daughter's good fortune. In the general air of excitement the only person who appeared worried was Robie. Stunned by the news at first, he found a terrible doubt gnawing at his mind.

'Why have you agreed to marry him?' he asked Crystal bluntly when they were alone, his pale blue eyes dark with suspicion.

'Why, Robie,' she exclaimed, trying to hide her alarm. 'What a strange question!'

'Which,' he persisted grimly, 'you have not answered. Are you in love with Damien Granville?'

'But of course I am!' she cried gaily. 'Why else should I want to marry him?'

'I don't know,' he said, frowning. 'Unless . . . it is something to do with the cancellation of the debt. Is it?' His face went white.

'Oh, Robie!' She pretended to be hurt and annoyed. 'How *can* you even consider such a thing? I . . . fell in love with Damien the . . . the moment I met him. He was so gentle, so understanding. He offered to cancel the debt immediately he learned of our circumstances—before there was any hint of . . . of marriage!'

'I . . . see,' he said slowly, examining her face minutely. She met his scrutinising look with no sign of agitation. Her eyes were clear and innocent. He loosened a little. 'Well . . . I just thought I'd ask. It would be diabolical of him to . . .', he bit his lip in embarrassment. 'What I mean is, he appears such a hard, ruthless man without any semblance of . . . of feeling that it seemed impossible he would cancel the debt without . . .' He stopped again and laughed apologetically as if ashamed of the thought.

Crystal heaved a silent sigh of relief and promptly launched into an impassioned recital of Damien's many virtues, disgusted with her own duplicity. Nevertheless she realised that, if ever Robie came to learn the truth, it would destroy him utterly. He would be mortified beyond redemption and would surely take his own life rather than face the disgrace of his sister's sacrifice.

Robie listened to her recital in silence. Naive and gullible, he was only too willing to be convinced of Damien Granville's fine motives. His sister's performance appeared to satisfy him completely. His frown disappeared and he smiled in relief.

'I'm glad you do love him, Crys,' he said with a laugh. 'I must say, he does seem an awfully decent chap after all. He has already cleared matters up with the gaming-house, I'm told. I was very wrong in my earlier opinion of him. I realise now.'

It was the same painstaking performance that Crystal put on day after day as they were wined and dined by Delhi society in celebration of the forthcoming nuptials. No one watching her cool, serene face, the heightened sparkle in her eyes and her ever-smiling mouth could ever have doubted that she was anything but completely happy. Her face ached with the effort of that smile, but she never allowed her façade to slip. Within her heart, however, she could not stop shedding bitter tears, hating passionately the man who had forced her into submission so unscrupulously.

Damien Granville himself, in spite of his utter dislike of the social process, was always the epitome of confident charm. His unfailing courtesy towards his radiant fiancée, everyone decided, could not be faulted. If, at times, he appeared arrogant and with a touch of impatience, indeed, this served only to heighten his desirability in the eyes of the onlookers.

As the day of the wedding approached, Crystal became more and more panic-stricken, the hunted look in her eyes more pronounced. On the night before the wedding, she decided to make a last appeal to Damien Granville, begging to be released from the monstrous bondage in which he had placed her.

'How can you make me go through with this . . . this charade?' she cried in anguish. 'I do not love you.'

Damien regarded her quite unperturbed. 'You will,' he said calmly, 'once we are married.' He seemed to consider the matter so casually that she exploded with rage.

'Never!' she clenched her fists. '*Never!* Oh, how can you accept the prospect of a wife who hates you as much as I do?'

He laughed. 'Love . . . hate . . . these words are meaningless to me! The world is not made of black and white. There are many shades of grey in between.'

She was aghast at his cynicism. 'You do not think it important that a man and woman should love each other before . . . before they wed?'

'No,' he said coldly. 'There can be . . . other reasons for marriage.'

She looked bewildered. 'Other reasons?'

He seems to struggle with himself for a moment, then said abruptly,

'You need not concern yourself with those for the moment.' Defeated, Crystal subsided in sullen silence.

The wedding ceremony, short and simple in accordance with Damien's wishes, was attended by only those close to the family. From the bridegroom's side there was only Gulab Singh, his private secretary, who was best man, much to the discomfiture of Delhi's snobs. Damien dismissed their comments scornfully. 'Gulab Singh is also my friend, and twice the man any of these Delhi *sahibs* can ever be. I don't care a damn for their opinion.' The bride was given away by her brother.

The reception, held on the spacious lawns of Khyber Kothi, was a more lavish affair attended by the city's cream. A military band was in attendance. All, some reluctantly, agreed that the bride and the groom made a striking couple indeed. If anyone observed the deathly pallor of the exquisite bride as she danced the first waltz in the arms of her dashing groom, they put it down to perfectly natural wedding-night nerves. Far more deserving of attention was the bride's magnificent antique

Indian jewellery studded with diamonds, emeralds and pearls—a wedding gift from her doting groom, worth a king's ransom. 'What a pity it is all wasted on Crystal,' whispered Betty Smythe *sotto voce* to her daughter, 'when she has not the faintest idea of elegant fashion.'

A suite of rooms had been prepared to receive the Sarkar's bride, adjoining the Sarkar's own apartment. An impressive retinue of servants lined up deferentially in the hall to welcome the Sarkar as he proudly bore his bride home. Crystal's personal staff was to consist of a plump, elderly woman with robust cheeks called Sharifa and a very young girl with shy eyes who was introduced to her as Sharifa's niece, Rehana. Both had been summoned from Damien's Kashmir household in order to supplement his all-male staff in Delhi.

Rock-faced and pale with nervous exhaustion, Crystal sank into the brocaded upholstery of a sofa in her sitting-room. The suite was lavishly appointed and consisted of a bedroom and two small antechambers, one a dressing-room and the other for storage of her boxes.

'I hope the rooms are to your satisfaction?' Damien asked as he opened cupboards and drawers and inspected the fittings.

'Perfectly,' she replied without interest, wanting only to be left alone—if such a luxury could now be had at all!

'This is only a temporary arrangement, as you know,' he said. 'We shall be leaving for Kashmir in a week. You will find things at Shalimar more to your taste, I hope.'

She made no reply, feeling too fatigued and apprehensive even to have the energy for idle conversation. If Damien noticed her wretched state, he refrained from comment. Instead he said, 'There is some work I have to complete downstairs. I may be late in coming up.'

Her heart leapt with pathetic relief. Even an hour or two more of blessed solitude would constitute a merciful reprieve. 'But,' he added immediately, 'come up I will.' An enigmatic smile played on his lips as he opened the door and went out.

Miserably, Crystal set about some desultory unpacking. Sharifa and her niece fussed around making the enormous four-poster bed and arranging the toiletries in the bathroom. On top of her clothes in the trunk was Crystal's beautiful nightgown and peignoir, a frothy, diaphanous affair ordered by Emma Covendale from the most expensive lace-maker in Delhi. Had it not been for so distasteful an occasion as her own wedding-night, Crystal would have considered them ravishing. But now she shivered.

'*Memsahib* cold?' Sharifa asked anxiously.

Crystal shook her head and smiled thinly. 'No. Somebody just walked over my grave, that's all.'

'Please?' asked Sharifa, puzzled.

Realising that the woman's English was limited, Crystal immediately changed to Hindustani. 'I am not cold, thank you. Just tired. I shall not require either of you any more tonight. You may leave. Goodnight.'

Sharifa's eyes shone with approval. '*Memsahib* speaks our language very well,' she said with new respect, 'That is good. In Kashmir very few people speak English and almost none at Shalimar.' Grasping Rehana's hand, she withdrew.

Crystal unpinned her hair slowly, allowing it to tumble to her shoulders. With a sigh of relief she kicked off her shoes and slid out of her stiff, formal gown. One by one she removed the pieces of jewellery with no more than a cursory glance at each. She repacked them in their velvet-lined boxes and pushed them to the bottom of her trunk, vowing never to wear them again. Did he think he could buy her love with pretty baubles? If he did, then he was more unthinking than she had assessed.

She washed, then observed herself in the mirror. She could hardly recognise herself! Underneath the golden tan, her skin looked tired and blotchy and her eyes lacked lustre. There were dark rings under them, and her body, naturally tall and lissome, seemed even thinner. The tensions of the past weeks were all too evident on her face and in the dull stoop of her shoulders. Dismally, she slipped into the beautiful apricot nightgown, noticing how little it did to improve her demeanour.

For a long while Crystal sat by the open window, brushing her hair with automatic, absent strokes. From the courtyard below came the muted sounds of singing to the accompaniment of drums and tinkling bells. The servants were celebrating the Sarkar's happy nuptials! Crystal grimaced, listening with only half an ear. She was lost in pondering a problem that had been causing her considerable concern lately. A problem that she had not foreseen at all.

That she disliked Damien—her husband—intensely, there was no doubt about in her mind. She could never, never, forgive him for the heartlessness with which he had forced her into this ludicrous marriage. Yet there was something about him that she was beginning to find—disturbing. She had steeled herself against his shallow charm, determined to show nothing but indifference. Of late, however, he was beginning to stir her in a manner that she could not understand. There was not in him, she knew, a single streak of tenderness or of concern for her. He had married her out of perversity, out of a desire to be cruel, nothing else. Yet she found herself reacting to his touch, however casual, with a response that was alarmingly strong. His violent kiss in the rose-garden had left her trembling and weak, much as she had been revolted by it. But each time their bodies came in contact with each other—a touch of the shoulder, a light brush of his lips on her hand, when he held her casually to dance—her legs seemed to turn to water and the blood raced through her veins making her pulsate with a strangely unrecognisable excitement.

Once, when he had offered her his hand as she alighted from his carriage, she had not been able to repress a shudder. He had glanced at her sharply, his eyes clouding with quick anger.

'Why do you recoil at my touch?' His face had turned white with temper and the scar on his cheek had stood out like a whiplash. 'Is your dislike of me so uncontrollable?'

She had bitten her lip in distress. How could she tell him the real reason for her reaction? She would rather die than have him know that he attracted her at all! Making her voice as scathing as possible, she had retorted, 'Yes. But no doubt time will teach me to keep it well leashed!' Her sarcastic reply had made him even angrier and he had turned sharply on his heel and left in a fury. She had smiled after him triumphantly, rewarded that her arrow had again found its mark.

Now, as she sat at the window waiting for her husband—how strange the word sounded!—on the first night of their marriage, she was filled with a cold dread. If the touch of his hand was enough to send her pulses racing—what would happen when he kissed her, caressed her, made love to her . . . ?

With a dry sob she rose abruptly to her feet and paced up and down the floor in mounting agitation. Damien must never find out that she felt anything but cold indifference to him! He must never have the reward of knowing that he could move her even by an inch. It was the only revenge she could wreak, the only way in which she could pay him back for her abject humiliation. Whatever happened, she mustn't weaken—or his triumph would be total!

He did not come up until nearly two o'clock in the morning. Sitting tensely by the window, watching the flickering lights of the river-boats, Crystal stiffened. Hardly daring to breathe, she heard his soft footfall pause by her door—then pass on. She let out her breath in a gasp of relief. Maybe he would not come tonight at all. Maybe he had changed his mind—O God, let it be that he has changed his mind! she prayed.

But it was not to be so. A few minutes later she heard the click of a latch. The connecting door between their suites opened and Damien walked in. He had removed his jacket, and the sleeves of his white ruffled shirt were rolled up to his elbows, the buttons down his chest carelessly undone. Without a word he sat down on the sofa and stretched his legs casually across a low stool before the fireplace.

'Come and sit here,' he commanded, but his voice was not harsh.

Fearfully, her throat dry and her heart thudding painfully, she did as he ordered. He watched her silently, taking in the slender figure outlined by the scanty pieces of lace and silk and the rise and fall of her half-exposed breasts. Quickly, she drew her peignoir closer around her neck, raising her head defiantly, her eyes unable to hide their fear. Suddenly he leaned forward, and with a gentle movement covered the small, clenched fist in her lap.

'Why are you frightened of me?' he asked unexpectedly. 'I am not known to bite . . . unless invited to!'

She flushed and involuntarily stiffened, trying to withdraw her hand, but he would not release it. 'I am not . . . frightened of you,' she whispered. 'I merely . . . detest you.'

He frowned in annoyance and let go her hand abruptly. 'Why? There is not one woman in Delhi who would not be delighted to share my bed!'

His arrogance made it easier for her to regain her courage. She shrugged. 'There is no accounting for female perversity. It is a curse of our sex!'

He stared at her for a moment, then his brow cleared and he threw back his head and laughed. 'By George, you are brave!' he chuckled. 'Not many women would dare to answer me back like that. But then,' he mused, 'that is why you appeal to me. You are different from any Englishwoman I have ever met in India.'

'I do not appeal to you at all,' she said miserably. 'You forced me to marry you for a reason I have not been able to divine.'

'You really don't know why I married you?'

She shook her head. 'No. But I know it is not for love, since you find the word meaningless.'

He observed her thoughtfully and rubbed his chin, a habit he had, she had noticed, when considering a difficult question. He rose from the sofa brusquely and walked towards the window. For a moment he stood gazing out without speaking. Then he turned and faced her.

'I am thirty-one years old, as you know. I am the last surviving member of my family. I have no brothers and sisters, which also you know. If I die, my estate will go to strangers. That is unacceptable to me. It is therefore necessary for me to have a son.'

Crystal rose slowly from her seat, her eyes absolutely incredulous. 'You married me only . . . for that?' Why, it was monstrous!

'It is as good a reason as any other,' he shot back lightly, his lips twisted in a sardonic smile.

'But for that . . .' she said bewildered, 'you could have married any woman you wished in India. Why *me*?'

He moved back towards her and stood so close that she could feel his breath on her face. She tried to step back, but the fender obstructed her retreat. His hand rose slowly and he stroked her neck with his fingertips. She clenched her teeth to stop the faint gasp that came to her lips, and closed her eyes so that she need not look into his.

'Because, my Crystal,' he whispered, 'you have everything I would like in the mother of my son. You have spirit, you are vastly intelligent and you do not cower in fear of the petty barbs of ignorant public opinion.' He took a deep breath and, although his eyes looked into hers, he appeared not to see them. 'I want my son to love his land like I do. I want him to grow up proud of his inheritance, part of the people around him. I want him to speak their tongue and understand them, to treat them like human beings and equals. All this you will be able to teach him, for you have learned it yourself. Indeed, you will be a fitting mistress for Shalimar, a perfect mother for the son I want. Also . . . ,' his tall, lithe body loosened suddenly and his voice became flippant, 'also you are the only woman I have ever met who does not bore me to tears!'

He lowered his hand abruptly and stepped back, leaving her shaken by the ferocious intensity of his words. 'In all this,' she breathed tremulously, 'not one word about love.'

'Love?' he laughed scornfully. 'Yes, I have heard that such a thing exists! But there is not one single woman in the world whom I have met who is capable of it. I have no time for your kind of love—*my* kind I have had in plenty.' His mockery was remorseless.

'Your kind of love!' she flung back, appalled by his cynicism. 'Surely, you mean your kind of *lust*!'

He seemed to find her comment highly entertaining, and laughed. 'Does it matter what you call it? It is pleasant. It engages the senses without disturbing the heart.'

She stared at him despondently. 'And that is all that you want of marriage? To engage the senses without disturbing the heart?' Somehow his words wounded her more than she cared to admit.

He shrugged. 'Why not? Or—do you plan otherwise?' The taunt was unmistakable. He had no illusions about her feelings for him!

Unable to tolerate any more of this cold-blooded conversation, she brushed past him quickly and walked to the window. 'I have no plans where you are concerned.' She kept her back towards him. 'You may have bought my body with your reprehensible bargain, and that I cannot deny you, much as I would want to. But,' she turned and faced him defiantly, 'you will never own other than that, I promise you.'

He covered the distance between them in a few rapid strides. His hand tightened around her wrist. 'But I shall never let you forget that I *do* own your body,' he said with such cold menace in his voice that she shuddered. 'Not for a solitary moment, that *I* promise *you*!'

She snatched his wrist away from him with a single movement. He did not object. 'I do not doubt it,' she said contemptuously, meeting his thunderous gaze without flinching. 'But it will be an act of rape given the sanction of the law—and you well know it.'

He laughed softly, unabashed. 'I have never yet taken a woman against her wish—nor shall I you.' His hand rose and he stroked her cheek with the back of it. 'You are very lovely, Crystal,' his voice was like a caress, 'and I like you best when your eyes spit flames as they are doing now . . .' His lips brushed her brow as light as thistledown. Startled, she tried to step back, but his arms were already round her waist. She felt his lips against her neck as he drew her to him without seeming to make any effort at all.

Panic-stricken, she struggled to release herself, but he laughed against her mouth, covering her face with kisses as fragile as a butterfly's wing. For an instant she stood still, knowing it was useless to try and match his superior strength. Deliberately, she made herself like stone, her heart crying out in torment but her face giving him no indication of the turmoil within. With a whispered oath, he drew her even closer as he brought his mouth down on hers and his tongue probed for entry. Her mind recoiled in horror, in outrage, but she seemed unable to withdraw, as though transfixed by a force beyond her capacity to resist.

Very slowly, propelled by something terrible and uncontrollable, her body began to dissolve as if it were made of mere wax. Weakly, her arms made an attempt at release but, even as she struggled, her mouth opened under his like a flower thirsting for the sun. She felt her legs crumble under her and his arms strengthened and tightened until she was next to his heartbeat. The blood gushed and pounded in her ears, and her body raged with tumult. She knew she was sinking, sinking, into some dark fathomless pit without an end. She tried to stop herself, gasping for breath, but it was too late.

With a single movement, he tore at the fragile cloth over her body, sending it floating to the ground like mist. His hand curled round her breast, making it spring to life, and every nerve-end in her being cried out in an agony of feeling so delicious that she whimpered without knowing that she had made a sound. The last vestige of her resistance crumbled. Even as she cried out silently in outrage, her arms lifted and wound themselves round his neck. He gasped and, without releasing her mouth even for an instant, lifted her as easily as a leaf and bore her to the bed. As his face loomed above her in the half-darkness, she made a last attempt at resistance.

'Damien, no . . . ,' she moaned, 'wait . . .'

But he was past hearing. His frantic hands caressed every inch of her body as his mouth found her breast and she cried out in unbelievable rapture, almost too much to bear. Her entire being burst into flames, willing him, wanting him to go on . . . And when he took her, it was with such force that she cried out in pain, but a pain so precious, so enchanting, that she seemed to revel in it. His passion was overpowering, the strength of his body frightening, but unable to leash her disarrayed, enflamed senses, she matched him kiss for kiss, caress for caress, giving herself to him in surrender that was complete, yet hating herself through every moment of it.

It was as if his love-making would never end. Expertly, a master of his craft, he made her scale mountains, lingering on heavenly peaks, soaring, soaring even higher, then sliding dreamily into valleys that were warm and languorous and filled with peace. She lost all count of time, all sense of reality, as she floated through mists of half-consciousness, wanting never to retun to earth. She did not know when she slept, but when she awoke, her head lay on his shoulder and she could feel his warm hand caressing her back with his finger-tips.

She raised her head and looked at him as if in a dream. His eyes were open. She lay back on her pillow, filled with pain, and winced. He turned on his side and, cradling her in his arms, kissed her gently on the lips, once. She gazed up at him through a mist, unable to see his face clearly.

'Damien . . . ?'

'Hush, my darling, go to sleep . . .'

He spoke with so much tenderness that, without knowing it, she smiled and closed her eyes, falling instantly into a deep, dreamless slumber. When she woke again, she knew not how much later, he was gone. She was alone in the dark.

CHAPTER FOUR

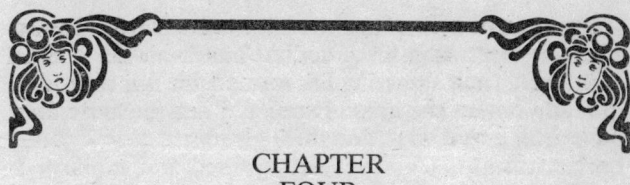

THE NOON sun stood high and bright in the blue heavens when Crystal opened her eyes again. Flinching against its brilliance as the sunshine poured in through her windows, she pulled the coverlet over her head and lay back with her eyes closed. She lay bathed in an unfamiliar langour for a while, wafting through a state of dreamy half-wakefulness, not sure whether she was still asleep or not. Momentarily, she could not quite remember where she was but then, as recollection seeped back through her befuddled senses, she was truly awake and her breathing seemed to stop.

Like a douche of iced water, the memory of the night came surging back. She lay numb for a moment, unable to move as waves of quick shame closed over her. Her face went crimson with the mortification of remembering her own participation in Damien's passionate attack on her body. Her whole being throbbed with a dull ache, but that she hardly noticed. What shattered her most of all was her own nefarious capitulation to her base instincts. More than Damien, she hated herself for having surrendered to him with such shameless abandon. Furious at the easy dissolution of all her resolves of last evening, she buried her face in her pillow and wept. Oh that her body could have betrayed her so cruelly!

Softly and for a long while she sobbed, unable to stem the tears of remorse, the pangs of shame. How fickle were the minds of women, how fragile their resolutions! He had demolished her defences in no time at all, made as easy a conquest of her as he undoubtedly had of his other women. He had taken her knowing that she had no love for him, using his practised hands on her like an expert musician caressing life into a lifeless instrument. In that moment she hated Damien Granville more than ever before.

The storm of tears left her drained and exhausted. Perhaps she slept again, she neither knew nor cared. But by the time her eyes re-opened, the tempest had passed. All that remained was a dull, physical discomfort, a painful testimony to the fact that she was no longer the girl she was yesterday. Damien Granville had seen to that!

Dully she rose and, in a trance, made her way to the bathroom to wash her red-rimmed eyes with cold water. Her beautiful nightdress lay on the floor in tatters, torn beyond repair. She picked it up and tucked it back in her trunk to keep it from Sharifa's curious eyes. Then she arranged her hair neatly and slipped into a cool dress of muslin. Composing her features into a mask of dignified composure, she rang for Sharifa. Of Damien there was neither sign nor sound, for which she was grateful. The thought of having to face him again—as she must!—brought an agonising sob to her throat. After last night—how could she bear to gaze into his eyes again? He would lacerate her with scorn, knowing how easily he had scored and how effortless had been his victory.

A soft knock on the door heralded the arrival of Sharifa and her niece. They stood deferentially waiting for orders, but Crystal could see the knowing look in Sharifa's eyes. For an instant she felt annoyed, then realised how unreasoning her anger was against the kindly woman.

'I would like some tea, please, Sharifa,' she said, pretending to be busy with arranging the pleats of her dress.

Sharifa bowed. 'I will fetch it immediately and Rehana will stay with you in case you need something else. I will also bring some breakfast . . .'

Crystal stopped her with an impatient gesture. 'I do not want anything to eat, thank you. Just some tea will do.'

Sharifa nodded her head knowingly. 'Very well. Perhaps *memsahib* should rest today. She must be very tired.' She looked concerned.

'I am not at all tired,' Crystal said with more sharpness than she had intended. 'I am just not very hungry.' For a moment she wondered if she should ask where Damien was so that she could be prepared for a visit from him, if at all. But then she decided against it. Wherever he was, she had no desire to see him immediately, and an enquiry from her might reach him and bring him up. As it happened, her ponderings were unnecessary.

'The Sarkar has gone out for the morning,' said Sharifa. 'There are some people who have come from Kashmir. He is with them.'

Relief sprang in Crystal's eyes. 'These visitors . . . will they be staying for luncheon?' she asked hopefully. If they were, then Damien certainly would not come up to lunch with her!

'I do not know,' said Sharifa, 'but I will ask Gulab Singh.'

'It does not matter,' said Crystal tiredly. 'It was just an idle question.'

She spent the rest of the morning, what remained of it, sitting on the large balcony that overlooked the river. The banks of the Jamuna were always humming with brisk activity, and this morning was no different. In the room, Sharifa and Rehana brought order and cleaned and dusted. For a while Crystal chatted with them, asking questions about their homes and families, something that pleased Sharifa greatly. She had come to Shalimar as a very young bride of one of the cooks, and had been there ever since. 'The Sarkar used to play in my lap when he was a little boy,' she said proudly.

'And where is his mother?'

Sharifa's eyes immediately fell. 'The big *memsahib*

'. . . left many years ago,' she said confusedly.

'Left?' asked Crystal. 'Left for where?'

Sharifa looked very embarrassed and cast a quick glance over her shoulder. 'The Sarkar has not . . . told you?'

Crystal shook her head. 'Told me about what?'

Sharifa took a deep breath. 'The big *memsahib* went away with . . . another *sahib* when the Sarkar was only ten years old.'

'Oh!' Crystal was shocked at the revelation. Why had Damien never spoken to her about it? Perhaps it was a subject that still caused him pain.

With a sudden start of surprise, Crystal realised just how little she knew about the man who was her husband. He had talked very seldom about his family or his background or, indeed, about himself. For instance, she had no idea how an Englishman came to own an estate in Kashmir in the first place. Kashmir was a state of turbulence and mystery that very few Europeans had visited until little more than thirty or forty years earlier. She knew it had been the cause of bitter battles between the British and the Sikhs, and had had a bloody history under successive oppressors. In fact, the first white woman to have had the courage to go up to this wild, beautiful paradise had been the intrepid Honoria Lawrence in June 1850, long before the railway to Amritsar had been opened. Her husband, Sir Henry Lawrence, had had a great deal to do with establishing a peaceful settlement in the Punjab and Kashmir with the Sikhs, and had travelled extensively with his family in the region.

Crystal recognised with a pang of guilt that her ignorance of Damien's life was largely her fault. Even so, he was a man of reticence who did not reveal himself easily. Determined always to keep him at arm's length, she had refused to lower herself by seeking information about him, preferring to remain in the dark. Now she felt vaguely uneasy at her lack of interest—or her pretence of it. Perhaps, she felt, she should make some effort to discover more about him—though her quest would in no way lessen her dislike of him!

Damien did not return for luncheon and no one seemed to know where he was. A merciful release, indeed! From the bookcase in her sitting-room she took out, with interest, an English translation of the travel diaries of the French Jesuit, Bernier. She knew that Bernier had accompanied the Moghul emperor Shah Jehan on a journey to Kashmir and now, lingering over her luncheon of boiled rice, chicken curry and yoghurt, she read his account of it eagerly. After lunch, she stretched luxuriously, feeling much more at peace with herself. She carried the book to her bedroom, intending to indulge in the luxury of reading in bed, but before she had completed even one page the book slipped from her hands and she was fast asleep.

It was as she was enjoying a welcome cup of evening tea after a long, restful nap that there was a loud, peremptory knock, and, without further ado, the door opened. Looking tired and dusty, Damien stepped into the room. Her cup half-way between the table and her lips, Crystal froze and her heart somersaulted in apprehension.

He flung himself on the sofa and, taking a handkerchief out of his pocket, wiped his forehead. 'It's devilish hot outside,' he said crossly. 'Absurdly so for April.'

She said nothing, continuing to drink her tea while keeping her eyes firmly fixed on her book. The remembrance of last night returned with renewed force, and she lowered her head even further, knowing that her face had crimsoned involuntarily. But if he noticed her agitation or, indeed, had any recollection at all of the night, he gave no indication. He was sitting casually, with his legs stretched out in a favourite position, gazing with an absent frown into the middle distance, hardly seeming to be aware of her presence.

The door opened again after a soft knock, and his

personal bearer, the *khidmatgar* she had seen on her first visit to the mansion, appeared carrying a tray with a tea-service and cups. He hesitated for a moment then, confidently, placed the tray on the table beside Crystal. Now that the Sarkar had got himself a wife, he appeared to indicate, it was only proper that the *memsahib* should pour. With a slight bow, he withdrew. Crystal waited for a moment uncertainly, then asked, 'Would you like some tea?'

He nodded absently without looking at her, and resumed his solitary meditations. She poured out a cup, then paused uncertainly again. Did he take milk and sugar? She had never taken the trouble to notice. She frowned and was on the point of asking, when she heard him say, with some amusement, 'Very little milk. No sugar.' She flushed as she realised he must have been watching her deliberations. She rose and, cup in hand, went to where he sat and placed the cup before him. She made to return to her seat, but he said gently, 'Come and sit beside me.'

'I . . . have my book on the table . . .' she mumbled, unable to look him directly in the face.

'Damn your book!' he snapped. 'You will have two whole weeks without me. You can read as much as you like, then.'

Her heart leapt. 'Two whole weeks? How is that?'

'I have to leave for Kashmir tonight,' he said brusquely, stirring the tea. 'I have had a message to say I am urgently required back at Shalimar.'

She did not ask him why. 'And . . . I am to stay on in Delhi?'

He looked at her silently, taking in the sudden spark of joy in her eyes. Then he said drily, 'Much as it distresses me to dash your hopes to the ground, no. You will follow me in two days' time. Gulab Singh will make all the arrangements and will be your escort.'

The spark of hope died, and she averted her face so that he could not see the despair on her countenance.

Two days! That was all she had left in Delhi within easy reach of her beloved friends and family. After that she would be transported into the far, far, wilderness of Kashmir with only her hated husband for company!

'The prospect of being without me for two weeks does not please you?' he asked sarcastically, knowing precisely what was passing through her mind. The note of mockery in his voice infuriated her, bringing back all the resentment of the morning. She realised that his lovemaking had meant nothing to him. The flashes of tenderness, the velvet-soft caresses, had been nothing more than those he lavished on all those who had shared his bed.

'On the contrary,' she flung back, 'it delights me! It is the prospect of then being *with* you that leaves me less than joyous!'

His eyes glinted ominously but he did not raise his voice. 'In that case,' he said with light derision, 'the performance you put on for my benefit last night pays tribute to your excellent histrionic abilities!'

She had been expecting his taunt all along, knowing that he would not rest assured until he had made it. Nevertheless, she went scarlet with embarrassment. But without batting an eyelash, she countered sharply, 'You already know that I am a good actress! Why, all Delhi is under the impression that I am madly in love with you!' She laughed scornfully at so ludicrous an idea.

'And . . . aren't you?' he asked softly.

Her smile could not have been more acidic. 'If you believe that, it is your own pride that blinds you, not any action of mine.'

'Even after last night?'

She controlled herself with admirable success and managed to shrug nonchalantly. 'It was pleasant,' she said carelessly. 'It engaged the senses without disturbing the heart—exactly according to your requirements!'

Her eyes flashed with jubilation as the barb went home. His bronzed complexion deepened further and the scar on his cheek became livid, as she knew it did when he was very angry. He looked at her hard with thunder in his eyes, hoist by his own petard, but then, unexpectedly, he relaxed and leaned back. He stretched out a languid hand and placed a finger under her chin. 'One day,' he said in a voice as soft as silk, 'it will disturb your heart like nothing ever has before. I will wager my life on it.'

She did not move her head, keeping it firm and proud. 'And if you do,' she scoffed, 'you will lose, even though as a gambler your prowess is said to be unparalleled.'

Very firmly, he drew her close and whispered against her ear, 'You have no idea with how much impatience I will await your arrival at Shalimar.' His arms closed round her waist. She did not—could not—resist as his rough cheek grazed hers.

'But you will no doubt find many willing substitutes to fill the lonely hours until then,' she retorted sarcastically, holding herself as stiffly as she could.

'Perhaps . . .'

His mouth was on hers before she could turn away. She closed her eyes tightly, determined not to give in this time. His hands were as tender as rose petals and his lips soft, as they lingered over hers, kissing the corners of her mouth, nibbling agonisingly. She clenched her fists, her knuckles white with the effort. But, with all her defences on the alert, she could not stem the waves of passion that were beginning to rise within her and threatening to overflow. Despairingly she realised that there was no protection from his devastating caresses, no hope of salvation from his determined onslaughts.

But salvation, when it arrived, did so from an unexpected quarter. There was a knock on the door.

He made no move to release her, seemingly unconcerned with the threatened interruption. She stiffened even more, petrified in case someone walked in and caught them like this.

'There is someone at the door . . .' She made a move

to free herself from him, but he held on maddeningly.

'Let them wait!'

'No . . .' She breathed in panic. 'Let me go, Damien.'

He laughed under his breath. 'Are you nervous of being seen in the arms of your husband?' he teased.

'Yes . . . no . . . oh, do let me go!' With a lightning move she broke away from his grasp and stood up, panting.

He laughed again. 'I can see flames in your eyes that are not those of anger,' he said. 'Or am I to take this as another performance?'

With an angry toss of her head, she walked away from him, not deigning to reply. But to her chagrin she discovered that her hands were trembling disgracefully.

'Come in!' Damien called out loudly. Gulab Singh entered, and bowed stiffly in Crystal's direction.

'We need to hurry,' he said to Damien. 'The train is due to leave in half an hour.'

'Then why the devil didn't you tell me earlier?' he said irritably and, it appeared to Crystal, unreasonably. But Gulab Singh remained unperturbed, obviously used to the Sarkar's mercurial temperament. 'Has everything been loaded?' Damien asked.

'Yes, Sarkar.'

'Good. I shall be downstairs in a moment.' He turned to Crystal as Gulab Singh withdrew. His entire appearance had changed. The tenderness of only a few minutes ago had vanished. His face was again rock hard and his eyes cold and distant. 'I shall see you in two weeks' time, approximately,' he said briskly. 'Gulab Singh has made all the arrangements for your journey. You will no doubt wish to spend time with your family before you leave, but I would be obliged if you would also supervise the packing of all my belongings here, especially my books.' The line of his jaw became taut. 'If you have any designs about delaying your departure, I would advise you to abandon them. You will leave the day after tomorrow, as planned.'

Without another word, without even a gesture of farewell or any sign of affection, he turned on his heel sharply and left the room. Crystal stared after him blankly for a moment. She had never known any man who appeared to have as many facets to his nature as Damien Granville—and, for better or for worse, she was married to all of them!

It was uncommonly soothing to be once again in charge of her own destiny, even if it was only for a short while. The constant tensions of the past weeks had left their mark, and Crystal revelled in her brief release from what she considered no better than bondage. Feeling light and cheerful, she had a frugal supper soon after Damien departed, then retired to her bedroom to complete her reading of Bernier's diaries, which she found enthralling. She read until past midnight, unable to put the book down, then fell fast asleep, exhausted. It seemed such a relief to have her soft comfortable bed all to herself, but she found, to her irritation, that all her dreams were of Damien and of the land of snowy peaks and wild valleys to which he was bearing her off so unwillingly.

She woke to the sound of Sharifa drawing the curtains aside from the windows and to the tinkle of a cup of tea which Rehana put on her bedside table. It was most agreeable sitting up in bed and sipping her steaming hot tea while perusing a copy of the local English paper which Sharifa placed beside her. Crystal yawned and smiled.

'I am hungry this morning, Sharifa. Perhaps I shall have a good breakfast today. Was my . . . was Mr Granville in time for the train last night?'

'Yes, *memsahib*,' the maidservant smiled, 'but only barely. The train was already moving when they reached the railway station.'

'Oh? Then how did they manage to climb on?'

'The Sarkar asked the guard to stop the train.'

'And the guard did?' Crystal said, surprised.

Sharifa looked shocked. 'Of course, *memsahib*! Nobody ever disobeys the Sarkar!'

Crystal smiled grimly. Nobody except his wife, she thought, pursing her lips—but that was something Mr Damien Granville had not yet had time to learn!

After she had bathed and changed into a cool dress of printed linen, Crystal asked for breakfast to be served on the balcony overlooking the river. It was a flawless morning, warm but not yet unbearably hot as Delhi would be in summer.

'What is Gulab Singh doing?' she asked, as she sat down to her meal of papaya, wheat cereal with cream and molasses, and a glass of fruit-juice.

'He is in the Sarkar's study with the coolies arranging the boxing of the Sarkar's effects.'

Crystal remembered that Damien had asked for her to supervise the packing but was well aware that Gulab Singh could safely be left to the task and would do it as efficiently as he did everything else. She had decided to spend the day at Khyber Kothi with her mother and with Robie, knowing how little time she had left in the city.

Suddenly she noticed a packet lying half-concealed under a napkin on the table. 'What is this?' she asked Sharifa.

'The Sarkar asked me to give it to you at breakfast-time.'

'Oh?'

Wonderingly, Crystal undid the parcel. Within the outside wrapping of red paper was something soft rolled up in several layers of tissue-thin paper. Slowly, she pushed aside the layers—and her eyes widened. In her hand she felt a fabric which was the softest she had ever touched. She unfolded it and could not suppress a gasp. It was a shawl of the finest *pashmina* wool, which felt like silk in her hands. On it, all over, were embroidered the most delicate patterns she could imagine. Indeed, so fine were the stitches that they looked like the lines of a paintbrush, this whole shawl giving the impression of an exquisite painting done in the warm, glowing colours of autumn.

'It is a *jaam-e-war*,' said Sharifa, her eyes shining with approval.

'What is a *jaam-e-war*?' Crystal asked, running her fingers over the rippling folds that felt so fragile but were uncommonly warm to the touch.

'It is a very special type of shawl made only in Kashmir,' she explained, her voice full of awe. 'It is woven of the wool taken from the under-fleece of the Angora goat found in the high mountains. It is,' she said proudly, 'the most beautiful craft of the Kashmir valley.'

'Yes,' said Crystal in admiration, 'I can see that.' The shawl was embroidered in an intricate pattern of paisley and the traditional *chinar* leaf she had seen on many Kashmiri articles. There was not a knot to be seen, so the shawl could be worn either side out. It was an object worthy of presentation to a queen, utterly exquisite. She had never possessed an article of clothing that felt so luxurious, so enchantingly rich, and yet so like gossamer against her skin.

Standing before her mirror with the *jaam-e-war* draped around her shoulders, Crystal felt the unpleasant twinges of conscience. She would never have imagined Damien capable of such a generous thought, a gesture of such delicacy. Her eyes clouded momentarily as she recalled the harsh sentiments that had passed through her mind about him last night. What disturbed her was not that he had given her a gift that was so expensive— but that he had thought of giving her a gift at all. She was touched by his consideration and marvelled at yet another side of this complex man with whom she had exchanged such meaningless vows.

The two days passed almost before Crystal knew they had gone. Before she could turn round and breathe, it seemed to her, she was standing on the platform at Delhi station, surrounded by mountainous baggage, ready to embark on the first leg of her journey. The parting from her mother and Robie had been tearful. Kashmir was such a distance away, almost in another age and another space. She had no idea when she would see her beloved ones again. The knowledge that her mother was now so much better gave her much relief, and Robie promised faithfully to look after her well. There was no doubt that he was a much reformed, much chastened man. He had sworn never to go near the gaming-tables again, and Crystal was reassured that this time he meant to keep his promise. His eyes filled with moisture as he stood on the platform waving her goodbye.

'I shall not disappoint you, Crys,' he mumbled in a choked voice as the whistle blew and the guard waved the green flag. 'I . . . I hope you are happy in your life. Give my regards to Damien.'

Crystal nodded, unable to trust her voice. Robie would be joining his regiment soon. How she prayed silently that God would keep him safe.

The long train journey to Amritsar, where the railway-line terminated, was hot and dusty. The square wooden boxes, that were the bogies, shook and rattled all the way, unable to retain their balance as well as they should at the high speed of the train—almost twenty miles an hour. Sharifa and Rehana, attending upon her in her compartment, were as solicitous as always, and Gulab Singh, travelling in an adjoining bogie with two of the male servants, was the epitome of concern, coming into their compartment at every stop to enquire after their well-being.

Crystal knew the Punjab well, having been on several excavations with her father, and the dull, flat countryside did not interest her much. By the time the train staggered tiredly into Amritsar station the next day, she felt rough and soiled with the dust. Even though Gulab Singh had arranged for a tub of ice to be placed in the compartment to provide relief from the persistent heat, she felt drained and her head ached dreadfully. There was, she knew, a long journey still ahead across the plains and then up the Pir Panjal range to the Banihal Pass, but the thought of a good 24-hour rest in Amritsar would settle her admirably. Crystal had always been a good traveller, having been in all kinds of rough terrains with her father. The hard living of the mofussil and the wilds had never deterred her, although now she longed for a cool bath and a bed that did not shake and rattle like the one in the train.

Amritsar was Gulab Singh's home town, being a centre of the Sikhs, and after having installed them comfortably in the *dak* bungalow and having made arrangements for the day's meals, he begged permission to visit his family. They were to leave early the next morning, and Crystal contented herself through the day with recovering her lost sleep and going for a carriage-ride through the city once darkness fell and the air turned cool.

The horses, mountain ponies and teams of coolies who were to make up their caravan arrived at dawn the next morning at the *dak* bungalow. Much refreshed, Crystal was up with the lark, looking forward, not so much to the journey across the dusty plains, but to her first sight of the hills and mountains that lay beyond. She noticed with some amusement that Gulab Singh had thoughtfully ordered for her both a palanquin and a litter in case she wished to be carried for part of the way. She wanted neither, informing him in no uncertain terms that she wished to ride like him on a horse and had no intention of allowing herself to be carried on men's shoulders like a sack of coals. Gulab Singh was a little put out by her comment, having never yet known a woman who preferred to ride on horseback rather than travel in effortless comfort. But he acceded politely to her wishes and immediately ordered a horse to be saddled for her. Sharifa and Rehana, much awed by the *memsahib*'s show of determination, agreed to occupy the palanquin instead, although uncomfortable at the arrangement.

Crystal was amazed at the assortment of their conveyance. There were altogether twenty-six carriers and a further eight hired to carry the palanquin and the litter. There were three grooms, four horses, five Punjabi mules, two goats to provide milk on the way, two *khidmatgars* to serve meals and, of course, Gulab Singh. The mountains of baggage containing Damien's possessions from the Delhi house, as well as her own belongings, were mounted securely on top of the mules, the lighter boxes being carried by the coolies on their heads. They were all sturdy hill people who, Crystal knew from experience, were extremely fleet of foot and capable of carrying tremendous loads without a care. The horse that Crystal was to ride was a beautiful blue roan mare with gentle eyes. She had never been comfortable riding side-saddle, much preferring to sit astride and had garbed herself accordingly, much to the silent horror of the men. But, approved or not, she was not prepared to suffer discomfort for the sake of an impractical convention.

Crystal had travelled this region before with her father, when he had been involved with some archaeological studies at the ruins of Taxila up in the northwest. It was from Koh Murree, just beyond Taxila, that she had first seen the Himalayan snowline and the mountains that surrounded the Vale of Kashmir. It had been a sight never to be forgotten, and her pulse quickened at the thought of penetrating beyond that childhood glimpse, beyond the cold fortifications of the Kasmir valley.

For some time they followed the bed of a small river with not a hill in sight across the dustbowl that was the Punjab plain. The day was hot, but a pleasant breeze blew across the corrugated landscape, making the journey not unpleasant. The smells of the river and the coarse scrubland around revived the many memories of her childhood spent in similar plains, and Crystal allowed herself to dwell silently on the past. Behind her, keeping a watchful eye all round, rode Gulab Singh barking out frequent instructions to the men and seeing that none strayed off course or lagged behind.

As dusk fell, they halted and surprisingly quickly a camp was pitched on the river bank. Before long, a kettle bubbled on the paraffin stove, a goat was milked and a welcome cup of tea arrived to whisk away the tiredness. The meal, cold meats, rice and lentils, was eaten by the river in a hum of conversation that provided the only sounds to break the vast silence of the plain at night. The hustle and bustle of the camp, so like the ones in which she had spent years of her childhood, was pleasant, and Crystal felt her spirits soar at the thought of the rest of the open-air journey that lay ahead.

'Is there anything else that Madam requires?' She heard Gulab Singh's voice behind her as she sat on a boulder by the water's edge.

'Thank you, no,' she replied, smiling. 'You have traversed this way many times, haven't you?'

'Yes. I know it well.'

'And my . . . the Sarkar?'

'The Sarkar also. He was born in my home town of Amritsar, as Madam knows, but was transported to Srinagar, the capital city of Kashmir, when only a year old. This area is as much home to him as it is to me.'

Crystal had not known, but did not say so. 'His father was in the Army, was he not?'

Gulab Singh nodded, and said with a shade of hesitation, 'Until he was married.'

'Oh?'

'Then he resigned, of course.'

Crystal had no idea why the 'of course', but he was presuming she knew the reason and she questioned him no further on the subject. Instead, she looked around. 'Do we arrive at the hills by tomorrow evening?'

'Perhaps. But it is still some time before we reach the Pass. Is Madam tired of riding?' he asked with quick concern.

Crystal laughed. 'Not at all! I have spent many years of my childhood on horseback, Gulab Singh. I do not tire that easily.'

He allowed himself a stiff smile. 'I have arranged for guards to watch your tent during the night. You may sleep without fear.'

'I always sleep without fear,' countered Crystal lightly. 'In any case I am in the habit of carrying my own firearm which remains under my pillow.' Her eyes twinkled. 'I assure you I am quite adept in the use of it.'

'I do not doubt it,' said Gulab Singh quietly. 'If I may say so, Madam is a very brave and very unusual lady.' He bowed and, overwhelmed by his own daring, walked off quickly.

There was no road, as such, to Kashmir, but the track was well used and on the journey they passed stray groups of people coming down into the plains. During the days of the Moghuls, Crystal knew, Kashmir was a much-favoured holiday resort for royalty wishing to escape the hot winds of the plains in summer. In those days, the Moghul emperors made spectacular journeys across these very paths, taking with them retinues of thousands with hundreds of elephants laden with their requirements. Every ten miles or so there were resting-places called *caravanserais* for the comfort of travellers. Each rest-house was built in the same style, a large open quadrangle, corridors serving for stables along two sides, and a suite of rooms facing the main entrance for the royal household. Crystal had read about them in Bernier's diaries, but coming across them now, she was shocked at their state of decay. Most were in sad ruins and some had been washed away by successive river torrents, leaving only the foundations. There were some fairly new halting-places built, said Gulab Singh, by the first Dogra king of Kashmir about thirty years ago, but these were rough when compared with the splendour of the earlier ones.

The route up to the Banihal Pass was spectacular

indeed, but the view from the top and the final descent into the Kashmir valley took Crystal's breath away. The Pass was perched high over the Kashmir valley, and the air was icy as the freezing winds raged and whistled around them. But Crystal was aware of nothing except the unbelievable panorama that lay spread out in the far distance. They began the descent, watching the Vale of Kashmir unfold before their eyes. It was a breathtaking sight.

'There is no place on earth,' said Gulab Singh with pride, 'where one can see a complete circle of snowy mountains surrounding a plain the length and breadth of this valley.'

Crystal nodded. 'Enclosed on all sides like a precious jewel . . .' she breathed, recalling the description she had read in a book by a sixth-century traveller in Kashmir. *'Learning, lofty houses, saffron, icy water and grapes,'* the traveller had written ecstatically. *'Things that even in heaven are difficult to find.'*

At the foot of their descent lay a vast carpet woven in a thousand shades of green interspersed with all the colours of the rainbow from pale lavender to vibrant browns and blues. Threading their way in between were shimmering streams concealed intermittently by a crouching mist. Embracing the lush valley on all sides were the snowy mountains reaching high into a sky of pure azure. It was like a shop-window so laden with beautiful wares that one did not know where to look first.

They soon left the icy winds of the Pass behind and entered a land of eternal spring with fruit-trees heavy with blossom—apple, pear, peach, apricot, cherry and mulberry. Sprawling meadows of emerald-green grass covered the rolling slopes like velvet, and all round were waving fields of rice, saffron crocuses and wild flowers such as Crystal had never seen before. It was as if the ground were enamelled with colour and the entire scene prepared by some divine paintbrush. Bernier had described this Vale as 'the terrestial paradise of the Indies'. Crystal now knew what he had meant.

Watching her, Gulab Singh asked softly. 'Madam is impressed?'

With her eyes wide in disbelief at so much beauty concentrated in one blessed valley, Crystal swallowed hard. 'Madam is . . . dumbfounded!'

They halted for a meal in a meadow covered with violets and narcissus growing wild alongside a babbling brook. The air was scented with the perfumes of a thousand blooms and herbs that intoxicated the senses and made one drowsy. As they ate, Gulab Singh pointed out to Crystal the peaks that were considered holy by the Hindus of the region: Harmukh to the east and Mahadeo to the south. To the east and north rose the ranges of the Himalayas and beyond stood the Zaskar and Ladakh ranges, and the Karakorams.

'Many of these peaks have never been scaled,' said Gulab Singh. 'Perhaps they never will.'

'It would be heresy to put a human foot on such fragments of heaven. It would defile the incredible purity of those chaste snows,' said Crystal in awe. 'They are made only for the gods.'

It was as they were almost upon the town of Srinagar, and could already see glimpses of the Dal Lake upon which it stood, that Crystal asked, 'Is Shalimar situated within the town?'

Gulab Singh laughed and shook his head. 'The Sarkar would never consent to live in any town, even one as beautiful as Srinagar. The estate is about ten miles outside the town on the road to Gulmarg.'

'And is it very large?' She was suddenly filled with excited curiosity to know more about her home to be. All this while she had closed her heart and mind stubbornly to everything connected with Damien. Now, with a vision of Kashmir before her eyes, she realised with a sense of shock that nothing had prepared her for what she saw. That Kashmir was beautiful she had heard from many and read about in books. But the extent of its beauty was something that had taken her completely by surprise. It was like being poised at the very gates of paradise!

'Yes,' said Gulab Singh in answer to her question. 'Shalimar runs to about five miles in one direction and four in the other.'

'Twenty square miles!' she exclaimed. 'Why, it is like a little kingdom, then.'

He nodded solemnly. 'Yes, it could be called that.'

'But surely it is rare for an Englishman to own land in Kashmir? How did my husband come to acquire such a vast estate?' She flushed as she realised how ignorant she must seem to Gulab Singh about the man to whom she was wed.

'Indeed, it is rare,' he explained patiently. 'The Sarkar's father, the late Colonel Edward Granville, was of considerable service in administrative matters to the late Maharaja Gulab Singh who had ascended the throne a few years before Colonel Granville came to Kashmir. Furthermore, Colonel Granville had a dream to breed the finest *pashmina* goats in Kashmir itself. Until then, the best wool came from the goats of the Tibetan mountains. As a reward for his services to the state, and in order to encourage the breeding of these rare goats in Kashmir, His Highness gifted him Shalimar.'

'And has the breeding of goats improved as a result of Colonel Granville's efforts—and my husband's?'

Gulab Singh's chest expanded visibly. 'Certainly. In fact, under the present Maharaja, the shawl industry has not only flourished, but our shawls are now to be found all over the world. Some of that credit goes undoubtedly to our efforts at Shalimar.'

'I see. And it was Gulab Singh, the first Maharaja of Kashmir, who paid the British seven and a half million rupees for Kashmir in 1846 after the conquest of the Punjab by the British?'

'Yes. My father served with the Maharaja at the battle

of Subraon, and,' he coloured slightly, 'I was named after His Highness.'

Crystal pondered all this information. 'My husband loves his home and Kashmir very much, doesn't he?' she asked thoughtfully.

'Yes,' said Gulab Singh quietly. 'They are his life.'

It was almost dark by the time they arrived in Srinagar, the ancient city founded by the emperor Ashoka in the third century BC. The rest were to go on to Shalimar. Gulab Singh, Sharifa and Rehana, and one *khidmatgar* were to stay on with Crystal, and escort her to Shalimar the next morning.

'My husband has a house in Srinagar?' Crystal asked, pleased at the prospect of exploring, even for a brief while, this tiny jewel of a town that was the capital of the state.

Gulab Singh allowed himself the luxury of a smile. 'Not a house, Madam, but a house*boat*.'

'A houseboat!' Crystal exclaimed. 'Oh, how delightful! On the Dal Lake? Why, I can hardly wait!'

Once within the town she dismounted and, with Gulab Singh and Sharifa on either side, decided to walk. It was the hour of dusk and the narrow cobbled streets were filled with jostling crowds, chattering away like crowds in India do. There was brisk selling in the stalls that lined the streets, and the Kashmiris in their fitted skull-caps and turbans and their flowing garments cast many a curious stare in her direction, still not being used to the sight of white-faced women in their midst.

'What on earth do they all carry inside their clothes?' Crystal asked, noticing the curious bulge in their garments.

'Their *kangris*,' said Sharifa. 'To keep them warm.'

'*Kangris?*'

'Yes, little mud pots in which they carry live coals.'

Crystal laughed in amazement. 'You mean they carry *stoves* under their clothes? How very odd! I should be frightened to death of burning myself to cinders!'

At the jetty made of thick wooden planks, they embarked in a tiny *shikara* boat that was to carry them to their own houseboat. The waters of the lake were alive with the lights of the town reflected in their depths, and the surface was thick with lotus-leaves and blossoms. The air on the water was cold, and Crystal pulled her thick fleece-lined jacket closer around her. The western horizons were still touched with faint streaks of orange and pink, and the white caps of the mountains were tinged with colour, making them glow like luminescent cones.

Damien's houseboat was huge, very long and low with a flat terrace on top. A wooden stairway reached down by the side of the *shikara* as willing hands helped Crystal on board. It was a houseboat such as Crystal had never seen or imagined. It had a large cosy sitting-room, two bedrooms with a dining-room by the side. It was beautifully furnished and pleasantly warm, with the walls hung with paintings, and everywhere the signs of attention and care. She noticed that it was called *Nishat*.

Crystal laughed delightedly. 'Why, it is like a little floating palace with every convenience imaginable! Does my husband stay here often?'

'Whenever he passes through Srinagar,' Gulab Singh said. 'He has many business interests in town.'

In the master bedroom, Crystal's travelling bags had been arranged neatly on the table. This was obviously the room that Damien used when he stayed in town. Unlike the furnishings in the Delhi house, the materials used here were light and flowery and the furniture of pale walnut wood. The large bed dominated the room, and the vases were filled with spring blossoms. On a desk stood a pipe-rack filled with pipes, and the bookcase bulged with volumes of every description. Some of Damien's clothes hung in the large *almirah* and a pair of fleece-lined slippers peeped out from under the bed. The room carried a faint scent of tobacco, such as she had smelt on her first visit to the Delhi mansion.

All the innocuous mementos of Damien's powerful personality made Crystal realise that the pleasant interlude would soon be at an end. Tomorrow, she would be with Damien again, once more a slave to his commands, expected to fulfil his every whim. The prospect of his overwhelming nearness filled her with unwelcome turbulence. Oddly enough, she dreaded his presence—yet wanted it at the same time! Very irritated with the confusing contradictions of her wayward heart, she sat down to a simple meal of Indian bread and lamb chops grilled in spices, and fresh fruit. However unwelcome the prospect of seeing Damien again might be, there was no doubt that it was also strangely exciting.

At Crystal's insistence, the journey to Shalimar was postponed to later in the morning.

'I would like to explore the town,' she said firmly, 'and this appears to be an excellent opportunity to do so.'

Gulab Singh looked uneasy. 'But the Sarkar has ordered that . . .'

'The Sarkar will understand my anxiety to become acquainted with Srinagar,' she said sharply, 'and a few hours will make no difference.'

Gulab Singh capitulated with a sigh. 'Very well. I will ask for a palanquin . . .'

'I shall walk,' insisted Crystal. 'It would be a crime not to do so, considering all the delights of this town.'

In the brilliant light of the morning sun, the Dal lake shimmered like a cloth of gold, and the large pink and white lotus-blossoms bobbed and undulated with the ripples. There were a number of *shikaras* about, and Crystal could see many other houseboats moored along the banks. However, none was as splendid as the *Nishat*, painted white with green roof and railings. The tiny jumbled wooden houses lining the narrow cobbled lanes all seemed to have pointed roofs and latticed windows with intricate shutters. The town looked incredibly quaint and very old. As there was not much time, Crystal decided that she would like to visit at least one of the famous Moghul gardens for which the country was famous. At one time, she had read, there were as many as seven hundred such gardens of varying sizes in Kashmir. The two most famous, said Gulab Singh, were the Shalimar Gardens and the Nishat Gardens—after which Damien's estate and houseboat, respectively, had been named—and the Chashma Shahi, garden of the royal fountain.

But Gulab Singh extracted his pocket-watch and consulted it meaningfully. 'The Moghul gardens are not such that they can be visited in a hurry. To appreciate them fully one must spend time there.'

'But surely we can spare an hour or two now?' protested Crystal.

'The Sarkar will be expecting Madam at luncheon,' he said firmly, 'and it would not be wise to keep him waiting. Besides . . .' he coughed, 'the Moghul gardens are the pride of every Kashmiri. It is likely that the Sarkar would wish to escort Madam around them himself.'

Crystal opened her mouth instinctively to disagree, but then decided against it. Even in the matter of seeing a garden, she thought to herself irritably, it appeared that the Sarkar's will had to prevail! Nevertheless she accepted Gulab Singh's suggestion that she should, perhaps, inspect some of the bazaars of the town instead, as they contained much that was worth seeing. Crystal had seen many beautiful things from Kashmir in the shops of Delhi, but no doubt there would be much more variety to be had in Srinagar. Besides, the remembrance of Damien's gift of an exquisite *jaam-e-war* caused her momentary unease again. She had not thought to buy him anything in Delhi. Indeed, in her bitterness against him, the idea had not even occurred to her. Perhaps it might be polite to now return the compliment.

Once again, with Gulab Singh and Sharifa walking determinedly on either side, Crystal strolled with fascination along the narrow cobbled lanes lined with small, dark shops that seemed filled with people. She inspected one or two but found that she could hardly make out anything in the gloom. On learning that she was searching for a gift for the Sarkar, Gulab Singh immediately led the way along winding lanes to an emporium where goods of high quality were to be found. They entered a house through a low doorway, crossed a stone courtyard filled with potted flowers and greenery and climbed a stone staircase into a large airy room filled with tastefully arranged handicafts. There were shawls, carpets, papier mâché objects, walnut-wood carvings, silver trinkets and cupboards full of coats and jackets. The owner of the emporium, a short, plump Kashmiri called Hyder Ali, bowed low when he learned of her identity.

'A gift for Mr Granville?' he asked, rubbing his hands together in anticipation. 'I have just the thing Madam seeks.'

Since Crystal had not the vaguest idea of what it was she sought, she said nothing but waited curiously to see what he would produce. He disappeared into an inner room and appeared almost immediately with a large leather box. But before opening it he arranged his important customer comfortably on a thick mattress on the floor lined with bolsters, and rapidly ordered cups of tea. Then he opened the box and, from within, extracted the most beautiful embroidered woollen jackets Crystal had ever seen. They were without sleeves but had small high collars, and two pockets on either side. The wool was as soft as down and as smooth as satin, and the embroidery, bold and colourful, was striking. The inside was lined with silk and they were indeed very well finished.

'Is it *pashmina* wool?' asked Crystal.

Hyder Ali looked shocked. 'But of course, Madam! I would not dare to offer anything but the very best for a gentleman of Mr Granville's calibre.'

Crystal looked at Gulab Singh uncertainly. 'Do you think my husband would like a jacket such as this?'

Gulab Singh nodded. 'The Sarkar is indeed very fond of these jackets,' he assured her. 'In fact, he very recently destroyed one by absent-mindedly putting in its pocket a pipe that was not fully extinguished. He was extremely upset at the loss.'

'Oh, good,' Crystal said, satisfied. 'I will take this one, then.'

While the jacket was being parcelled, they sipped their tea and made polite conversation. Hyder Ali subtly tried to interest Crystal in the further purchase of a shawl so unusual that she was almost tempted. It was like a fragment of mist, incredibly warm, yet fine enough to be pulled through a ring from one's finger. Crystal marvelled at such delicate weaving and fingered it wonderingly.

'Our shawls go back to the time of the first Moghul emperor,' Hyder Ali said, 'and now they are to be seen even in Europe, is it not so?'

Crystal answered that she did not know, but had heard that Napoleon had bought Kashmiri shawls for his Josephine and had thus made them very popular in France. Hyder Ali was delighted with the information, promising to pass it on to his select clients.

Finally, all the transactions completed, they rose to leave. Hyder Ali bowed even lower than before. 'My heartiest felicitations to you, Madam, and to Mr Granville, on your marriage. It is indeed a match made by the angels of heaven!'

Or the devils of the other place, thought Crystal drily as they descended the steps to the street. The future would soon tell to which of these the credit—or otherwise—should go! In the meantime, Shalimar, and the Sarkar, awaited. It was a prospect about which she was beginning to have decidedly confused feelings.

CHAPTER FIVE

SHALIMAR!

The wrought iron gates, tall and painted black, loomed ahead. On either side was a small lodge, neat and covered in creepers with tumbling white blossoms, meant obviously for the gate keepers. Soundlessly, the gates swept open as their cavalcade arrived, and the attendants, clad in dark green liveries, touched their splendid yellow turbans with their hands in a salute. Crystal peered excitedly through the curtain of her palanquin, longing for a better view of what lay ahead but unable to get it from her cloistered seat. The palanquin had been a subject for much discussion between her and Gulab Singh in Srinagar, but this time he had remained firm. It would not be seemly, he insisted, for the bride of the Sarkar to arrive at Shalimar sitting astride a horse. The Sarkar would not approve and the staff would be shocked. Reluctantly, Crystal had given in. She had, after all, had her own way until now and to argue about so minor a matter would seem childishly stubborn.

Fleet-footed, the palanquin-bearers swept down the winding drive with confidence. From what little Crystal could see, on either side of the broad avenue were tall, lush *chinar* trees with vast parklands beyond. There were flowering shrubs everywhere and clusters of blooms in well-ordered beds at which gardeners worked. As the palanquin passed, they rose and eyed it curiously, folding their hands in greeting. Here and there she could see small spotted deer nibbling at the grass. Of the house itself she could see nothing.

The avenue began to rise gently and soon they arrived in what appeared to be a vast pillared portico. Gently, the palanquin was set down, and, crouching uncomfortably, Crystal stepped out to find she was confronted by a series of wide steps that led up into a hallway with glass doors. The steps were lined by about a hundred people, standing in hushed silence, all staring at Crystal with open curiosity as she stepped out into the portico. There were women and children, several men in the same dark green livery and yellow turbans and many without, all with folded hands.

Crystal looked at them and smiled nervously. 'Who are all these people?' she asked Sharifa, who stepped out from the palanquin behind.

'Some are the Sarkar's staff and their families and the others live and work on the estate.' In her favoured position of chief maidservant to the new bride, Sharifa now proceeded to shout out brisk orders, very much aware of her seniority and importance.

But of the Sarkar himself there was no sign.

As the baggage began to be off-loaded, Gulab Singh led the way up the steps amidst the hum of muted comments, some of which Crystal could understand. 'She is beautiful,' said a woman's voice as she passed. 'But then that is only to be expected of the Sarkar's wife.'

'And how brown she is!' commented another voice. 'Almost like a Kashmiri.'

'Surely, she is not a white woman,' remarked a third. 'She is not at all like the others.'

Flushing with embarrassment at being the unwilling object of so much curiosity, however well meaning, Crystal quickly followed Gulab Singh into the house. The hall which they entered was enormous, with polished wooden flooring covered partially by rich Persian carpets in glowing colours. There were great clusters of flowers everywhere, arranged beautifully in tall vases either of brass or of porcelain and glass. Crystal had no idea what the exterior of the house looked like but the interior showed unmistakable signs of elegance and refinement—and wealth. On the pale cream walls hung oil-paintings and fine tapestries, each one selected with care and in impeccable good taste. Did all of Damien's wealth come from the working of his estate, Crystal wondered again, or from other lucrative pursuits such as—gambling? It was a thought that had caused her unease before, and now, confronted by evidence of his riches, she felt disturbed again.

Her own apartment was on the first floor and she could not suppress an exclamation of pleasure as she stepped inside. The sitting-room, large and rectangular, was airy with sunshine pouring in from the huge glassed-in windows. It was very different from the room she had left behind in Damien's rented house in Delhi. Instead of being exotic and overwhelmingly opulent, it was restful with muted furnishings and signs of the same quiet elegance noticeable elsewhere. Not a single object overpowered the senses, each chosen with thoughtful care. Unlike the Delhi mansion, this gave the indication of a home, luxurious yet restful, designed to be lived in. To one side of the room was a sprawling open fireplace in which burned a leaping log fire filling the room with a scent of pine. Adjoining was an equally large bedroom, also warm and sun-drenched, a dressing-room and a bath with excellent modern fittings.

But it was the vista presented through the glassed-in windows that ran the length of the apartment that held Crystal's attention and made her tremble with wide-eyed wonder. The land sloped gently into a valley clothed in a patchwork of fields, with tiny villages nestling amid clumps of bottle-green trees. Shades of yellow, brown and cinnamon ran gaily into each other and one side of the valley was carpeted with a riot of wild flowers. Away in the far distance, at the bottom of the valley, the grass fell gently into the waters of a winding stream bestrewn with mossy boulders. All this is the jealous, never-failing embrace of the majestic mountains capped with snow and shining white against a sky of pure sapphire.

It was a sight of such splendour that Crystal could only stand and stare. To awaken to this every morning! Oh, it was too incredible for words!

A discreet cough in the background drew her sharply back into reality. 'If there is anything else Madam desires,' said Gulab Singh, 'Madam has only to ask. Sharifa and the girl will be, of course, in constant attendance.' Noticing the look of silent enquiry on her face, he added, 'The Sarkar is away at the moment, I understand. They expect him back tomorrow.'

Crystal felt a sudden stab of something—but was not sure whether it was relief or disappointment! 'So much for our undue rush in getting here today,' she said acidly. 'We could well have stayed on in Srinagar and visited all the gardens!'

'Perhaps,' said Gulab Singh calmly. 'But the Sarkar's orders were quite clear. They had to be obeyed.'

The Sarkar's orders! It was a phrase of which Crystal was becoming increasingly weary. Why, he was like a despot from the middle ages! But, however much she wanted to, she decided not to express the stinging retort that sprang to her lips. Instead, she merely said, 'I shall be very comfortable here, Gulab Singh, thank you. It is a beautiful apartment.'

'The Sarkar's apartment adjoins Madam's,' he said, walking to a door that she had noticed before. He flung it open for her. 'This is the Sarkar's sitting-room.'

Curious, she stepped into the room. In size and shape it was like her own, but its other aspects were completely different. It was, very strongly, a man's room with books lining the walls from floor to ceiling, leather armchairs and furnishings in unadorned block colours. Nevertheless, it was by no means stark, giving the impression of comfort without fussiness, elegance without any desire to overwhelm. The room exuded the same powerful aroma of sweet tobacco, and she noticed a shining brass hookah set beside an easy chair by the open fireplace. Even though Damien was not here, a low fire burned in the grate, obviously to keep the room warm for his return.

For a fleeting instant, overwhelmed by souvenirs of his presence, she felt a longing for him to return. Then, shocked and startled at the waywardness of her heart, she replaced it with a surge of anger. How thoughtless of him to allow her to step foot in Shalimar without being here to receive her! Surely nothing could be so urgent as to demand his attention at so important a moment in her life? Perhaps he had not even remembered that she was to come here today. Perhaps to him her arrival was only a detail to be lost in the general business of his everyday life.

Feeling suddenly very alone and depressed, she dismissed Gulab Singh and wandered miserably about Damien's apartment. His bedchamber next door was filled with his belongings that she remembered from Delhi. On a hook behind the bathroom door was his silken robe; by the side of the washbasin rested a pipe, half-filled and forgotten. A pocket watch, one of many, undoubtedly, lay ticking on his dressing-table. The dove-grey suit he had worn for the wedding hung neatly in his clothes cupboard filled with the aroma of his powerful masculinity. She felt her eyes moisten, but then she shook herself impatiently, appalled at the silly fantasies of her mind. If Damien Granville could not even be bothered to remember that she was arriving today, why should it cause her any concern? She knew he cared nothing for her and the fact that her own thoughts were veering towards him constantly was a matter of ignominy. She determined to think of him no more and instead start to acquaint herself pleasurably with the prospects of Shalimar.

Sharifa had already started to unpack her belongings

and was sorting out the clothes that were to go for washing and pressing. It was well past two o'clock and Crystal ordered for herself a light lunch of lamb kababs with a salad, and a bowl of fresh peaches. Then she sent for Gulab Singh and enquired if he were otherwise occupied.

'No, Madam. I am at your service,' he said.

'In that case, would it be possible for me to be shown round the estate? I am most curious to see it.'

'Certainly,' Gulab Singh bowed. 'I will order the horses.'

Crystal changed quickly into her riding-habit, a deep indigo with a tight bodice, a collar like a man's jacket, fitting sleeves and a long straight skirt. With it she wore her shining black riding-boots. It was a habit meant for riding side-saddle, a compromise Crystal felt inclined to make, considering the conservative attitudes probably prevailing on the estate. Whatever her differences with Damien, she felt she could not undermine his position by being unnecessarily rebellious. In any case, she was well used to the side-saddle and knew it would cause her no hardship. On her head she wore a silk scarf. Her father had once explained to her that, to Indians, a woman with an uncovered head was indecent. Certainly no Indian woman would presume to go around bareheaded without invoking scorn.

Down in the spacious stables, filled with horses and ponies, Gulab Singh had selected for her a light brown mare called Yasmin. In the adjoining stall stood a splendid shining black horse with flaring nostrils and the devil's own eyes. He glared at Crystal angrily and snorted, scraping the floor with his hooves.

Gulab Singh laughed. 'That is the Sarkar's other mount. He is called Shaitan, the Devil, because he has a temper as fierce as one. Only the Sarkar can handle him. The one he is using now is a bay gelding which is more amenable to company.'

Watched by Gulab Singh and some of the grooms,

Crystal stepped on to the mounting-box and swung herself elegantly into the saddle. It felt comfortable and she smiled with pleasure. Gulab Singh nodded approvingly. Obviously, today he could not fault either her feminine apparel or her demure, dignified behaviour! He himself mounted his own horse, a piebald called Sikandar, the Indian name for the Greek king Alexander.

They started off at a slow trot, in the direction away from the entrance gates. As the distance between them and the house increased, Crystal saw it clearly for the first time. It was double-storeyed, symmetrical in design, and appeared to be uncommonly large, almost like a small palace, which it had once been. It was painted white, with the windows picked out in green.

They travelled first through a field of delicately tinted purple flowers of saffron, which was a monopoly of Kashmir from ancient times. Used in worship from time immemorial by the Hindus, Greeks and the Romans, saffron yielded a perfume which, legend said, the Greeks sprinkled in their public places, and the Romans in the streets each time the emperor Nero entered the city. All over India, the saffron was mixed with rice dishes to give them added colour and scent.

They passed through orchards bursting with fruit, and Gulab Singh explained that in Kashmir the seasons changed at every thousand feet of elevation. The valley could therefore be blessed with snow, spring blossoms and summer fruit all at the same time, depending upon where one happened to be. They arrived at a small cluster of huts thatched with reeds from the lakes. Under the shade of spreading trees, sat groups of weavers working their looms. As they approached, the men rose and bowed in greeting.

'What are they weaving,' asked Crystal. 'Shawls?'

'Yes. In the olden days the finest *pashmina* wool had to come from the Tibetan mountains. But now we breed these special goats here at Shalimar and they are,' his chest expanded visibly, 'the finest in the whole valley.'

'And Kashmiris have made these beautiful shawls for centuries?'

'Indeed yes, but the industry was developed commercially under the Moghuls. They used to wear in their turbans a jewelled ornament known as the *jigha*, shaped like an almond. On top of this *jigha* was an aigrette of feathers. One of the old weavers imitated this design in a scarf he made for the emperor Babar, the first of the Moghuls. It was so well liked that this design was adopted all over India, and also in Persia, and it is to be seen also in carpets. The *jigha*, the *chinar* leaf, the paisley shaped like a young mango, all these are motifs much favoured in Kashmir, as you can see in these shawls the men are weaving. The Sarkar himself has done a great deal to encourage . . .' He broke off abruptly, as one of the grooms rode up through the trees. They exchanged a few words, then Gulab Singh frowned, appearing suddenly ill at ease.

'Some visitors have arrived to see Madam,' he said tersely.

'Visitors?' Crystal was surprised. 'Who are they?'

'Mrs Adele Hathaway and Captain Saunders. The Sarkar is . . . acquainted with them.' He looked very uncomfortable indeed. 'Mrs Hathaway is a widowed lady who has been living in Srinagar.' About Saunders he said nothing.

Much put out by the interruption in what promised to be an enjoyable exploration, Crystal reluctantly turned her mount and followed Gulab Singh back to the house. However, she could not resist lingering pleasurably in the warm sunshine, loath to abandon the glories of Nature on all sides.

'These mulberry trees are for breeding silkworms, aren't they?' she asked, pausing at one. 'Kashmir has lovely silks, I know.'

Gulab Singh smiled. 'Madam is unusually well informed. It is a rare virtue in women and one that the Sarkar regards highly.'

Had Crystal not been riding a horse, she would have undoubtedly stamped her foot. How maddening that all conversations should inevitably lead back to the Sarkar—and how condescending Gulab Singh sounded, just like his employer!

They returned to the house by a slightly different route, skirting the neatly tended kitchen-gardens at the back and the vineyards with great clusters of grapes hanging in purple profusion.

'Shalimar is self-sufficient in its requirements as far as food is concerned,' Gulab Singh said with complacent pride. 'The Sarkar has seen to that. During the famine we were feeding hundreds every day.'

'There is so much that I want to see here,' said Crystal crossly, 'and I am annoyed at these people arriving without prior intimation.'

'Mrs Hathaway is rather a . . . forceful lady,' said Gulab Singh uncomfortably.

'And this Captain Saunders?'

Gulab Singh seemed to stiffen. 'I would not like to comment upon Captain Saunders,' he said coldly. 'The Sarkar does not like him.'

'Oh, I see.'

Much amused and instantly curious to meet them both, Crystal dismounted outside the stable door and handed over the reins to the groom. Her first visitors at Shalimar! Well, she thought, it might turn out to be an amusing afternoon after all, and the very fact that Damien did not care for Captain Saunders immediately predisposed her towards him!

She took a few minutes to freshen her face and hair and change into sandals and a silk dress. The visitors had been seated in the formal drawing-room on the first-floor wing opposite the private apartments. The room, which she had not had occasion to see before, was like an audience hall in some luxurious imperial palace. There were rich hangings and Kasan carpets on the walls, with fine French furniture, gilt mirrors and Belgian glass chandeliers. The wooden floor was completely covered with exotic Bukhara carpets and there was a profusion of beautiful clocks and porcelain. On one wall hung large oil portraits of a man and a very delicately featured woman, both in western clothes.

Crystal stopped and gazed in amazement, not at the splendour of the room, but at Mrs Adele Hathaway. For some reason, she had presumed her to be an elderly lady. The vision that confronted her now was not only young but also startlingly attractive. She was tall, but slight of figure, and her grooming could not have been faulted even in the drawing-rooms of London and Paris. For a moment Crystal remained poised in surprise. Then, recovering her manners, she smiled and stepped forward, hand outstretched.

'Mrs Hathaway? I am Crystal Cov . . . er . . . Granville,' she bit her lip vexedly at the inadvertant slip.

Adele Hathaway took the proffered hand in her own and subjected Crystal to a long, penetrating stare. For some reason that Crystal could not divine, the scrutiny did not please her. Her lips tightened a little and a hard look came into her pea-green eyes. However, when she spoke, her voice was warm and friendly.

'My dear Mrs Granville, how delightful to meet you at last! We have been hearing all kinds of accounts of you, haven't we, Henry?' A tall figure, whom Crystal had not noticed before, detached itself from a far window and came forward. 'Mrs Granville,' Adele Hathaway continued, 'may I present Captain Henry Saunders? We are both old friends of Damien.'

Crystal shook hands dutifully with Henry Saunders, who was thin and angular with sandy hair and very pale blue eyes. She could not help feeling a little bewildered. 'I am very pleased to meet you, but . . . what kind of accounts of me have you been hearing, and from whom?'

Adele Hathaway tinkled with amusement with a laugh like the sound of very tiny bells. 'Ah!' she exclaimed coyly. 'That would be telling . . . but we do have friends in common in Delhi.'

'Indeed we do,' echoed Henry Saunders. 'The Smythes.'

'Oh.' Crystal subsided into momentary silence. She could well imagine the accounts they had received of her from them!

'And how do you like being in this wonderful, wonderful, place, my dear?' asked Adele.

Crystal looked her straight in the eyes, not liking her very much but without being able to decipher the reason. At close quarters she was much older than she had looked from a distance. There were small lines around the eyes, and the effort to conceal them with skilfully applied cosmetics had not been completely successful.

'I haven't really had a chance to see very much of it yet,' she replied, adding pointedly, 'Indeed, I was on a tour of the estate when you arrived.'

Adele Hathaway took the remark in her stride by ignoring it. 'Oh yes, the estate. Damien is so proud of it, isn't he, Henry? It is a place that I have always loved. So peaceful, so away from the noise and dirt of Srinagar.'

'You know Shalimar well?' asked Crystal, not knowing quite where the conversation was leading.

'Of course!' Adele's large eyes opened wide as if in surprise. 'Why, I have seen every inch of it with Damien. Oh, he is so in love with his Shalimar, isn't he, Henry? He hardly has time for anything else!' She laughed again as though the fact was in some way displeasing to her.

'Well, if I had an estate like Shalimar,' said Henry Saunders, suddenly making his second comment of the evening, 'I wouldn't have time for anything else either . . . er . . . except my lovely wife, of course!'

'How right you are,' sighed Adele. 'Damien is away,

isn't he?' Crystal nodded. 'He promised to come and see me in Srinagar last week and never did. I shall have words to say to him when I see him!'

The door opened and a liveried bearer wheeled in a large trolley loaded with tea-things and fruit. Crystal heaved a silent sigh of relief. Pouring out tea would give her something to do while the idle conversation proceeded. She busied herself with the teapot while the bearer handed out the cakes and sandwiches.

'Did you have time to see something of Srinagar?' asked Adele, nibbling delicately on a sandwich.

'Not very much,' said Crystal with a rueful smile. 'But I hope to return soon and make a thorough investigation of everything. It seemed a delightful place.'

'Oh yes, it is, if you can ignore the dirt in the streets,' said Adele, crinkling her perfect nose in distaste. 'And the people are so . . . coarse, somehow.'

'Do you think so?' asked Crystal in surprise. 'That was not the impression I got. I thought some of the people I saw in the streets were extremely handsome.'

Adele shrugged carelessly. 'Yes, there are some that could be taken almost for Europeans with their light eyes and pale hair. Well, like Nafisa, for instance. She could pass for a European easily if she were to change her mode of dressing.' She picked up another sandwich to nibble at while Captain Saunders looked acutely embarrassed.

'Who is Nafisa?' Crystal asked innocently.

Adele's eyes dilated in sudden horror and her hand flew to her mouth. For an instant she said nothing. Rising abruptly, Henry Saunders went and stood by the window.

'Oh, my dear!' Adele Hathaway gasped. 'Oh, I *am* sorry! I thought you . . . knew . . .'

Crystal stared from one to the other in perplexity. 'Knew what?'

'About Nafisa . . .' She took out a tiny fragment of lace and dabbed her eyes quickly.

'But who *is* Nafisa? I'm afraid I do not recognise the name. Should I?'

'Nafisa is Damien's . . .' She shook her head in distress. 'My dear, you must forget what I have said. It was . . . quite unthinking of me! I thought you must know because, well, everybody in Kashmir knows . . .'

An ugly suspicion was beginning to form in Crystal's mind, and her hands went suddenly cold. But, with supreme effort, she retained her composure and said as coolly as she could manage, 'Well, I'm afraid I don't quite know what you are talking about. There are many . . . friends of Damien's that I have yet to meet.' In fact, she had not met any at all, but she certainly was not going to tell Adele Hathaway that. There was something about Adele that was already confirming her dislike. She wondered, uncomfortably, just how well Damien did know her.

Plunging into the conversation in an effort to redeem it, Captain Saunders said quickly, 'I know Srinagar well, and should you ever wish to make a chukker of it, I would be honoured to escort you. That is, if Damien will allow it.'

'Oh, I'm sure Damien will escort me himself when he returns,' she said calmly. 'After all, he does know this area like the back of his hand.'

'Of course, of course,' he said quickly. 'But I know how busy Damien is . . .'

Changing the trend of the conversation, Crystal asked politely, 'Are you stationed in Srinagar, Captain Saunders?'

'Yes, but only temporarily. I am here on special deputation from the Punjab Army headquarters in Lahore.'

'Oh?' Crystal made an effort at polite interest, although her mind was not in the subject at all.

'Yes. There is a fear at headquarters that the Russian influence in this area is growing. Some strange people seem to be infiltrating into Kashmir through Gilgit and Tibet in the north.'

'Really?' Crystal had heard the subject discussed in Delhi.

'Oh yes,' he said, warming to his theme. 'The problem is, of course, far more acute in Afghanistan, but then that isn't very far away, is it?'

'You mean there are Russian agents coming into Kashmir?' she asked with a disbelieving laugh.

'Don't pay any attention to Henry, dear,' said Adele with scorn. 'He sees Russian agents behind every *chinar*!'

Henry Saunders flushed. 'That is not true, Adele. It is well known that the Russians have some very profitable connections in this area. It is not, I assure you, a matter to be laughed at!' He sounded quite angry.

Very tactfully, Crystal again diverted the trend of the conversation, not wanting to plunge into a political discussion with strangers whom she did not much like. 'No, I am sure it is not,' she said soothingly. 'I have heard it mentioned frequently in Delhi. But tell me, Captain Saunders,' she said, leaning forward and giving him her entire attention, 'since you do seem to know this area so well, what are the places that one should see in Kashmir? Would you recommend the Wular Lake, for instance?'

Flattered, Henry Saunders's eyes lit up and he immediately launched into a rather tedious monologue on areas that Crystal had already read a great deal about. But she listened wide-eyed and apparently fascinated, her mind occupied with something else entirely. Adele Hathaway listened to his recital with ill-concealed impatience for a while, then, taking advantage of a gap in the monologue, stood up.

'Come on, Henry,' she commanded imperiously. 'It really is time we started back. Mrs Granville has arrived only this afternoon and I'm sure she would like to rest.'

Immediately, Henry flushed again, sprang to his feet and said awkwardly, 'Oh, I do apologise for . . . for having got carried away . . .'

'Not at all,' said Crystal graciously, rising as well, and much relieved that they were finally leaving. 'I have learned a great deal from you this afternoon.'

'You and Damien must come and dine with me one evening soon,' said Adele at the door of the drawing-room. 'He says my cook makes the best *gushtav* in Srinagar. It is his favourite dish, you know.'

Crystal had no idea what *gushtav* was, but refrained from enquiring. She could easily get the information later from Sharifa. Captain Saunders paused briefly before an oil-painting which hung at the far end of the room, and Adele hastily took the opportunity to whisper in Crystal's ear, 'You must forgive me for my slip, my dear, and please don't ask Damien about . . . Nafisa. He would be furious if he knew that I had told you, when he has not himself.'

In her eyes was a faint glimmer of triumph, which Crystal did not miss. Nevertheless, she smiled composedly. 'There are very few secrets between my husband and myself. If he has not told me, I'm sure it is only because it is of no consequence.' The lie came easily to her. She had no intention of allowing Adele the satisfaction of knowing just how deeply she had succeeded in disturbing her.

Henry Saunders, very properly, bent over her hand briefly. 'If you do decide to come to Srinagar and will allow me the privilege of showing you the city, a note addressed to me at the *dak* bungalow will reach me.'

'Thank you,' Crystal smiled. 'I shall remember that.'

Outside the door, Gulab Singh hovered unsmiling. Very courteously, he escorted them downstairs, his rigidly straight back eloquent with disapproval.

Slowly, Crystal returned to her apartment, disquieted by the unexpected visit. It was obvious that Adele

Hathaway was well known to Damien. How well known? Was she one of the many women in Damien's life? And . . . Nafisa? She had never heard that name from him either. But then, there really was so much about his life that she was not aware of. *Everybody in Kashmir knows*, she had said. Who was this Nafisa who was involved with Damien in some way? Crystal was surprised to see just how agitated she had become! She could not understand the reason why. After all, she was only too well aware of Damien's reputation with women—what did it matter to her? Their marriage was only a farce with no love lost on either side. Why should she care which other women he was involved with?

But, oddly enough, care she did. The violent emotion she was feeling now she recognised very easily as— jealousy! The realisation appalled her, and she felt disgusted with herself at stooping so low. If Damien Granville was beginning to occupy her thoughts rather more than necessary, then he had to be exorcised forthwith! About that there was no doubt in her mind at all.

The sun was setting, and the beautiful Venetian glass lamps in her apartment were being lit and the fire stoked and fed from baskets of pine-cones. Crystal opened the glass door into the small balcony off her bedroom and watched the sun go down behind the mountains. It was a sight of unforgettable splendour. The entire mountain range seemed bathed in flames as the snowy mantles across their peaks shone like luminous rubies. The brilliant hues of the valley dulled and then faded as they merged with the night. For a long while Crystal stood on the balcony, gazing sightlessly into the darkened distance. But try as she might, she could not get it out of her mind that she had to find out who this Nafisa was! She knew that she would not be able to rest until she had done so—much as the compulsion disgusted her. But she had no idea how to set about it. She could hardly ask Gulab Singh! And Sharifa would know immediately why she had asked. She would be embarrassed and frightened of what the Sarkar might say, and would lie.

Trying to find a solution to the delicate problem that was gnawing away at her heart, Crystal wandered up to the bookcases in Damien's sitting-room to find something interesting to read. She knew that Kashmir had known many excellent poets and, since she was well able to read Urdu, the poems would hold more meaning for her than English translations. Searching through the bookcases, she suddenly came across a book in a script that she recognised as Russian. Inside was a scrawled inscription with no date which read, 'To my darling with all my love.' It was signed 'Natasha'.

Crystal's heart lurched and then plummeted even lower than it already was. Natasha! Not another one of Damien's earlier lady loves? Earlier? Present? And why—Russian? She had never received any hint that Damien knew Russian . . . It was distinctly odd. Carefully, she replaced the book in its place, frowning. For a moment she felt utterly disconsolate. How many dark areas were there in the life of this unfathomable man whom the wheel of fortune had forced her to marry?

It was as she was having her supper by the fire that Crystal had a flash of inspiration. Sharifa had gone down to the kitchens to prepare herself some kedgeree, complaining of an upset stomach. Looking after her needs at the moment was Rehana, her niece.

Crystal eyed her curiously for a while, taking in the innocent face and the naive expression of the little girl who was no more than fourteen. 'Where do you parents live, Rehana?' she asked.

Rehana flushed in alarm at being addressed directly by the *memsahib*. She lowered her lashes shyly and whispered, 'In Srinagar.'

'And how long have you been at Shalimar?'

'Two years.'

Crystal's eyes gleamed. Deliberately she launched into a bright conversation intended to put the child at her ease. She plied her with questions about her home, her family and her interests. Very soon, her shyness forgotten, Rehana was chattering on gaily about herself without inhibition. The chatter was interspersed with much laughter, as Crystal tried to speak a few words of Kashmiri. When she felt Rehana was quite at ease, she asked, 'And where is your house in Srinagar?'

'Not far from the Shalimar Gardens.'

'And,' Crystal threw out very casually, 'does Nafisa live close to you?'

Without hesitation the child replied, just as casually, 'Oh yes. Her house is two streets away from ours. Next to the mosque.'

Crystal's heart leapt! Her ploy had worked! She felt a little ashamed of extracting information from Rehana through subterfuge, but this had seemed to be the simplest way to get it. Suspecting nothing, Rehana prattled on about Nafisa, who was obviously well known to her. Crystal bit her lip, wondering how she was to ask the question to which she really wanted the answer, but she need not have worried. Suddenly, Rehana said quite innocently, 'Nafisa's house is very nice. The Sarkar has given her a lot of pretty things for it.'

Abruptly, Crystal stood up and walked to the window. So, her suspicions were right after all! Nafisa was Damien's mistress—why else should he fill her house with pretty things? For a moment she paced up and down, agitated. Also there was no doubt that Adele Hathaway knew Damien extremely well—how well, she had no idea, but it would not be difficult to guess! Damien seemed unable to keep his hands off any woman he met. How evil! And how utterly degrading for her, his wife!

She seethed with anger—and a strange kind of pain. She was staggered at how jealous she felt. Again and again the vision rose before her eyes of Damien making tempestuous, passionate love to Nafisa . . . to Adele. It was a vision that she almost could not bear. It was abominable, abhorrent! She felt utterly miserable, not only because of Damien's amorous philanderings, but at her own startling reaction to them. Was it possible that she was beginning to fall in love with this odious man who happened to be her husband? Oh, it could not be true, it *must* not!

Dully, unable to concentrate on her book, she changed into her night-clothes, turned the lamps down low and sat, in near-darkness, by the window. The flames of the low fire threw strange patterns on the ceiling and an orange glow filled the room. Her mind raged with torment; she had never felt so alone in her life.

How long she sat thus, lost in her own turbulence, she did not know, but suddenly, when the fire had almost burned out and the house seemed still and silent, she heard a familiar voice.

'Why are you not asleep?'

Like a startled deer, she jumped from her seat with a strangled gasp. Damien's voice came from the doorway, where he stood outlined against a faint glimmer of light. For a moment she could not believe the evidence of her ears or her eyes. Surely he was not expected back until tomorrow? He came into the room and walked up to her. In the half-dark he peered closely at her face. 'You look . . . troubled. Are you?'

His eyes were searching and his voice was so soft that, for a fleeting instant, she had the wild impulse to fling herself into his arms and seek solace from her wretchedness against his chest. But then, mercifully, the feeling passed as rapidly as it had arisen. Without saying a word, she moved away and very deliberately turned up the lamps. The room was flooded with light. He followed her slowly to the fireplace, where she was placing a fresh log on the dying flames.

'I tried to get back this morning, but was delayed unavoidably. I'm . . . sorry that I was not here when you arrived.' She was surprised at the apology—and not displeased. So he had not forgotten that she was due in the morning! 'Did you have a comfortable journey? Did Gulab Singh look after you well?' He sat down by the fireplace and patted the seat beside him. Pretending not to notice the gesture, Crystal sat down opposite.

'Yes, thank you, on both accounts. There was nothing to complain of.'

If he did notice her strange demeanour and the waxen look on her face, he did not make any comment. He was, indeed, in high spirits. 'Well, what do you think of my Kashmir? Does it please you? Are you not thunderstruck at all this beauty?' He waved his hand in the direction of the window.

'Indeed I am,' she said, but without excessive enthusiasm, unable to match his buoyancy. 'It is a place of rare charms.'

'Charms! Is that the best you can do when faced with the delights of heaven?' he laughed. 'And what do you think of Shalimar?' His eyes glistened with pride. 'Is it not the most perfect place on earth?'

'You have answered your own questions,' she said, not intending to sound sharp but not able to repress the retort.

He looked surprised, but leaned forward and took her hand in his. 'I have missed your presence here,' he said, not with emotion, but in a very matter-of-fact voice. 'Watching you at the window, I felt that you belonged here.'

'And that is why you could not bestir yourself to be present this morning?' She was determined not to let his charm overwhelm her, knowing how shallow it was.

'I have already apologised,' he said abruptly, releasing her hand. 'It could not be helped.' He paused, then continued in a low voice. 'I very much want you to be happy at Shalimar.'

Oh, how hypocritical he was! Happy at Shalimar! How could he expect her to be happy, surrounded by evidence of his debauched life, reminded constantly of the countless women who occupied his heart and mind?

'In that case,' she said coldly, 'you must ask your mistresses not to make it a habit to call upon me!'

He raised his eyebrows quizzically, and his eyes showed a flicker of amusement. 'You mean Adele? Yes, I heard that she had called upon you this afternoon—with that young jackass Saunders!'

There was not even the pretence of a denial! How easily he accepted the truth about his shameful relationship! He laughed lightly. 'You must not let Adele upset you. She means no harm—and has her uses from time to time.' He seemed not the slightest bit perturbed by the situation.

'Oh, I am certain she has her uses from time to time, as you so delicately put it! As, no doubt, have I!'

'You put yourself in the same category as Adele Hathaway?' he asked, genuinely taken aback. 'You are my wife!'

'And she is your mistress!' she flung back, unbearably incensed by the nonchalance with which he treated the matter. 'Can you deny it?'

'No,' he said with disarming, disgraceful frankness. 'I cannot deny the relationship. My only objection is to the grammatical tense you use. I have not had anything to do with Adele Hathaway since I left for Delhi. She *was* my mistress at one time, yes. It was of no great consequence.'

She felt choked with anger and humiliation. 'And you can admit it to me with so much brazenness? With not a shade of shame?'

'Would you rather I lied to you?' He shrugged and spread out his hands. 'I have not been a saint. Which man has? It would be hypocritical to pretend. Surely you are old enough to know that men do have . . . appetites that demand to be satisfied?' His attitude was that of a very patient parent trying to be reasonable with a wayward child. It drove her to further fury.

'And would you accept the same excuse from me about . . .' she blurted out the first name that came into her head, 'Henry Saunders, for instance?'

He stiffened immediately and his face became thundery. 'By gad, I would *not*! I'd horsewhip him from here to kingdom come if he so much as laid a finger on you . . . Has he?'

She laughed. 'Don't be absurd! He has not had a chance . . . yet!' She had no idea why she said it. She had not given Captain Saunders even a passing thought, but the sight of Damien's face, dark and angry, and the calmness with which he dismissed his own philanderings, drove her into a state far from reasonable.

He leaned back in his seat and observed her reflectively through narrowed eyes. 'Don't play those kinds of games with me, Crystal,' he said with deadly calm. 'You already know my views on how to treat wayward wives!' He put his hand in his pocket, withdrew his pipe and, from a leather pouch, began to fill the bowl with tobacco. Once again he appeared to be in perfect control of himself. 'Women like you are not meant to fiddle with fire.'

He was not really taking her threat seriously, she knew. On his lips was a smile of complacency. She longed to reach out and wipe it off, to wound him so that he would awaken to her own misery.

'And what about women like . . . Nafisa?'

Very briefly, his hand stilled in the act of filling the pipe. For a second it remained suspended in mid-air. He did not look at her. Then he resumed his activity, giving it his full concentration. It was only after he had placed the pipe in his mouth and, picking up a burning stick from the fire, lit it to his satisfaction, that he asked casually, 'Who told you about Nafisa?'

Not a word in refutation! Not the whisper of an excuse! Crystal let out a long, slow breath and slumped back in her chair in misery, unable to sustain her anger any more. He had admitted everything; it was like the ultimate degradation. She stood up quickly. 'I am very tired,' she said flatly. 'I would like to go to bed.' Oh, how she prayed that he would accept her excuse and leave her alone with her wretched thoughts!

But Damien seemed far from inclined to retire meekly, no matter how tired she felt. He uncoiled himself slowly in his seat and rose, towering above her. Very deliberately he laid his pipe on the mantelpiece and cupped her face with both his hands.

'I have already told you that I have had many mistresses in my life,' he breathed softly. 'Why does the fact now upset you so much?'

She met his gaze as coldly as she could without moving. 'You appetite for mistresses bothers me not a bit! You are welcome to as many as you wish, as far as I am concerned!'

'Ah, but it does bother you . . .' The hateful black eyes were actually laughing! 'It couldn't be, could it, that the uncaring, unbridled Crystal Covendale is actually jealous?'

'Jealous?' Her voice was shrill and over-emphatic, 'Oh, what insufferable pride you have!'

He chuckled softly. 'Well, we shall soon see . . .' He bent down swiftly and, with his arms encircled about her waist, kissed her hard on the mouth. She stiffened her back into rigidity and clenched her fists, making her heart like stone. Her face became carved out of granite and she gave him not the whisper of a response. It was an effort that drew all the breath out of her but, miraculously, she succeeded.

He stepped back and frowned. 'I see that your acting abilities seem to have improved considerably during my absence!' he breathed, and she could see that he was becoming angry.

'Not a bit!' she retorted with a triumphant smile. 'It is you who still refuse to accept that you are not totally irresistible to *all* women!'

Before he could think of an answer, there was a loud

knock on the door. With a muffled oath, he strode over and opened it. 'Yes, what is it?'

Gulab Singh stood outside and coughed apologetically. 'The men are downstairs waiting for an answer. They want to know if you have come to a decision about the harvesting tomorrow?'

'Damn! I had forgotten about that. Come, let us settle the matter now.' Without a backward glance, he walked out of the room slamming the door behind him.

With a massive sigh of relief, Crystal sank into the chair and buried her face in her hands. She felt herself begin to tremble. Oh, what a damnable life she would have with this profligate, this man who had not a tinge of decency in his soul! How he would torture her with his debaucheries and his bare-faced philanderings! She would be the laughing-stock of all Kashmir—helpless to retaliate in any way, having to submit to his inhumanities in abject surrender. And how demeaning that she should now be able to find in her heart love for a man such as this!

Crystal paused in shock as the thought flashed through her mind. Love! For Damien Granville? Why, the very idea was obnoxious! And yet she could in no way deny the frantic leapings of her disobedient heart. She was in love with Damien! Mournfully, and in utter desolation, she admitted to herself the horrible truth—knowing that, rather than let him receive even a hint of it, she would prefer to cut off her right hand!

With new-found determination, she extinguished the lamps in the sitting-room, quenched the fire and, firmly, turned the key in all the doors to her apartment. The thought of lying in his arms again, thrilling to his caresses, feeling the softness of his lips against hers, hearing his heartbeat against her own . . . oh, it was not to be considered! She would not be able to tame her own passions, she would overflow with all the love pent up inside her, and he would know that he had gained such a victory as could not be reversed.

With all the entrances well barred, she lay down in bed, exhausted, snuggling into the warm bedclothes and willing sleep to come.

CHAPTER SIX

But, pursue it as she might, sleep would not come. She tossed and turned, trying to blot out the ragings of her mind, but without success. It was as she counted the chimes of midnight from the porcelain clock on her desk in the sitting-room that she first heard the sound that she feared: the rattle of a doorknob! With a frightened sob, she sat up in bed, pulling the bedclothes up as she shivered. The knob rattled once, then fell silent. For a moment she listened, without daring to breathe, but the sound was not repeated. Slowly her body loosened and, with a sigh, she was about to slide under the bedclothes again, giving voiceless thanks to heaven, when there was the loud report of a shot and the sound of splintering wood. With a strangled cry she leapt out of bed, intending to flee into the dressing-room next door but, before she could move more than a step, he strode into the room, his face contorted with fury and in his hand a still smoking pistol.

He walked up to the bed and stopped, legs apart, his hands on his hips. It was as if all the hounds of hell had been unleashed within him. For a moment he said nothing, his eyes boring into her like iron rods. She stared at him in horror, terrified of what he might do. Groping blindly for the bed behind her, she sank back into it and pulled the bedclothes up to her neck.

'Leave me alone,' Damien,' she whispered as the sobs caught in her throat. 'Oh, leave me alone . . .'

He ignored her pleas. Indeed, it was as though he had not heard them at all. 'Don't ever again,' he ground out between clenched teeth, his voice all the more terrifying for its menacing softness, 'lock the door upon me . . . or you will not live to see the sunrise.'

With a cry, she buried her face in the quilt. 'Go away,' she breathed against the sheet. 'Go *away*! Can you not see that I do not want you near me . . . ?' Oh, how she longed for him to gather her in his arms, kiss away the agony from her heart, tell her that he loved her just a little . . .

But Damien did none of these things. Instead, he replaced the pistol carefully in its holster around his waist. 'There is not a door built yet that can detain me against my will. You will remember that in future.' She did not reply, gazing up at him in mute anguish. He appeared unmoved by her look and walked slowly towards the window, turning his back. 'I have never taken a woman against her will,' he said with icy quietness. 'Indeed, I have never needed to!' He turned round sharply and faced her. 'I shall not come to you again . . . ,' he paused briefly, 'until you ask me to. I promise you that!'

Crystal swallowed hard. Instead of relief, her heart filled with despair. With a supreme effort, she forced her mouth into a bare smile. 'I shall never ask you to, *never*!'

'We shall see.' A sardonic smile played upon his lips. 'I shall make a woman out of you yet!'

'Why should you trouble?' she hurled back. 'You have plenty who give you all you need?'

He did not contradict her. Instead, he fingered his chin reflectively. 'There is a great deal you still have to learn,' he said, amused.

'Then perhaps you could get your mistresses to give me lessons!' she retorted, her breast heaving with anger.

'You would benefit from them, no doubt,' he burst out without remorse. 'A woman of discernment knows when to have spirit and when to be . . . soft. That is something Nafisa could teach you well.'

She started as if stung. 'Then *go* to your Nafisa!' she

stormed. 'Leave me to my own inadequate devices!'

Without another word, he walked towards the door. Before going out, he turned and looked at her. 'Perhaps I shall,' he said under his breath. 'Perhaps I shall . . .'

And then he was gone.

For a long, long, while Crystal sat transfixed, immobile her mind a sudden blank. Then, with a deep sigh, she slipped again under the bedclothes. Covering her head with the quilt, she smothered her mouth in her pillow and, for an inordinate length of time, she wept.

Over the next three days, she did not see Damien. She had not any idea where he was. That he was at Shalimar she learned from Sharifa. She explained that it was harvesting-time and there was much to be done. He was spending all his days out of doors, supervising the many jobs that had to be done, collecting rents from tenants, listening to complaints and implementing plans for the constant improvements he sought on his land. That she did not see him at all, Sharifa was not aware. Crystal took care to send for her only after the sun was high, preferring to breakfast late rather than have the maidservant—and through her all the servants—learn that the Sarkar did not care to sleep with his wife! It would become a topic for much active discussion at Shalimar, and Crystal cringed at the thought of such public disgrace.

The terrible scene with Damien had left its scars. Had she let them do so, her thoughts would have kept her submerged in the depths of an inky depression. However, she was determined not to allow that to happen. She convinced herself that it was indeed a relief to be finally free of Damien's presence and attempted to keep herself as busy as she could. She wrote long ecstatic letters to her mother and to Robie, extolling the beauties of her new home, praising her husband. She told them how happy she was, how perfect life was in every respect. She described in detail the many activities at Shalimar, fabricating events that she felt would please and reassure her mother. It was all very hollow and artificial, but the lies had to be told for the sake of her family's peace of mind. Whenever she could she worked on her father's uncompleted papers.

Learning that Damien had gone up to Gulmarg, some thirty miles miles from where they were and where he also owned a house and some land, Crystal felt it safe to venture forth once again on the estate. She was anxious to complete the tour that had been so rudely interrupted by Adele and Captain Saunders, but had been hesitating, loath to meet Damien accidentally in her wanderings. She sent word to Gulab Singh that if he were free, she would appreciate his guidance on the tour.

When she went down to the stables, she was surprised to see him standing by a horse that she had not seen before. It was a beautiful glossy chestnut with a light beige mane and tail and large, soulful eyes.

'I haven't seen this one before!' she exclaimed as the mare nuzzled her shoulder.

'It is for Madam. The Sarkar reared her from the finest stock, at his place in Gulmarg, and he has trained it himself. She is very gentle, but as fast as the wind. Her name is Sundari, which, as Madam knows, means Beauty.'

Crystal stood still, absent-mindedly stroking Sundari's head, unable to say a word. She recalled with a guilty start that she had not even thanked him for his previous gift of the fabulous *jaam-e-war*, nor had she remembered to give him the jacket that she had bought for him in Srinagar. She flushed with quick shame at her own lack of manners, but her heart thrilled to know that he had not forgotten her completely, that he did think of her still!

Unaccountably, her spirits soared, and she was smiling as she mounted her new mare and adjusted herself comfortably in the beautiful leather saddle. This was not a gift she could ignore—not that she wanted to. She would make a point of seeking out Damien on his return from Gulmarg to thank him for his thoughtfulness. Secretly she was pleased that she would have an excuse to speak to him. She was surprised at just how wretched she had felt over the past three days because of his cold rejection of her.

It was another glorious morning such as she had come to take for granted in this wonderland of Nature. Yet she had not become blasée about her enchanting surroundings. They rode this time through great banks of rhodedendrons spilling over the countryside as though cast down at random by some divine hand. The air was balmy and warm, unfailing touches of the eternal spring that prevailed in the Vale. The estate was vast, very well planned and appeared to be self-sufficient in its fertility. She watched the harvesters cut and thresh the paddy that would produce fine rice for the most fastidious tables of India, and learned how the wool of the long-haired mountain goats was sheared and carded to produce the exquisite softness of *pashmina*. Wherever they went they saw evidence of plenty, with happy, smiling faces beaming in greeting and welcome. In one of the huts they were invited to have a cup of *qahwa*, the spiced Kashmiri tea served from a gleaming samovar. From a shyly smiling housewife in another she managed to secure a recipe for the traditional dish of *gushtav*, the meat-ball curry made with mint and favoured by Damien. All in all, it was a most exhilarating morning and she was more than delighted with the gentle Sundari. Damien had obviously trained her well, and she felt very moved by his thoughtfulness.

It was as they were returning to the stables that Gulab Singh mentioned he was leaving for Gulmarg early in the morning and would be away for two days.

'Will my husband also be away for two more days?' she asked, her heart sinking with disappointment.

Gulab Singh smiled. 'With the Sarkar it is difficult to tell. He comes and goes as he pleases.'

'What is the house in Gulmarg like? Is it large?'

'No indeed. It is a log cottage which the Sarkar built himself for occasional sojourns when he wanted privacy and quiet.'

She felt a stab of jealousy. With Adele or Nafisa or Natasha perhaps? It was a painful subject and she quickly changed it. 'I notice there is a coach in the barn. Surely it is not possible to use coaches in Kashmir? There are hardly any roads!'

'It is a whim the Sarkar had once. The very first coach the Kashmiris had ever seen was brought up by the Lawrences in 1850. Hundreds of people gathered to see it, although it never could go anywhere!'

Crystal laughed. 'But that was thirty-two years ago. Surely a coach could go at least to Srinagar now, although I agree it could not squeeze through the streets. They are so narrow.'

'Oh yes, it could go to Srinagar. However, the journey is not very comfortable. The road is not much more than a wide track, even now.'

The idle conversation started in Crystal's mind the genesis of an idea which remained with her stubbornly through the evening. Damien's cruel taunt that night was not something she had been able to forget: A woman of discernment knows when to have spirit and when to be soft. *That is something Nafisa could teach you well*. The remark had been rankling in her mind incessantly. What did he mean? The wounded anger of the time had been replaced by a consuming curiosity that she was not able to cast aside. She seemed devoured by a desire to find out more about this Nafisa, to see for herself what it was about her that made Damien admire her so. She cringed at the idea of coming face to face with her, but knew that she would not be able to rest until she had done so.

Early the next morning she sent word to the stables that she would like the coach to be prepared. Gulab Singh, she knew, had already left for Gulmarg, so there was no fear of objections from that quarter. In his absence, there was no member of the household who would dare question her orders. After her breakfast of cereals, milk, honey and grapefruit, she waited until Sharifa was out of the room. Then she said to Rehana very casually, 'It would be pleasant to take a drive down to Srinagar. Would you like to come with me? You could, perhaps, visit your family.'

Rehana's eyes immediately lit up, and she nodded eagerly. 'But I shall have to ask my aunt first.'

'I shall ask her for you,' said Crystal kindly. 'She will not refuse.'

Sharifa was surprised to be asked the question, but immediately said, 'Yes, certainly Rehana may go, and I shall come too. It is a long time since I saw my sister.'

'No, Sharifa,' said Crystal smoothly, 'you have not been well. The journey in the coach will only serve to upset your stomach more. I insist that you stay and rest. Perhaps next time I will take you, when you are feeling better.'

Reluctantly, Sharifa saw the wisdom of the advice and nodded. 'You are right, *memsahib*. In truth, I do not feel I can face it.'

Elated at the success of her little scheme, Crystal readied herself for the trip. She dressed with unusual care, choosing a very smart velvet dress of chartreuse which had a chic bonnet to match. She did her hair with care, brushing it until it gleamed and twinkled with coppery highlights. She treated her face to a light patina of cosmetics and was pleased to note how well she looked. Whatever virtues Nafisa might have, she was determined to prove that she could at least match them!

The Shalimar coach, small and dainty, was kept in mint condition, as were the sprightly ponies that pulled it. Crystal would have far preferred to drive it herself, but she knew that this would be viewed with horror by the staff and by people in Srinagar. The liveried coachman, not very experienced in the art of driving and nervous of the responsibility of transporting such precious cargo as the Sarkar's lady, started off clumsily but soon rallied. Out on the main road the carriage gathered reasonable speed, although the rough tracks made it a journey that could hardly be called comfortable. Enthralled with her very first ride in such a splendid vehicle, Rehana clung to Crystal nervously, her eyes shining and her round face flushed with excitement.

They reached the outskirts of Srinagar in fair time. Asking the coachman to take them as close to the Shalimar Gardens as he possibly could, Crystal reclined back in the plush upholstery try... not to allow her nervousness to become too ...ent. It was a very bizarre visit she had set ... ...morrow, perhaps, she would not remem... ...could have possibly had the courage to make it.

They ...ied up in a by-lane bordering the Gardens, and ...ana let out an excited gasp. 'This is where I live,' ...e exclaimed. 'Just round the next corner.'

'Well,' said Crystal, 'before you run off home, you must first show me the mosque that is two streets away from here. Do you remember that you mentioned it the other night?'

'Oh, yes,' said Rehana, surprised. '*Memsahib* wishes to go to the mosque?'

'I hear it is very old and very quaint. I have an inclination to see it for myself.'

Unsuspectingly, Rehana led the way down the narrow cobbled streets through which people jostled, headed for their morning's business. As she passed, they all stopped to stare in wonder. Crystal gritted her teeth determinedly. I have come so far, I must not flinch now, she kept repeating to herself doggedly. It might be a wild-goose chase, but I cannot go back now! The mosque appeared at the end of the lane. There were crowds of people about. Rehana looked at Crystal uncertainly, and a worried frown appeared on her forehead.

'*Memsahib* would like to go inside? It is not advisable without an escort.'

Crystal smiled reassuringly. 'I can take care of myself, Rehana. Besides, I do want to have a look at some silver jewellery. See, there is a jeweller's shop. I will go in and browse for a while.'

Rehana agreed to leave her, but her reluctance was apparent. 'I shall wait for the *memsahib* near the carriage when I have seen my family.'

'Yes,' said Crystal. 'I shall not be more than half an hour.'

Without delay, Crystal entered the first shop opposite the mosque. It was small and somewhat dingy, but the silversmith did have a modest array of ornaments in his showcase. He was delighted to see such a fine *memsahib* in his establishment and, anxious to make a sale, spread out all his wares on the counter.

Crystal toyed with a few items, admiring the fine filigree work, half-heartedly asking questions to which she already knew the answers. Was this traditional Kashmiri work? Was it very old? The silversmith, overwhelmed by her interest, waxed expansive. Hastily she bought a chain and pendant, thinking to give it to Rehana as a surprise, then asked, just as she was on the way out, 'Oh . . . I have to visit someone in this street, a lady called Nafisa Sultana?' she paused expectantly, her heart beating with suspense.

The man immediately smiled. 'Oh yes, Nafisa Begum's house is next to the mosque. I shall send my son to show you.' He looked slightly surprised, but made no further comment, giving quick instructions to his son.

The house was tall and narrow and painted pale lemon. Without pausing, the lad opened its small wooden street door and entered. Heart thumping wildly, Crystal followed, wondering again at the mad impulse that had brought her here so rashly. Supposing this woman was rude, hostile and offensive, as was highly likely? Supposing she refused to see her at all? Crystal had no idea what she was going to say to this Nafisa, and suddenly she recoiled at the prospect of facing her. But it was too late to retract.

In the flagstone-lined courtyard an elderly woman, fat and ungainly and chewing betel-leaves, sat sunning herself on a string cot. Seeing them, she rose with an enquiring look. The lad whispered something to her quickly and, with a brisk nod of his head to Crystal, vanished back into the street. Pulling herself up to her full height, Crystal handed her card and said coldly, 'I would like to see Begum Nafisa Sultana.'

The old woman obviously could not read, for she looked at the card blankly and then at Crystal, up and down, with frank curiosity. Her large mouth, stained red from the betel, stopped munching for a moment as she conducted her silent appraisal. Then, without a word, she turned and waddled up a narrow stone staircase that led to the upper floors. Crystal looked around. There was a series of rooms opening out of the downstairs courtyard in which she stood, and from each doorway she could see curious eyes staring at her. From the veranda on the first floor, several heads appeared over the balustrades to gaze downwards. Crystal felt her nervousness return and her heart beat painfully. It was an insane impulse that had brought her here, she knew. What would Damien say if he ever found out—as well he might? The thought made her palms clammy with sweat. Besides, she had a horrible suspicion as to what this house was!

The old woman waddled back down the stairs and made a signal to Crystal to follow. The first-floor veranda was now deserted. They walked to one end and passed through a curtained archway. They were now in a room that was very large and very beautifully decorated. There was hardly any furniture in it, but an exquisite Persian carpet covered the entire floor. To one side were laid thick mattresses covered with red velvet *masnads*, gold-embroidered coverlets such as those used by the very rich on their divans. Matching bolsters surrounded the *masnad* and, in one corner, stood a selection of traditional musical instruments.

Crystal's heart took a quick leap; her face became red, her suspicions confirmed. It *was* the house of a singing-girl—and Nafisa Begum was obviously a woman of easy virtue! It was unforgivable that she had not guessed that earlier—all the indications had been there. But, of course, it was far too late to turn back now, as momentarily Crystal was vastly tempted to do.

They entered a smaller room that was furnished as a sitting-room in the Western style. There were chairs and tables, a sofa, and a low divan on which sat a very young girl. She was dressed in the traditional flowing Kashmiri garments and on her head was a veil of thin gauze. She rose as Crystal entered. She was not very tall but there was a grace about her movements as she stood up that gave the impression of a very delicate swan. She bowed in greeting.

'Please be seated, Mrs Granville,' she said in English. 'I am honoured that you have chosen to call on me.' She turned to the old woman and, with a touch of imperiousness, ordered a samovar of *qahwa*. It was obvious that she was used to being obeyed.

Crystal sat down on a chair, momentarily tongue-tied, but from under lowered lashes she observed the woman closely. She was astonishingly young, perhaps not much older than herself. She had very pale grey eyes and light brown hair that was thick and glossy, woven into a plait that reached down almost to her knees. Her skin, the colour of wheat ripened in the sun, was smooth like a peach, and her lips, full and sensual, were coloured a delicate shade of pink. She was extremely beautiful.

She conveyed no signs of discomfort at all, appearing supremely poised and at ease. Observing Crystal's silence, she smiled, revealing a row of perfect white teeth. 'I have heard a great deal about you, Mrs Granville,' she said, and her voice was soft and musical. 'I have been wondering if we would meet.'

Crystal stared in surprise. 'A great deal about me? From whom?'

Nafisa's eyes widened. 'Why, from the Sarkar, of course.' She spoke without any sign of self-consciousness or embarrassment.

But Crystal coloured, hardly knowing how to conduct a conversation such as this. Before this wraith of a girl, she felt large and clumsy, almost devoid of grace. Nafisa appeared not to notice her discomfort, talking as though they were, indeed, old friends.

'How does my country appeal to you?' she asked. 'There are not many Europeans here, but those who have been are always lyrical in their praise.'

'Yes, it is very beautiful,' Crystal said stiffly. 'Kashmir has indeed been favoured by the gods.'

Nafisa smiled, and there was genuine warmth in her expression. 'And . . . Shalimar? Is that not a wondrous world in itself?'

Crystal froze. 'You . . . know it?'

Nafisa gazed at her silently for a moment, then shook her head. 'No. I have never been there. It would not be . . . correct for the Sarkar to take me to Shalimar.' There was in her tone a hint of sadness. 'His home is the honoured preserve of . . . his wife.' She said it very simply, without any sign of rancour or discontentment.

Unaccountably, Crystal felt her heart warm. There was something very lost and innocent about this lovely girl. As the old woman came in again, bearing the samovar on a tray with small cups, they sat lost, each in her own thoughts, not speaking. It was after the woman had left and Nafisa was pouring out the spiced tea that she said suddenly, 'He told me you are very beautiful. I can see that he was right.' Again, it was said without any expression of envy, merely as a fact.

Crystal reddened and immersed herself in sipping the delicious tea. She had come to put this woman in her place, to investigate her not with kindness but with anger and raging jealousy. Now she found it impossible to revive her earlier feelings about her. She was so gentle, so modest and so openly friendly that it was difficult not to respond to her warmth.

'How long have you known . . . my husband?' asked Crystal impulsively, realising how clumsy the bald question seemed amidst these delicate surroundings.

'Two years.'

Two years! Crystal's heart again throbbed with jealousy. Damien had been making love to her for all that while, long before he had even known of her own existence! The thought was suddenly very painful.

Nafisa was observing her silently, taking in the heightened colour of her face, the flash of anger in her eyes. 'You are embarrassed to meet me,' she said quite unexpectedly but without any emotion. 'Please don't be. It is a situation that women in the West find difficult to understand. Or accept. But in the East . . .' she spread out her hands and smiled, 'in the East we know that there are many compartments in a man's life, each separate from the other.'

Crystal frowned, not quite sure what she was trying to say, but surprised that Nafisa had, so quickly, arrived at the heart of the matter. Emboldened by her complete lack of subterfuge, her obvious willingness to answer any question, Crystal asked, 'How did you meet Da . . . my husband?'

Nafisa looked into her cup reflectively for a moment. Then she sighed. 'Through my profession.' Once again, there was no hint of embarrassment, only a tinge of sadness. She sighed again. 'For women like me, there is no alternative.' She noticed Crystal's look of puzzlement and continued, 'I was born of an English father and a Kashmiri mother. They were not married.' Her tone was very flat. 'My father was an officer in the Army on leave from Peshawar. My mother was a very young innocent girl who worked as a washerwoman in the *dak* bungalow. She was very beautiful.' For a moment she sat lost in thought, her eyes distant. 'A child born out of wedlock and belonging fully to neither culture—and to both—has little future in India. For girls it is worse.' For the first time, a note of harshness entered her voice. 'There is no choice for them but to . . .' she broke off, and Crystal noticed, with surprise, that her eyes were moist.

Crystal made a gesture as if to stop the painful reminiscences, but Nafisa suddenly smiled. 'You have a right to know,' she said simply. 'You are his wife.' She paused to refill their cups, glad for the few moments in which to recollect her composure. 'I have been luckier in my life than most,' she continued. 'I have had the great fortune to belong to only one man, and he has been kind to me. But on my part I have been foolish.'

'Foolish? Why?'

'I have committed the great crime of . . . coming to love him. In our profession, it is not allowed . . .'

Her eyes again filled with tears and, watching her, Crystal felt inexplicably moved. It seemed an extraordinary reversal of everything she had envisaged about the visit. She had not come here with the intention of commiserating with her husband's mistress—but that was precisely what she was beginning to do!

Nafisa wiped her eyes with the edge of her veil. 'You may return with peace in your heart,' she said, and suddenly her dove-grey eyes were proud and filled with hauteur. 'Your husband belongs to you and to you alone. He will not come to me any more.' She looked at Crystal with a faint flicker of amusement. 'That is what has been troubling you, has it not?'

Dumbly, ashamed at how easily this young, beautiful girl had read her own heart, she nodded. Then, clearing her throat awkwardly, she asked, 'And . . . you?'

Nafisa lowered her head. 'I can never give myself to any other man,' she said. 'In seven days I leave for Lahore, where my mother's sister lives. I shall start a school to teach music.' Her face became melancholy. 'I have given Damien pleasure,' she whispered, using his name for the first time, 'but on his heart there is not a single mark left by me. His heart is for you alone.' She spoke without bitterness, only with a sorrow that was painful to watch.

Crystal shook her head, unable to pretend before this remarkably open-faced girl, so wise for her years. 'His heart,' she said achingly, 'is, perhaps, for no woman.'

Nafisa's eyes immediately softened in compassionate understanding. 'It is possible,' she said soothingly, 'that the forcefulness of his manner deceives you, for he is indeed a man of violent tempers. But,' she stretched out a delicate hand and laid it on Crystal's, 'to disagree with him one must agree first. Within, he is like honey, warm and sweet.' She peered earnestly into Crystal's downcast face. 'And I have seen what lies in his eyes. It is love for you.'

Crystal laughed ruefully, but could not bring herself to tell Nafisa the truth. For all her wisdom, how wrong she was about that! What would she say if she knew how coldly, how finally, Damien had rejected her?

Slowly she rose to her feet, preparing to leave. She looked at Nafisa's wistful little face with a flash of pity. 'I had come prepared not to . . . like you,' she said frankly, surprised at her own words. 'But I cannot help doing so. Perhaps we could even have been friends if circumstances had been different.'

'Why not?' asked Nafisa calmly. 'We have much in common. After all, we both love the same man.' For the first time during the interview she appeared to be on the verge of breaking down. But, with an effort, she collected herself. 'I hope, Mrs Granville, that you give him many sons. I would have laid down my life to give him but one.'

Crystal's vision blurred as she fumbled her way down the stairs. It was as though the pain in Nafisa's heart was also in her own. All her petty jealousies against her vanished and she felt overwhelmed by a sense of deep compassion for the broken, bewitching girl she had just left behind. How agonising it was to love and not be loved in return! Suddenly, she knew exactly how Nafisa must feel.

The coach awaited her return patiently, but there was still no sign of Rehana, for which Crystal was grateful. She wanted desperately an opportunity to be silent and to be alone with her conflicting emotions. With a quick word to the coachman, she slipped into the Shalimar Gardens through a side gate, intending to calm her senses with a solitary walk. Her mind was divided in equal parts with surging relief that Damien did not love the girl he had had as a mistress for two long years, and pity for the girl who still adored him so completely. It was truly a selfless love that Nafisa bore, a love that demanded nothing in return. Suddenly Crystal felt ashamed of her own petty thoughts. Compared to the sacrifice Nafisa was prepared to make for her love, how churlish appeared to be her own behaviour! She now knew exactly what Damien had meant when he had flung Nafisa in her face so cruelly. Crystal was honest enough to admit that he had been right. This morning she had indeed learned a great deal from Nafisa . . .

'Mrs Granville? I say, Mrs Granville . . . !'

Crystal turned round in surprise as she heard her name being called. Waving at her from the end of the path was Captain Saunders, and rapidly he walked up to join her.

'Why, Mrs Granville, what a very pleasant surprise! Are you alone?' He looked round anxiously.

'Good morning,' Crystal said a little coldly, displeased at having her solitude disrupted so unexpectedly. 'Yes, I am alone.'

His face lit up immediately. 'Then do you mind if I walk with you?'

As a matter of fact she did mind, but could hardly say so. 'No, of course not,' she smiled as cordially as she could.

'These are extraordinary gardens, aren't they?' he

asked, looking around. 'I believe they are unique in all India.'

For the first time Crystal became aware of her surroundings. She had been so immersed in her own thoughts that she had hardly noticed where she was. Now, belatedly, her eyes lit up with pleased amazement. The unique garden after which Damien's estate was named was formed in terraces between the mountains on a slope. A stream flowed down the decline in an artificial channel lined with gigantic *chinars*. At each terrace the water cascaded down in a little artificial waterfall, and the entire length of the stream was studded with fountains. Leading from terrace to terrace were flights of steps crowned with pillared porticos. Two tiny islets, connected by a bridge, terminated the view downhill and beyond this lay the placid jade-green Dal Lake into which the stream flowed. Everywhere was a kaleidoscopic profusion of flowers and of grass in every shade of green one could imagine. It was like a rainbow fallen to the ground by accident.

'The gardens were carved out of the hillside by Asaf Khan, who was the Moghul emperor Shah Jehan's father-in-law. The empress Mumtaz Mahal, his wife, is the one who lies buried in the Taj Mahal.'

'No,' said Crystal gently. 'The Shalimar Gardens were designed by the emperor Jehangir. It is the Nishat Gardens that were the inspiration of Asaf Khan about the year 1620, I think.'

Henry Saunders looked deflated. 'Well . . . perhaps you are right. You are extraordinarily well informed for a woman,' he said admiringly.

'I would take that as a compliment, except for the last three words,' she replied coolly, wishing he would go away. 'I have lived in India all my life; why should I not be well informed about it?'

He shrugged. 'Well, so many aren't. I hear you also speak the lingo like one of them?'

'So does my husband,' she said, mentioning Damien

deliberately so that Saunders should remember to keep his place.

His face became thoughtful. 'Yes . . . your husband speaks many languages well, doesn't he?' His manner became suddenly somewhat tense. 'Including Russian, I believe.'

Crystal stared at him in casual surprise. 'Russian? Oh, I hardly think that is likely. What an extraordinary idea!'

'Yes, it is,' he said quietly. 'Extraordinary, I mean. You didn't know?' He looked at her curiously. She shook her head. He laughed in a manner that was very strange. 'Your husband is obviously a man of many talents—some not always visible!'

There was a sneer in his voice that irked her. 'Is it necessary,' she asked sharply, 'to wear all one's capabilities on one's sleeve?'

'Not at all,' he said smoothly. 'In fact, some are best kept hidden.'

She frowned, her irritation mounting. There was something in his tone that made her suddenly dislike him. 'Captain Saunders,' she said impatiently, 'are you trying to tell me something I am perhaps too obtuse to understand? If so, I would be obliged if you could speak plainly. I am not used to innuendo!' Two bright red spots appeared on her cheeks as, inadvertently, her voice rose.

Her show of temper did not seem to ruffle him. He smiled maliciously. 'There are indications,' he said bluntly, 'that your husband has dealings with the Russians. Certainly, he appears to be well-equipped to do so.'

Crystal stopped dead in her tracks and gaped at him. For a moment she struggled with words, unable to mouth them. Then, as her voice returned, she blurted out, 'Are you quite mad, Captain Saunders?'

'Not at all,' he said coolly. 'I am completely sane and know what I am saying. I have no proof, of course, but intend to procure it . . . with your help, perhaps.'

'With *my* help?' she laughed. 'Now I know that you *are* mad! First, I do believe you are raving, and second, even if you are not, what makes you believe that I would ever help you in deceiving my husband?'

Henry Saunders's smile widened. 'Because,' he said, 'there are rumours that there is not a great deal of love lost between you and Damien. In fact, I believe on reliable authority that there is no love lost at all!'

Had they not been in a public place, Crystal would have had no hesitation in slapping his hateful face. As it was, she merely stared at him agape, then swung on her heel and walked away, too furious to listen to any more. She heard his voice call out softly behind her. 'Tell me, Mrs Granville, is it true that Damien won you in a game of dice?' He laughed. Crystal's footstep faltered but she did not stop. Neither did she look back. She couldn't. She was thunderstruck at what he had said—so much of it being not very far from the truth!

At the coach, Rehana was waiting patiently, surrounded by members of her family, all of whom had turned out to pay their respects to the Sarkar's lady. Crystal acknowledged their greetings in a daze, hardly able to raise a smile. She conversed with them for a brief, moment not knowing what she said, then hastily climbed into the coach. All she could think of was the despicable Henry Saunders and all the horrible things he had managed to discover about their marriage. His charge about Damien being a Russian agent she dismissed as utter nonsense, of course. For the moment all she could consider was—how on earth he had succeeded in finding out so much so close to the truth? Had he heard it from the Smythes in Delhi? But how had they known? Surely their relationship and the bizarre circumstances of their marriage could not be common knowledge! But if they were . . . She cringed as she thought of the terrible effect it might have on Robie and her mother's health.

Raging with confusion and despair, she hardly noticed the journey back to Shalimar or listened to Rehana's constant patter. All she wanted was the privacy of her rooms, where she could sit and ponder these dreadful new revelations, and send off another falsely comforting letter to Mama.

It was not until many hours later, when she had managed to calm herself down somewhat and could dismiss Henry Saunders and his scurrilous conversation as nothing but malice, that she suddenly remembered something. It had been niggling at the back of her mind all afternoon, but she could not, however much she tried, put her finger on it. Now, as she sat by her window watching the spectacular sunset on the Himalayas, drinking in the beauty of the changing colours around, she remembered what it was.

It was the book in Russian that she had found in Damien's bookcase on her first day at Shalimar. The book given to him with such a loving inscription by—'Natasha'. It was a Russian name, she knew, and her heart sank in cold dread at the implication. Could it be that what Henry Saunders had said was true?

CHAPTER SEVEN

ALTHOUGH CRYSTAL'S sleep that night was frenzied and disturbed, interspersed with frightening nightmares, the morning brought a delight that was completely unexpected, but so welcome! When she rose, early, and stumbled out desolately into her sitting-room, she was astounded to see Damien sitting by the crackling fire, casually going through a pile of mail by his side. For a moment she could hardly believe her eyes, wondering if this was some strange apparition that had overstayed from her dreams of the night. But Damien was very real indeed, garbed in a casual shirt and with his strong, hirsute chest half exposed.

He looked up at her as she entered. 'Slept well?'

Quickly she nodded, all the disturbances of the night forgotten in an instant. He smiled and looked her up and down. 'Well, you don't look as if you have. What have you been doing—fighting all the demons of hell singlehandedly from your bed?'

She remembered that she had neither washed her face nor paused to brush her hair, and her night-clothes were disarrayed about her. Hastily she ran back to her room to perform the necessary ablutions, her heart singing with delirious happiness. One would have thought that she had not seen him for weeks!

Scrubbed and brushed, clad in a new lace peignoir which she hastily abstracted from her wardrobe, she stepped sedately back into the sitting-room, her face deceptively calm. 'Did you return from Gulmarg during the night?' she asked.

He nodded briefly and tossed an envelope in her direction. 'Letter for you,' he said. 'If it's from your mother, I hope she is well and not too worried about the fate of her daughter carried away into the wilderness by a big bad wolf.' He was in high spirits.

Crystal laughed and opened the letter impatiently. It was not from her mother but from Sally Hawthorne. Over tea served by Damien's *khidmatgar*, she read it avidly. It was full of chit-chat and pieces of news about their mutual friends. Crystal giggled as she read certain parts written in Sally's usual humorous style. She stopped to pick up her cup and saw Damien watching her. She coloured self-consciously. 'It's from Sally . . . Sally Hawthorne. Perhaps you remember her? She writes very entertainingly.'

'This is the first time I have seen you laugh with genuine amusement,' he exclaimed. 'That's good. I don't like you to look like a dying swan, as you usually do.'

'I thought you were going to say—like an angry goose! Temper is what you usually accuse me of!'

'Well, that too,' he conceded amiably, and laughed.

Crystal went back to her letter hastily in case he noticed the blinding light that shone from her eyes. The ugly scene of the other night seemed to have been forgotten. She had never seen him so light-hearted before and she rejoiced in it. Even the horribly mixed events of yesterday seemed to have receded in significance. Secretly she cocked a snook at Captain Saunders. What did it matter what people gossiped? Neither she nor Damien Granville cared a hoot about public opinion, petty and ill-informed as it could be. As for Damien being a traitor to his country—why, she had never heard such poppycock in her life!

They breakfasted on broken wheat porridge laced with quince honey from Shalimar's own hives, and goat-milk to which Damien was exceedingly partial because of its lightness. He had ordered huge clusters of grapes from the vineyard and explained that these were known as the *anab-shahi* breed from Persia and were uncommonly sweet. Indeed, he was so utterly charming to her that Crystal wondered, unkindly perhaps, if there could be a special reason for it. There was! And she had not long to wait before it became apparent.

'I shall be going to Srinagar today,' he said as they were finishing breakfast, still picking at the luscious grapes. 'Would you care to come with me?'

Crystal's heart turned a cartwheel. Obviously, he did not know that she had made a journey on her own yesterday. 'Th-thank you,' she stammered, taken by surprise. 'I would like to.'

'I have to see Hyder Ali about a business matter and after that we have a call to make on the Palace. His Highness has especially asked to meet you.'

So that was it! A request from the Maharaja of the state could hardly be turned down, and the charm had been invoked to ensure that she did not refuse! For a few seconds Crystal struggled with her disappointment at so obvious a trick. But then her spirits lifted again. What did it matter why he was being so pleasant? She would spend the whole day in his company—and that was a luxury she had never had before. A luxury not to be turned down!

'If we are delayed in Srinagar we can stay the night on the houseboat,' Damien said.

Crystal smiled without showing any overt expression of excitement. 'That would be very pleasant indeed.' Mention of Hyder Ali had suddenly brought to her mind the jacket that she still had not given him. She went into her bedroom and fetched it. Offering the parcel to him, she said, 'I . . . I bought you a jacket when we passed through Srinagar on the way to Shalimar. I hope that it fits you.' A hot blush coloured her cheeks as his face lit up in extreme surprise. He undid the parcel quickly and held the jacket up so that he could examine it properly.

'It is just what I require,' he said nodding, and she could see that he was very pleased. 'How did you know that I needed one?'

'Gulab Singh mentioned it when I was hunting for a gift.'

He put the jacket on immediately on top of his shirt, and it fitted well. 'There are indeed advantages in having a wife,' he said, 'if only so one can dispense with the hated business of shopping.' But she knew that he was only teasing, perhaps to cover his own discomfiture at receiving a gift so unexpectedly from her.

'I have not had the opportunity to thank you for the *jaam-e-war* that you left for me in Delhi,' she said, her nervousness making her voice sound stiff. 'And also the magnificent chestnut. I am very . . . pleased with them both.'

'Hmph!' he muttered, as if they were matters of no consequence. 'You need a horse of your own here at Shalimar.'

'But I may also ride it out on the roads?' she enquired anxiously.

'Yes, but only if you are accompanied. A woman gallivanting on her own is not considered favourably in Kashmir.'

'I thought you did not care what people said?' she could not help asking, disappointed at having her freedom limited like this.

'I don't, but I do not wish to hurt the susceptibilities of my staff and tenants. We are foreigners in Kashmir; we must do as they do. In any case,' he asked, 'where do you wish to go on your own?'

'Nowhere,' she replied, unable to hide her irritation at his persistence. 'It is just that I do not like to be hampered by clustering attendants.'

'There will not be any clusters. And I will instruct your single escort to maintain a discreet distance, if that is what you wish.' He picked up a letter from the table and started to make notes on its margins, thus signifying that the subject, as far as he was concerned, was closed. *To disagree with him, one must agree first*, Nafisa had said. Oh, how difficult that sometimes was!

She was surprised upon going downstairs to see that Damien had ordered the coach to be harnessed for their journey to Srinagar. Sharifa had packed a small bag for her in case they were to stay overnight and, with great excitement, had pressed and packed separately the clothes that Crystal was to wear for the meeting with the Maharaja. After much deliberation, Crystal had selected to wear a *sari*, rather than a Western garment. She had sometimes revelled in wearing one in the house and had learned to carry it with perfection. Seeing her pleasure in the dress, and commenting on how well she looked in it with her golden skin and being at home with all things Indian, her father had bought her for her last birthday a magnificent Benarsi *sari* of peacock-blue silk adorned with a wide border of gold embroidery. She had never yet had the occasion to wear it. She felt elated at how pleased Damien would be to see it on her.

To her delight, he chose to drive the coach himself, declaring himself extremely uneasy with somebody else at the reins. He invited her to sit next to him on the driver's seat, which she did with unconcealed pleasure. It was still not yet ten o'clock and a delicate, semi-transparent mist clothed the valleys like a veil. Some of the deeper ravines were coloured in patches of indigo and purple. Very soon, Crystal knew, everything would be blue and lavender deepening to bright sapphire and rich violet as the day wore on. In the evenings, of course, the hues would melt into pale pinks and apricots which darkened into flame and scarlet as the sun set behind the mountains. She marvelled at the ever-changing countenance of this fabled Vale, with a hundred varied aspects all in one day.

By her side, Damien drove slowly, knowing that she was enjoying the views around. He smiled. 'Are you surprised that I could not live anywhere else after this?'

he asked softly. She shook her head. 'Kashmir has ruined me for any other place in the world.'

She nodded. 'Perhaps,' she said dreamily, 'it will ruin me too!'

He turned to her in pleased surprise and chuckled. 'This is an evil place, really,' he said with amusement. 'It bewitches you until you cannot escape its spell. Do you know what the emperor Jehangir replied on his deathbed when asked if there was anything he wanted?'

'No.'

'He said—only Kashmir!' He chuckled again. 'This siren of a place had captivated him too!'

'I am told that Gulmarg is even more exquisite than what I have seen so far. I read that it has five hundred different varieties of plants. I would like to go there, especially as you have a house which . . .' she broke off suddenly, at the quick change in expression on Damien's face. It was, all of a sudden, very closed.

'It is not possible at the moment,' he said curtly. 'The house is under repair.'

Crystal wondered why her idle remark intended only to make conversation should have so much upset him, but refrained from asking. There were shades to his temperament that she could not fathom. Shall I ever know this man, she wondered inwardly? But after that she made no further remark about Gulmarg, and the matter was forgotten.

Leaving the coach in the hands of the *syce* who had accompanied them, following on a horse, they walked to the wooden landing-stage on the lake. Servants from the houseboat were waiting for them and Damien despatched them to fetch their luggage from the coach.

'I have to make one or two business calls,' he said. 'I'll leave you to your own resources until luncheon.'

'Where are you going?' she could not help asking, reluctant to lose him even for a short while.

He frowned. 'I have to see Hyder Ali, I told you, and one or two other people.' It was obvious that he disliked having to account for his movements to anyone, and for a moment Crystal felt a stab of jealousy. Could he be going to see Adele or Nafisa? The thought seared her like a pain but she was wise enough to take refuge in silence. If he were, he was hardly likely to tell her!

There was a samovar of steaming hot *qahwa* waiting for her when she reached the houseboat. The rooms looked sparklingly clean and there were great bunches of flowers everywhere. The dining-table had been laid with two places, and her own luggage, she was dismayed to find, had been placed in the bedroom adjoining Damien's. Were they to occupy separate bedrooms tonight then—or not? Her heart palpitated with suspense and the possibility of being in his arms again filled her limbs with an aching languor that was quite, quite, delicious!

On the Dal Lake there was brisk activity. Boats of every kind plied hither and thither, some swiftly, some taking their ease more slowly, others resting for a while. Fruit- and vegetable-sellers in their tiny *shikaras* hawked their wares from houseboat to houseboat, their minute craft laden with produce from the fertile soil. A shy little boy, no more than ten, rowed his *shikara* alongside the *Nishat*, where Crystal sat on deck sipping her *qahwa*. He looked up at her through long black lashes and smiled. She smiled back. Encouraged by his reception, he promptly held out to her a pink lotus-bud. Laughing and touched by the gesture, she leaned over the rail and took it. Without waiting for payment, he paddled off rapidly, frightened by his own daring.

The lake was dotted with islands, all covered in lush greenery and tall *chinars* or firs and pines. She was astonished to see some flat islands, lush with vegetables, moving placidly across the lake. These were the 'floating fields' of Kashmir, and they certainly did look odd, if equally enchanting.

Lost in her own thoughts, enjoying the various vignettes of life on the lake, Crystal was suddenly surprised to hear a loud female English voice at the entrance of the houseboat. 'Are the *sahib* and *memsahib* in? If so, please tell them Mrs Hathaway has called.'

Crystal's heart sank. Today of all days she had no desire to meet anyone at all, least of all Mrs Hathaway. It was not an intrusion she took to kindly, and was on the point of sending word that she had a headache, when Adele Hathaway stepped through the door onto the back deck.

'Ah, there you are, my dear! I heard that you and Damien had come down for the day and I felt I absolutely had to see you both.' Without ceremony she signalled to the *khidmatgar* to bring her a chair and, as it arrived, ensconced herself comfortably.

'How kind of you,' said Crystal warily. She wondered what was the reason for this visit. Last time, she had no doubt at all, it was only to inform Crystal about Nafisa's existence and to create trouble between her and Damien—as indeed she had. 'Would you care for some tea?'

Much to her relief, Adele shook her head. 'No, thank you, dear. I can stay only a short while. How long will Damien be?'

Hoping that he would be as long as possible so as to avoid meeting their unwelcome visitor, Crystal replied sweetly, 'He warned me he might not be back for luncheon. He has a great deal to do in town.'

'Oh?' Adele examined her shrewdly and her face took on a very cunning look. 'I wonder where he has gone?' she asked with pointed innocence, her voice, nevertheless, loaded with innuendo.

'*I* don't,' countered Crystal lightly. 'Damien's business matters are no concern of mine.'

'Oh, I see, it's *business* that's keeping him, is it?' Adele laughed.

Crystal flushed and quickly averted her head, pointing to something on the lake to divert the conversation. How she longed for Adele to leave! That she had been

Damien's mistress was a fact that still rankled, but Crystal had accepted his assurance that this was no longer so. Damien had dismissed Adele with sufficient unconcern to set her mind partially at rest. Nevertheless Crystal disliked her, fearful of what further mischief she was out to commit.

She continued to make forced conversation for a while, becoming more and more agitated, and was actually relieved to hear Damien's voice boom out across the lake as he arrived back on the houseboat.

'Ah!' exclaimed Adele, smiling. 'The great man himself!'

Damien strode through the doorway and stopped as he saw Adele. She jumped to her feet, ran up to him and presented a cheek to be kissed. He looked extremely taken aback and glanced quickly at Crystal, very embarrassed indeed. Crystal turned her head away. Deliberately ignoring her cheek, he shook Adele's hand instead.

'Well, well,' he said drily. 'A surprise indeed!'

Adele flushed at the snub and bit her lip. Then, rallying almost immediately, she said gaily, 'You broke your promise to me, you naughty boy!' She sounded very coquettish.

'Did I?' He came and stood by Crystal, leaning casually against the railings. Crystal could not help enjoying his extreme discomfiture at having Adele and his wife for company at the same time!

'You promised you would come to see me on your return from Delhi, and you haven't, not once,' Adele pouted.

'I have been busy,' he said curtly, turning to look across the lake.

His lack of interest was so apparent that Adele coloured and a look of malice flashed into her eyes. From under modestly lowered lashes she observed him shrewdly, then said, 'Oh, yes, that I know. Why, even your poor little wife had to do without your company yesterday.'

Damien turned and frowned in enquiry, and Crystal's heart seemed to stop beating altogether as her breath caught in her throat.

Seemingly unaware of the consternation she was causing, Adele continued, 'No wonder she was forced to come down to Srinagar on her own—the great man was too involved with making his millions!' Crystal went white and knew exactly what was coming, while Damien continued to frown and his eyes hardened. Adele laughed lightly. 'Why, had it not been for Captain Saunders, she would have had to do all her exploration on her own, isn't that so, Crystal?' She stared at Crystal piercingly, challenging her to deny it.

Damien said nothing and stood at the rails with his head averted, pointedly gazing in the other direction. Crystal closed her eyes in sick despair. So this was the purpose of Adele's seemingly cordial visit this morning! Watching Damien's rigid back already bristling with silent anger, Crystal could have wept. How successfully this wretched, malicious woman had wrecked what would have been an idyllic day together!

But worse was still to come. Noticing the sudden tension in the air, Adele's eyes widened in feigned surprise. She looked from one to the other in pretended shock. 'Oh!' she exclaimed, wringing her hands in remorse. 'Have I said something that I shouldn't have?' Her distress was commendable! 'Oh dear! I always seem to be putting my foot in it! I had no idea Damien . . . didn't know about . . . yesterday.'

While Crystal watched silently in numb horror, knowing how Damien would react to this little titbit of information, Adele extracted a lace handkerchief from her bag and dabbed her eyes delicately, exactly as she had done at Shalimar the other day. That this was all part of another nefarious scheme Crystal did not doubt.

But, to her utter astonishment, Damien turned round suddenly and she noticed his face was quite relaxed. 'What was that you said, Adele, about yesterday? Oh yes, it was indeed fortunate that Henry was on the spot to escort Crystal. She told me about it.'

While Crystal's mouth opened in amazement, Adele's lips clamped shut in disappointment, the purpose of her little visit coming to naught. She began to fumble. 'Oh in that case . . . er . . . I am so glad I didn't say anything. I didn't want to . . . cause trouble . . .' she faded out, flustered.

'Oh, I'm *sure* you didn't,' said Damien, his voice so silky that Adele abruptly rose to her feet. 'It would be so dreadfully unlike you!' His eyes scorned her coldly and Crystal's heart soared at how aptly he had put this terrible woman in her place. She felt grateful for his quick intervention but knew, nevertheless, with awful certainty that when they were alone this would not be the end of the matter!

Very pleasantly, he escorted Adele to the door as, without even a glance at Crystal and head held defiantly high, she made to leave. Crystal heaved a sigh of shuddering relief, but awaited Damien's return with apprehension. Nor was her fear unfounded. When he came back, a moment later, his face was set like cold marble and his eyes gleamed blacker than ever. He took in silently the tell-tale red flush on Crystal's countenance.

'I thought I had expressly forbidden you to have anything to do with this man,' he ground out through clenched teeth. 'Why did you not tell me you had been to Srinagar yesterday?'

'I . . . I meant to, but . . .' Her face was a picture of guilt, she knew, although not for the reason that he thought!

'You came down to meet Henry Saunders?' he asked sharply, his eyes stormy and his lips thin and tight. The scar on his cheek stood out livid white against his brown, weather-beaten face.

'*No!*' she cried, galvanised into self-defence against the unfair accusation. 'I did *not* come to Srinagar to meet him! Indeed, the encounter was purely accidental. I came down to . . . to have a look at the Moghul Gardens. Captain Saunders also happened to be there . . .' She tailed off as she saw the look of scepticism on his face. Suddenly her temper flared. 'Oh, don't believe me if you don't want to,' she flung at him angrily. 'It does not disconcert you that your mistresses—past or present, I know not—come to see you in my presence without shame; but I chance upon a man you do not like and you are ready to believe the worst of me! Well, believe what you like, it doesn't bother me a bit!' Sick with frustrated anger, she rose to her feet and was about to brush past him, when he caught her arm and held her.

He looked at her closely. 'I accept that you do not like me,' he said very softly with eyes narrowed. 'But I will not accept being made a fool of. I wish you to understand that quite clearly.'

She struggled to release her arm but his grip was like a vice. *I accept that you do not like me!* Oh, what a stupid, blind fool he already was! Tears of frustration came into her eyes. 'It is not I who have made you a fool,' she snapped. 'It is the hand of fate!'

His eyes narrowed even further and for a moment he struggled with his exploding temper. Then unexpectedly he relaxed, threw back his head and laughed! 'By gad!' he exclaimed releasing her arm, 'your tongue is as sharp as your wits. But,' he chuckled, 'I must admit I like it! It makes a pleasant change from the constant servility one receives as the Sarkar.' She made to walk past him, but with a nimble step he blocked her path. 'All right,' he added surprisingly. 'I believe you. Your face is such that it cannot harbour a falsehood without giving itself away.'

Without a word, she ran past him into the room. In spite of his acceptance of her explanation, she felt greatly agitated. Her strange conversation with Henry Saunders yesterday came flooding back. What would Damien say if he knew just what the insolent Captain had said? He would not only take out the threatened horsewhip, he would probably also put a bullet through the wretched man's heart! And what would be his reaction to her surreptitious visit to Nafisa? For sure, that would not please him greatly either! Just as well she had taken all the precautions she had.

Luncheon was a doleful meal with neither of them inclined to conversation. Silently she picked at the chicken pilaf and curry. She had no idea what was going on in his mind. As to her own thoughts, he obviously did not care. Miserably she pushed her plate away, excused herself and retired to the back deck alone. They were not expected at the Palace until five o'clock in the evening. She intended to use the intervening hours to regain her good temper. She wanted desperately to win Damien's favour again, but felt too proud to make the first overture. If only he knew just how despairingly she wanted his love—and how much of hers he possessed already!

To her surprise, he joined her after a while at the rails, his face impassive but not angry any more. They stood in silence, side by side, watching the boats. The afternoon was warm and filled with cheerful sounds from the lake. It was difficult to retain any semblance of ill-temper and, with his elbows brushing hers so casually, Crystal found herself relenting, especially since he himself appeared to want peace again.

'How many different kinds of boats they seem to have on the lake,' she said finally in an effort to break the silence.

'Dozens,' he agreed pleasantly. 'The waterways of Kashmir are very important in commerce. They are the lifelines for the carriage of much cargo.' He pointed to a large boat that was moving past them slowly. 'See this one here? This is a *bahat*, used to carry bulky loads such as grain and wood. It has a high prow and stern and those cabins on board also carry the boatman and his family, who live on board.'

'It looks so heavy and lies so low, it seems about to sink!'

Damien laughed. 'Not these boats. Like all the other Kashmiri boats, *bahats* are flat-bottomed and can carry as much as a thousand *maunds* at a time. These smaller ones are called *wars* and have a much lower prow, see? These other little ones are the *dungas* and the *shikara* you have already been in. Then we have the *kuchus*, which are very heavy and open-roofed. They carry stones, and this one here . . .'

As he made his explanations, Crystal listened in growing admiration. How learned he was about all things Kashmiri! There seemed to be nothing he did not know of first hand. Indeed, he was more a part of this wild, wondrous land than she would have thought it possible for any foreigner to be. She felt renewed respect for the man she had married, realising just how much more there was to him than she had first thought probable.

Finally it was time to change for the important occasion ahead. In the absence of Sharifa, her sister Zaitoon—Rehana's mother—had been summoned on board to assist Crystal in her toilet. The *sari*, well pressed and neatly folded, was laid out on the bed, together with a matching blouse and half petticoat. Crystal allowed Zaitoon to brush her hair, then coiled it into a smooth chignon at the nape of her neck. Around the chignon Zaitoon wound a fragrant garland of white jasmine flowers, as Indian women often did. In her eyes, to enhance their size and accentuate the translucent amber highlights, she applied a thin line of black *kohl*. Then, in a final effort to please Damien, she slipped on some of the beautiful wedding jewellery that he had given her. She had sworn she would not wear it again, knowing how much that would annoy and hurt him. But, suddenly, she was frantic not to do anything that might spoil this marvellous opportunity to win his favour, maybe even his love!

As Zaitoon watched, she draped the *sari* around her

expertly, taking care to fold the pleats so that they did not catch in her feet. She secured it over her shoulder with a pin, not wanting the heavy silk to slip.

Observing the expertise with which her fingers worked, Zaitoon clasped her hands in admiration. '*Memsahib* knows all the ways of our people!' she exclaimed. 'Just like the Sarkar.'

Crystal smiled at the compliment. 'I have lived here all my life, Zaitoon, and they are my people, too.'

Over her shoulders, when the *sari* was securely arranged, she draped the *jaam-e-war*. The light blues and pale yellows in the exquisite shawl matched the deep blue of her *sari* perfectly. Crystal stepped back and took a final look at herself in the full-length mirror. Just as she was slipping on a pair of gold leather sandals, there was a knock on the door that connected her room to Damien's, and he walked in. He took a step, then halted abruptly in his tracks, his eyes widening in astonishment. Silently he surveyed her from head to toe as she waited nervously for his comment. His eyes lingered a moment on the jewellery.

'Do I . . . look all right?' she asked uncertainly.

For an instant he did not reply, then he smiled his slow, wonderful smile and his gaze softened. 'You look . . . ravishing,' he said, the blackness of his eyes containing something indecipherable in their depths. She saw the desire in his look, the open admiration, and she began to dissolve with slow pleasure. How striking he looked in his scarlet suit and ruffled silk shirt! Her face glowed in response, but he suddenly turned on his heel and made to leave.

'His Highness will be delighted with your effort to please him,' he said in a matter-of-fact voice. 'You carry the *sari* well.' He went out abruptly.

It is not to please His Highness, she cried out silently after him, it is to please *you*, oh you fool! Surely he could see in her eyes what she felt for him? How could he be so obtuse! Yet she felt unbearably elated at his approval, joyous that he found her ravishing—and desirable!

Carefully she stepped into the *shikara* that was to take them to the landing-stage, worried in case her *sari* became soiled or crushed. Damien gave her his hand as she climbed off the stairs and into the little boat and, as her fingers came in contact with his, she felt the same electrifying thrill his touch always produced. She shivered.

'Are you cold?' he asked anxiously. She shook her head, drawing the *jaam-e-war* more closely around her shoulders.

On the jetty, she was astonished to see an entire cavalcade from Shalimar! There was Gulab Singh, two grooms, two goatmen, a small donkey-cart laden with a box, a superb black Arab stallion with nostrils flaring that looked like Shaitan, but wasn't, and had the most superb saddle—and, to her utter amazement—no less than twelve long-haired goats! A crowd of people surrounded this strange melange.

'Is all this part of our retinue?' Crystal gasped in disbelief.

Damien laughed. 'Indeed, yes. As you can see, it is to be quite a ceremonial parade!'

'B-but to what purpose?' she asked, bewildered. 'And why the *goats*?'

'Well,' said Damien, greatly amused by her expression of perplexity, 'it is a long story, but to cut it short, when Maharaja Gulab Singh was installed on the throne by the British in 1846, it was agreed that, in recognition of the supremacy of the British, he would present to the government each year certain gifts as a token of this recognition?'

'I see. But what does this have to do with you?' Crystal asked, still not clear in her mind.

'The gifts of a horse, this fellow here, twelve *pashmina* bearing goats of the highest quality—the ones you see laden so unhappily into that cart—and three long shawls of the finest wools, in the box, are all prepared at

Shalimar. It is an old tradition from my father's days.'

'Oh!' Crystal's eyes dilated in awe and she was much impressed. That such a great honour should fall upon Damien and his Shalimar! It was indeed something to be proud of. 'So, this evening we are going to deliver the gifts which will then be sent to the Viceroy?'

'Yes,' said Damien. 'These poor devils with large, patient eyes have no idea of the long journey that awaits them after being nurtured with loving care in the comforts of Shalimar. Now, come on, climb on to your magic carpet like a good girl. It wouldn't do to be late.'

By the side of the cobbled road stood a beautifully painted palanquin, its motifs and carvings picked out in gold. To bear it were four liveried men, their uniforms sparkling with as much spit and polish as were their eyes! Damien swung himself lithely into the saddle of the black stallion, holding down its rearing head with tightened reins. Crystal sighed and settled back into the plush cushions of the palanquin, too excited to protest about this hated form of transport. All she could think of was how extraordinarily handsome Damien looked in his formal clothes and how superbly he sat the horse that led their strange procession.

CHAPTER EIGHT

It was indeed an odd procession that wended its way slowly up the hill towards the Palace high above, and it seemed to cause great excitement among the crowd that followed it enthusiastically. All around Damien, leading the cavalcade on the splendid horse, were smiling faces and, as he laughed and exchanged banter with the people, Crystal again glowed with quiet pride to see how much at ease he was among them. It was obviously an occasion that was well known to the crowd, for many remarks were passed about the excellent quality of the animals and the undoubted fineness of the six shawls contained within the box on the cart. They were, indeed, splendid gifts from their Maharaja to the Queen of England, something all of Kashmir could be proud of.

At the gates of the Palace, sparkling white and guarded by a team of smartly uniformed guards, they were received by officials with due honour. They all seemed to know Damien well and, as he dismounted from his horse and walked with them down the drive, he was showered with compliments on this latest example of Shalimar's prowess at horse-breeding. Following at a modest distance behind was Crystal's palanquin and, as it passed down the drive, she had glimpses of beautifully-laid-out gardens and a breathtaking view over the town and the lake.

At the main entrance to the Palace, many hands were extended to assist as the palanquin was brought to rest in the hall. Damien helped her to descend from its uncomfortable depths, and introduced her to each of the officials in turn. It was a splendid hall, brilliantly lit by chandeliers, and there was a sense of occasion about their visit which set her pulses racing. Although no official would be daring enough to make a personal comment about her appearance, Crystal could see frequent admiring glances cast in her direction. In deference to local custom, she had covered her hair with an edge of the *sari*, knowing that this was something Damien would approve of, as indeed he did. Throwing an amused glance at her, not without quiet pride, he chatted casually in Kashmiri with the escorts, very composed and full of arrogant self-confidence.

Presently they were ushered into the personal apartments of the Maharaja whose name, Crystal knew, was Ranbir Singh, son of Gulab Singh, the first of the Dogra Maharajas of Kashmir. For a moment she wondered whether she was to be led away to the women's apartments to be entertained by the Maharani, and hoped that it would not be so. She would far rather stay with the men, as their conversation was bound to be more informative and enjoyable. But Crystal had read that women in Kashmir, unlike in other parts of India, were given considerable freedom, and there was no *purdah* or concealment of the features for women, except among the higher classes.

As they were ushered into the royal presence in a small, comfortable sitting-room beyond the formal salons, Crystal was struck by the informality of the man who ruled this impressive state. Maharaja Ranbir Singh was seated upon a divan covered with a crimson and gold *masnad* such as she had seen in many aristocratic Indian homes and more recently at Nafisa's house. He reclined against large, matching bolsters and was dressed very simply in loose white silken trousers and a shirt studded with gold buttons. As he was a Sikh, he wore a magnificent turban of bright green. His jewellery consisted of a single gold chain round his neck and a diamond ring. He had a pleasant, open face and a beard that was streaked with white. He smiled as they entered.

'Ah, Damien,' he said, his eyes lighting up with pleasure. 'It is good to see you again.'

Damien bowed and folded his hands in the traditional greeting. 'I am delighted to see Your Highness looking so well after your recent indisposition,' he replied. Glancing towards Crystal, he said, 'May I present my wife?'

The Maharaja stared at Crystal as she also folded her hands in greeting, and his eyes widened in surprise. 'I had not heard that you had married an Indian girl, Damien!'

Damien laughed as Crystal flushed and lowered her eyes in sudden shyness. 'Well, Your Highness,' he said lightly, 'I am sure she will take that as a compliment to her talent in dressing, but she is, surprisingly, as English as can be.'

'Is she?' the Maharaja exclaimed, then laughed as well. 'I find it difficult to believe, so perfectly Oriental are her features—and so perfectly beautiful, I might add.' He chuckled, indicating chairs upholstered in gold damask. 'Please be seated and let us talk, but before we do,' he chuckled again, 'I would like to compliment you on your excellent choice of a bride, Damien—not that I would expect anything else from you!' He turned to Crystal and said very seriously, 'I might tell you, Mrs Granville, that news of your marriage has left many hearts desolated in Kashmir! Why, in my own Palace, hint of a visit from Damien is enough to send the Maharani's staff rushing to the windows in the hope of catching a mere glimpse of him!'

Damien coloured in embarrassment and put a finger into his collar. Crystal smiled brightly, greatly enjoying his discomfiture. 'I am sure, Your Highness, that my husband is only too well aware of it—as his own talent in dressing will testify!' The Maharaja laughed loudly as Damien glowered at her, furious.

They had been using Urdu, and the Maharaja complimented her on how well she spoke the language. 'You have obviously been in India many years,' he said, 'for your accent is flawless.'

'I was born in India, Your Highness, and have lived here all my life. I learned Urdu long before I became fluent in English.'

He looked surprised. 'How is that?'

'My father was an archaeologist,' she explained, 'and I spent many years of my childhood wandering about the country on excavating trips.'

'What was his name?'

'Covendale,' said Crystal. 'Arthur Covendale.'

'Why, I have met him, then,' exclaimed the Maharaja, 'at Taxila, north of Rawalpindi. He did some work there, did he not?'

'Yes, indeed he did,' said Crystal, astonished at the coincidence. 'He was particularly interested in the Greek influence on Taxila and the Indus valley.'

'How extraordinary!' exclaimed His Highness. 'Isn't it, Damien? That I should have met the father of your bride, so many years ago?'

'Indeed, it is,' said Damien, reclining comfortably in the chair, listening to their conversation with interest. 'I never had the pleasure of meeting Dr Covendale, but I understand he was a highly learned man.'

'And what about you, my dear?' asked the Maharaja. 'Are you also interested in archaeology?'

'Very much so,' said Crystal firmly. 'It formed part of my earliest education.'

'In that case,' commented the Maharaja, turning to Damien, 'you must introduce your wife to all the ancient monuments we have in Kashmir. Our history, as you probably know, Mrs Granville, goes back to even before 2,000 BC. The temple at Martanda, for example, is worth seeing. You must take your wife there, Damien.'

Damien nodded and smiled slightly. 'Certainly. There is a great deal Crystal hasn't seen yet in Kashmir. I stand guilty of neglecting her shamefully.'

Crystal looked at him in pleased surprise. What a handsome admission! How wonderful if he did decide to remedy it now! The doors of the chamber were suddenly flung open and a succession of sprucely uniformed bearers appeared carrying a succession of trays of a variety of sweets and savouries, and the inevitable samovar of *qahwa*. There was a lull in the conversation as the trays were placed on dainty, ornately carved walnut wood tables, and bowls of walnuts, currants, dried apricots and almonds, all covered in wafer-thin silver-paper, were arranged. A bearer poured out the cups of spiced tea as another served them with the delicacies that soon filled their plates. Having performed their duties, the bearers withdrew, once again leaving them in privacy but hovering, undoubtedly, on the other side of the door in case they were needed again. Crystal was very impressed at the quiet efficiency with which a royal staff worked, but proud to remember that Damien's staff at Shalimar was just as well trained and expert as these.

As they ate, the Maharaja and Damien began to talk of other matters. Crystal noticed how relaxed her husband was with His Highness. Obviously they had known each other for some time.

'I am told,' said His Highness, 'that your gifts are as excellent this year as they have been every year. The stallion, especially, should please them in England.'

Damien accepted the compliment with a mere inclination of the head.

'I have been considering the possibility of changing the nature of these gifts, Damien,' the Maharaja continued. 'I intend to write to your Viceroy and suggest that we do away with the live animals and settle for some fine wool instead. What do you think?'

'Well, it certainly would be easier to transport wool! These very valuable goats are also damnably delicate and, as Your Highness knows, there have been unfortunate casualties. This business of taking them to England to breed them there is, I agree with you, quite ridiculous. Yes, I think it would be a good idea to make a presentation of wool instead.'

'I shall, of course, continue to send the three shawls that your weavers on Shalimar produce so exquisitely. I am told that these shawls are greatly appreciated by your Queen Victoria who, they say, already possesses quite a few.'

'And so she should,' agreed Damien irreverently. 'After all, the Empress Josephine owned no less than four hundred and started quite a rage for them in France. Which is why Kashmir seems to be dominated by French traders these days and I don't see why English merchants should be left behind.'

'Surely your English merchants are also doing well out of our weaving expertise,' said His Highness. 'After all, those Scotsmen in Paisley have taken our mango motif and even given it their town's name!'

Damien laughed as Crystal listened fascinated at how much detail lay behind a Kashmiri shawl that she had always taken so casually. 'Well, it is a matter of great incentive for our weavers to know that their work is appreciated abroad. After the tragic depletions during the famine, we need many more weavers to join the trade and be trained in it. It must not be allowed to die out,' Damien said emphatically.

'No,' remarked the Maharaja sadly. 'It would be a crime if it did. But they say a mere 4,000 weavers remain out of a previous 40,000, and our 1873 population of nearly 500,000 in the valley has been halved by the famine.'

'It is increasing,' assured Damien, 'as the next census will reveal. I am doing my best at Shalimar to encourage young lads to take up weaving and be trained by their elders.'

'Yes, I know,' said the Maharaja, 'and we are grateful for your efforts. Indeed, it was a fortunate day when your father accepted my father's offer of Shalimar and decided to settle here to help the industry. It was, of course, a matter of great personal sorrow to me when your dear mother . . .' He broke off abruptly and glanced at Crystal who was listening with attention riveted.

Before any more could be mentioned on the subject, however, Damien rose slowly to his feet. There was a subtle change in his expression which Crystal could not fathom. Very reluctantly, she was forced to rise too.

'Kashmir has given us far more than we can ever hope to give her,' Damien said with rare feeling. 'I think Your Highness is only too well aware of my own gratitude for that.'

The Maharaja rose to his feet, smiled, and put a detaining hand on Damien's arm. 'By the way, Damien, I received yesterday a young army officer from Lahore by the name of . . . Sanders, I think. No, Saunders. He appeared to feel that there is increased Russian activity in Kashmir. He said something about infiltrators. Have you heard anything?'

Crystal's heart jumped into her mouth and she noticed a quick tautening of Damien's jawline. But his manner did not change. 'Really?' he commented casually. 'No, no such case has been brought to my notice.'

'Neither to mine. Our agents are, as you know, quite alert and would have surely reported any incursion to me. This man Saunders feels that with the increased tension in Afghanistan and the growth of Russian influence there, they may feel confident to try entry through Gilgit now.'

'I doubt it,' said Damien dismissively. 'The British government,' he added with a curt laugh, 'is obsessed with fear of the Russians.'

Crystal was surprised at the unusually sharp tone of his voice, as his face suddenly set into grim lines. The Maharaja, however, appeared not to notice, merely shrugging his shoulders and saying with a smile, 'Well, I hope you are right. I would hate the British to find an excuse to send their troops into Kashmir.' Turning to

Crystal, he smiled with added warmth. 'I am delighted to have met you, my dear Mrs Granville. I regret that the Maharani is not in Srinagar at the moment, but next time she will be enchanted to meet an English lady with whom she can communicate without an interpreter.' He laughed. 'My father had the honour of meeting Mrs Honoria Lawrence in 1850. She was the first white woman to brave the journey, you know.'

'Yes, I have heard of her,' Crystal smiled in return. 'I understand she was indefatigable in her travels across India.'

'And you remind me of her,' the Maharaja chuckled. 'You appear to have the same spirit of adventure. I like it and admire it.' His eyes twinkled. 'I hope your husband does, too!'

Damien's smile was dry. 'It is difficult not to admire spirit,' he said, 'except when one is at the receiving end of it.'

The Maharaja laughed delightedly and clapped his hands. Immediately the doors opened and two bearers entered carrying between them a heavy wooden chest. Crystal recognised it as walnut wood and it was intricately and exquisitely carved. 'A small token for you and Damien,' the Maharaja smiled, 'with my sincere felicitations on the happy occasion of your marriage. I hope you are blessed with many sons and perhaps,' his eyes sparkled with humour, 'a daughter or two as lovely as their mother.'

Crystal blushed and, with shyly lowered lashes, thanked him for such a generous gift. She suddenly recalled, fleetingly, the reason Damien had given, on their wedding-night, for having married her. What would the Maharaja have to say if he knew just how fruitless their marriage was likely to be?

On the way back from the Palace, Crystal sat in her palanquin immersed in thought, only vaguely aware of the stunning view that lay below the hill. The mention of Saunders had upset her dreadfully—and Damien too, she guessed. Had Saunders told the Maharaja about his suspicions, totally absurd as they were? And why had Damien's mood changed so radically at the mention of the Russians? Was it only because of his strong aversion to Saunders? Or was it because he had something to conceal? Also the Maharaja's abrupt mention of Damien's mother and the effect of it on Damien—what did it mean? As she sat cogitating over all these questions, Crystal suddenly felt very uneasy. There seemed to be so many loose threads in Damien's life that she had not been able to tie up. Would she ever?

By the time they reached the landing-stage, Damien's composure was once again perfect, although he appeared to be uncommonly silent. He dismissed Gulab Singh for the night, but asked his *syce* to wait at the jetty with his horse.

'Will you be going out again tonight?' Crystal asked, trying to keep her disappointment from showing. It was already quite late and the thought of having to eat alone after the excitement of the evening did not appeal to her.

'Yes,' he said with no further explanation. He went into his room to change into more informal clothes. Crystal changed from her *sari* into a dress, feeling suddenly depressed. There was something undoubtedly troubling Damien. She longed to be taken into his confidence but knew that that was unlikely. The realisation doused her spirits even further. She sat on the bed, very desolate, and watched Zaitoon fold her clothes and put them aside for pressing later.

A curt knock heralded Damien's entry. He had discarded the stiff formal suit and was comfortably clad in dark trousers, a cotton shirt and a dark blue casual jacket.

'I shall be going out for a while. I shall probably be late in returning. You don't need to wait up for me.' He subjected her to a sharp look, taking in the downward tilt of her mouth, as disappointment showed plainly in her eyes. A sardonic smile twisted his lips, and he raised his eyebrows quizzically. 'You need not worry,' he said, completely misunderstanding the expression on her face. 'You will not be disturbed tonight.' With a sarcastic laugh, he was gone.

Crystal sat miserably for a very long while on the roof that night, watching the twinkling lights on the Dal Lake vanish one by one. There were the beginnings of a moon in the sky. The crescent still rode the crests of the mountain peaks throwing a pale, flickering light on the snows. Gradually, the lake became still and silent, but Crystal did not move, one single question repeating itself in her mind interminably. Where had Damien gone? She writhed in agony as she considered that he might have gone to see Nafisa. It was a prospect she could not bear and the tears stung like needle-points inside her lids.

Finally, too tired to stay awake any longer, she crept back into her room and slipped into bed. In spite of her tiredness, sleep did not come readily. She must have dozed off, however, for suddenly she woke with a start as she heard sounds of movement next door. Damien was back! She lay with bated breath, wondering if the adjoining door would open, if he would relent and come to her after all. Oh, how she prayed that he might! The scalding memory of those fevered kisses, the frantic caresses of his strong, confident hands and of the unforgettable feel of his skin next to hers, were all suddenly overpowering. But then, the ugly scene in her bedroom that terrible night returned in full force. *I shall not come to you again until you ask me to!* With what venom he had spat out his cruel promise to her! How well she knew that Damien was not one to go back on his words easily—and she would never ask him!

As the sounds in the bedroom next door subsided, the houseboat was once again cloaked in the silence of the night. Damien had gone to sleep. How she longed that she could do the same! For a while she chased oblivion fruitlessly. Then, dull and fatigued, she buried her head in her pillow and wept.

'Come and have some *sheera*!'

Damien was already at breakfast when Crystal rose the next morning, heavy-eyed and tired with an aching head. Dressed casually in shirt-sleeves, he appeared once again full of bonhomie, smiling at her as innocently as if there was not a trace of tension between them. Crystal sighed and settled herself at the breakfast-table laid out on the sun-drenched roof. She decided it was no use trying to understand the complex facets that went to make up the character of the man she faced. It would be far easier for her peace of mind to accept each day for whatever it might bring.

'What is *sheera*?' she asked, examining closely the array of dishes on the table.

'Vermicelli cooked in sugar syrup and milk. See? It has all the goodness needed to bring back the shine in your eyes!' His own, black and dancing with humour, were unusually amicable.

The *sheera* was delicious, laced with a variety of nuts and raisins. She ate with relish, the light meal at which she had picked last night, alone and miserable, having been long forgotten.

'Do we return to Shalimar today?' she asked, avoiding the subject of yesterday's visit to the Palace. It was possible he did not wish to mention it, considering how strangely he had been affected by some of the topics of conversation.

'I have to remain in Srinagar for another day or two, but if you would like to return, I shall arrange it with Gulab Singh.'

'Oh, no,' she said hastily. 'I would like to stay, too. There is so much to be seen. I haven't been to the Nishat Gardens yet.'

'How would you like to go to Martanda to investigate the old temples?' he asked suddenly.

Her breath caught with excitement. 'Oh, I would love

that—if it could be arranged.' She paused and lowered her eyes. 'Would you be able to come too, or do you have work to do?' She sounded so anxious that his eyes twinkled at her.

'No, I do not have any work to do. I merely await some information from Hyder Ali. I am entirely at your service today.'

The prospect of not only seeing the unique and famous temple complex, but also of having Damien all to herself for the entire day, sent Crystal into a paroxysm of joy. Secretly she hugged herself, but outwardly she merely smiled politely. 'That will be very agreeable,' she said sedately. 'I shall go and get ready.'

The journey to Martanda was not long, but Damien ordered a night of camping as well, and the thought added pleasure to her mood in no small measure. The Vale of Kashmir in the prime of spring, it seemed to her, was made for outdoor living. With the lush beauty of the land underfoot, the velvet black canopy of stars above and the pristine embrace of the white mountains all around, a night in the meadows promised a taste of pure heaven. Who knew, under romantic circumstances such as these, anything at all could happen—and how she prayed that it would!

Out on the landing-stage she was once again faced with a veritable cavalcade. There was Gulab Singh, two grooms, three donkeys laden with baggage, and their keepers, Damien's bay horse and her own Sundari. She looked at her lovely chestnut in surprise. 'How did Sundari get here?'

'I had her brought down, knowing that she might be needed,' Damien explained, and Crystal was suddenly very touched. How thoughtful he was sometimes—and how devastatingly charming he could be when he chose to!

Zaitoon was to accompany them to Martanda to look after Crystal's needs and Damien contented himself with but one servant, his personal bearer. Gulab Singh was to remain in Srinagar to await the information from Hyder Ali, but the grooms and the donkey-keepers were, of course, to go with them.

Riding demurely side-saddle, with a silk scarf tied over her hair, Crystal trotted dutifully alongside Damien as their party started on their way. On the outskirts of Srinagar, the river Jhelum, which was the lifeline of the valley, sparkled silver and blue in the brilliant sun and the heavenly gardens of the Moghuls looked spectacular as they passed by.

'I had no idea there were so many waterways in Kashmir,' Crystal commented as they went over yet another lovely wooden bridge.

'Oh, there are hundreds,' said Damien. 'Canals, lakes, streams, rivulets and brooks. There are said to be about 34,000 boatmen and their families making a living off these waterways. Do you know what one of the greatest pleasure of these waterways is?'

'No.'

'Trout-fishing! Ever done it?'

'Not really,' she said hesitantly. 'Of course, I have fished in ordinary rivers for ordinary fish, but not for trout, I believe this is something very special.'

'Indeed it is. Let's see. We may be able to find a camping-site near a fast-flowing stream, although the Lidder valley is best for trout.'

'Well,' said Crystal lightly, 'I believe in trying everything once! I look forward to instruction in trout-fishing.'

Damien laughed and once again Crystal was enthralled at how very attractive his face became when it lost its dark, brooding appearance, and how wonderfully white were his even teeth against the dark brown of his complexion when he smiled. If only he would remain this way for the whole of today, what a blessing it would be!

Looking down into the bottom of the valley, as they climbed towards the Martanda plateau high above

Srinagar, the rolling hills were again multi-hued with the vivid light greens of the rice-fields and the rainbow colours of the spring wild flowers. The soft blue haze of morning still clung to the bottle-green groves of clustered trees dotting the landscape, and the patchwork of fields showed an incredible variety of pastel shades.

Passing by a sparse collection of huts, Crystal suddenly gave a cry of excitement. 'Oh, Damien, do stop a moment. I would like to examine something I have seen.'

While he watched with tolerant amusement, she dismounted quickly and ran to a carelessly piled heap of broken stones that lay just by the side of the track. She turned one over and saw that it had an image carved on it. Four or five villagers gathered at a respectful distance to watch Crystal as she poked and probed among the stones.

'What are these, Damien?' she asked breathlessly. 'They appear to be very old relics of some sort.'

He joined her and, bending down on one knee, examined the stones. Then he shrugged. 'You find these sorts of collections all over Kashmir,' he said. 'Nobody has been able to give a correct explanation for them, but it is believed that, since this valley has always been dominated by Hindu and Buddhist influences, these are the works of bygone people meant for temples that have long since been destroyed.'

'Can I take one back,' she asked. 'It looks so beautiful and forlorn as if no one cared for it any more.'

He laughed and shook his head. 'Come on,' he said, taking hold of her hand, 'you will find thousands of these all over Kashmir I'll find you something really beautiful in Shalimar, I promise.'

He held her hand until they reached their horses and, for a moment, Crystal felt such piercing happiness that tears almost came to her eyes. She longed to keep it in hers for ever, but when he let it go, she silently mounted her horse again, content that she had him all to herself at least for another day.

They arrived at the Martanda plateau well before the time for luncheon. Right on top, in the middle of an even plain, stood the ruins of one of the most magnificent temples Crystal had ever seen. It was massive, towering above them, even in its decrepit condition a forceful reminder of its former glory. Crystal stood silently, watching it in awe. Despite the decay that the centuries had wrought, it commanded admiration for its size as well as centuries had wrought, it commanded admiration for its size as well as for the sheer beauty of its architectural design and ornamentation.

She bent down and picked up a piece of broken masonry. 'It's limestone, isn't it?'

Damien nodded. 'This was built by an eighth-century Hindu king called Lalitaditya, but you can see the influence of the Greeks in the surrounding colonnade of pillars.'

'My father used to call this style of architecture Arian, a combination of Aryan and what the Greeks called Araiostyle.'

He peered at her with head tilted and eyes squinting against the glare of the midday sun. 'You miss him very much, don't you?'

'Yes.' Her voice was suddenly small and sad. This was the first time she had visited any site of archaeological importance without him.

'There are some ruins at the southernmost end of Shalimar,' he said suddenly. 'I have always wondered about them. Perhaps you would undertake their complete excavation some day?'

Her eyes lit up. 'I would love that,' she said simply. 'I am never more happy than when in the company of old ruins.'

'Presumably,' he teased drily, 'I do not qualify yet! Who knows, in fifty years, when I do, your eyes will brighten when you look at me in the same way that they are brightening now before this heap.'

She bit her lip. Did he think that her eyes were alight only because of that? How obtuse some men could be!

As they wandered round the ruins, discovering all their delights, Crystal realised that, for all his flippancy, Damien was extremely well informed about antiquity, especially that in the Vale. He had read a great deal about Kashmir's ancient history and there were few sites of archaeological significance that he had not visited personally. Listening to him now relate the influences brought by the Greeks, the Buddhists, the Hindus and the successive waves of Muslims, she was fascinated.

On a shady slope underneath spreading walnut trees, the servants had prepared a simple luncheon of barbecued lamb ribs and flat unleavened bread baked on a hot stone. As always, there were piles of freshly picked fruit. It was a glorious meal. Crystal ate sitting on a large boulder that allowed an uninterrupted vision of the valley. By her side, Damien reclined on the grass, leaning on an elbow.

After luncheon she leaned back against a tree and closed her eyes, overcome by a deep, contented sleep. Damien laid his head back on the grass and stretched out languidly, lost in thought. There were few sounds except for the monotonous buzzing of the bees as they hummed their way from flower to flower, and the gentle whistling of the fragrant breezes rustling through the leaves overhead.

Deep in the recesses of her sleep, she suddenly heard Damien's voice. 'Why did you go to see Nafisa?'

Crystal awoke, startled, and sat up with a jolt. He had found out! How? For a moment she struggled for words to reply, her heart becoming heavy at what else he might say. 'I . . . wanted to meet her. How did you know?'

Without opening his eyes or moving his position, he smiled. 'There is very little that happens in this valley that I do not know.'

'Oh!'

'Well . . . why?' He turned over on his side and looked at her intently.

'Does it matter?'

He shrugged. 'No. But I am curious.' He appeared to show no particular emotion except that.

She laughed lightly, determined not to endanger this idyllic afternoon with even a hint of tension. 'It's a good idea, don't you think, for every wife to acquaint herself with her husband's mistresses? It might make for more . . . cordiality all round!' She said it with so much pleasantness that the words held no sting in them. If he noticed the touch of bitterness in her voice, he did not react. He did, however, look at her sharply, but only for a second. Then, rising quickly, he began to dust the grass from his trousers.

'Let's see if we can find a quiet stream at the foot of the plateau where we can fish and set up camp for the night.' Taking the conversation completely in his stride, he walked off.

Crystal stood up too, brushed her clothes and set out after him, full of thoughts. How had he found out that she had visited Nafisa? Could it have been from Nafisa herself? Is that where he had gone last night—and returned content and satiated? Her spirits drooped again at the vision of Damien wrapped in the arms of his beautiful Kashmiri mistress, whispering words of love. She felt riddled with hot stabs of jealousy all over again, and her face crumpled. How demeaning it was to be in love with a man who had not a kind thought to give in return!

The narrow heavily-wooded footpath that led down the side of the plateau was cool, and all round were the cries of chattering, cooing, twittering birds. Sudden flashes of brilliant colour sped past. At the bottom of the hill thundered a narrow stream that crashed and bubbled over the scattered boulders. Kneeling on a patch of open grass, Damien was gazing into the waters. He looked up as she joined him.

'Some good trout,' he said in approval. 'Not very many, but we may be lucky.'

Running back up the path, he called out to his *khidmatgar* to follow them down, then, hands in pockets, he paced up and down beside the stream, observing, to all intents and purposes, a gigantic yellow butterfly that hovered uncertainly over a clump of poppies.

The retinue arrived presently, and the fishing-rods were soon assembled. Damien looked at her hesitantly. 'You're not exactly dressed for trout-fishing, are you?'

'How should I be dressed?'

'Well, in trousers, really. You have to fish from mid-stream for trout and you'll need to put on waders, hardly suitable for what you're wearing now.'

The problem was finally settled with a compromise. Crystal was to sit perched on a flat, high boulder that jutted from the stream not very far from the bank and Damien would stay close at hand in case of a bite and if the fish had to be followed down stream. He watched critically while Crystal cast the line with fair competence.

'Not bad,' he nodded in reluctant approval. 'But take care next time that you don't hook the bushes on the other side and lose the fly.'

'All right,' said Crystal. 'But if I get a bite, I'll shout for you, so don't wander too far.'

In abject obedience, he stretched himself out on the grass, crossed his arms underneath his head and closed his eyes. Crystal smiled and sat back to enjoy the wait, hoping it would not be long. The retinue had moved further down the bank and up a small hillock, where the camp was to be pitched. Behind the hillock she could see fields of waist-high corn and scarlet splashes of poppies. Just below the hillock the stream dipped sharply, forming a small cascade which fell noisily on to the stones beneath.

Crystal's line, long and slack, suddenly gave a jerk. Quickly she sat up, much excited. The lines tautened and there appeared to be something at the end of it, tugging hard.

'Damien!' she shouted. 'I think I've caught something.'

He jumped up and nimbly leapt on to the boulder, taking the line, the far end of which was still jerking strongly. With long waders over his trousers, he jumped into the gushing stream, which came waist high. Slowly he began bringing in the fish, winding the line back steadily. He walked cautiously, as the bottom of the rivulet was slippery, but successfully made his way near enough to the fish to get a glimpse of it.

'It's a trout, all right. Not too big, but enough for dinner.' He took the long-handed net, kept at the ready and, quick as a whip, scooped the struggling fish out of the water, closing the mouth of the net rapidly. Crystal watched with wide-eyed excitement as she saw the handsome monster that, technically at least, was her catch. Damien jumped back on the bank, net in hand, and Crystal averted her eyes with a shudder as he stunned the trout.

'Is it dead yet?' she asked from a safe distance.

'Couldn't be deader!' he called back cheerfully. 'About three pounds, I would say, not exactly a world record but creditable for a first try.'

They hung it over a fire on a forked stick to cook. It was, without doubt, the most delicious fish Crystal had ever eaten. Dreamily, she picked at it with her fingers and even the charred fragments tasted exquisite.

'The last time I camped in such a pretty place was in the foothills below Simla, but it wasn't as beautiful as Kashmir.'

'Nothing is as beautiful as Kashmir,' said Damien complacently.

The white, peaked tents were pitched in a row except for two, larger and more elaborate, which were on a further hillock, presumably for Damien and herself. A roaring fire blazed in front of the servants' tents, and above it swung large cauldrons containing their evening meal. Crystal washed her hands in the ice-cold stream below, then strolled along its bank towards the cascade above which their own tents had been pitched. Dusk had fallen and, one by one, the stars came out, filling the vast expanse above with their faint, flickering glow. The moon was yet to rise but, even in the starlight, the mountain masses filled the horizons. It was getting to be chilly as the night winds began to blow and Crystal pulled her light shawl tighter round her shoulders. Watching the noisy waterfall at her feet, she did not hear Damien's soft footstep. She started as she felt something soft and warm draped round her. It was his jacket. She looked up at him, surprised at so concerned a gesture, and smiled. The barrier between them crumbled further.

Slowly, without talking, they strolled back to the top of the hill to their tents. There was utter peace in the evening. In the far distance she heard the howl of jackals. She shuddered.

'Is there danger from the animals here?'

Damien shrugged. 'No more than anywhere else. They are more frightened of us than we should be of them.'

'Oh, I know. Officers from the Army always used to come up here during their holidays for shooting,' she said. 'I heard them talk about it in Delhi and Lahore.'

'Yes, the shooting here is good, but one has to go higher to get the really big cats and even higher to get animals like ibex and markhor.'

'Do you enjoy shooting?' she asked.

He looked amused. 'It depends on what or—who.'

'I mean animals. Game-hunting.'

'I have done some up near Gulmarg. There is desolation for miles around and one sees a fair number of leopards there. Even tigers. But only when it's warm. In the winters they move down into the valleys.'

It was the first time he had mentioned Gulmarg since

she had asked to go there. He said it so casually that she was tempted to question him further, but hesitated. His mood was so mellow, almost benign, as he stood beside her leaning against the trunk of a tree, that she could not bear to say even one word that might break the fragile thread that seemed to bind them together. Watching the sharp profile of his aquiline features, the long sweep of his neck as it disappeared into his shirt carelessly unbuttoned at the top, and the smooth line of his legs, Crystal felt a wave of softness rise within her. She longed to stretch out and run her fingers through his unruly black hair blowing wildly in the wind.

But Damien appeared, suddenly, to be a thousand miles away, lost in another world—a world that seemed not to include her. With a barely audible sigh she made to turn away, annoyed at her own imaginings. Before she could move, however, his hand reached out and grasped her wrist.

'Where are you going?'

She stood stock still, not making any attempt to release her hand. 'It seems to me that you would prefer to be alone . . .' She bit her lip at the unwanted note of desolation in her voice.

Without appearing to, he moved and, very carefully, cupped her face in both his hands. For a trembling instant he gazed into her startled eyes. The black depths held no hint of mockery. Instead, they were disturbingly sensuous, smudged with desire. Crystal's throat went very dry, but she did not move. 'No,' he breathed against her lips, 'I do not prefer to be alone.' Unnoticed, his jacket slithered from her shoulders to the ground.

It seemed as if her breath would desert her for ever. He kissed her lips with infinite tenderness, then moved caressingly over her cheeks, her eyes, her forehead and around the corners of her mouth, lingering deliciously, agonisingly. His arm dropped until it encircled her waist, and he pulled her so close that she could feel the brass buckle on his belt bite into her flesh. The searing heat of his body surged through into hers. She heard herself gasp as her breath became shallow and ragged, and her heart soared into the starry canopy above.

He loved her, every nerve in her being exulted, he wanted her with all his love, all the wonderful tenderness in his body . . . With a broken cry, her arms reached up and drew his head down to hers. This time he abandoned all thought of gentleness, and his kiss, hard and crushing, claimed her mouth without mercy. Crystal felt the blood roar in her ears as she responded hungrily, wantonly, willing him never to stop. His hand curved possessively around her breast and her rapture was complete, awaiting now only total surrender. Her knees began to crumble.

Then, against her lips he whispered triumphantly, so softly that she almost did not hear. 'If you do not want me near you, you must give the necessary instructions to your wayward body.'

He pulled his face away and released his arms, very slowly, knowing that without them, she would fall. A smile of cruel satisfaction played upon the lips that only a moment ago had been seducing her so lovingly.

Crystal stumbled back a step and watched him with horror, as he stood enjoying the total rout of her dignity. He had set about arousing her deliberately, with the intention of no more than wreaking his revenge. Obviously he had waited impatiently for this moment when her defences would be lowered, when he had lulled her into a mood of mellow vulnerability. Oh that she had learned from experience not to fall into so transparent a trap!

'You are . . . ,' she breathed vehemently, white-faced and choking, 'a vile, sadistic *monster*.' That she could actually waste her love on someone as merciless as this!

He merely shrugged, accepting the charge with no change of expression. The smile did not leave his face, nor the gleam of victory in his eyes. 'Did you think that I would forget so easily?' The smile whipped off his face and his eyes narrowed. 'You hunger for my caresses, and you will hunger more. But you will not get them until you come crawling to me, begging to be taken—make no mistake about that!'

The extent of his vehemence shattered her. Blindly, burying her face in her hands, she ran stumbling to her tent. Mercifully, the servants were all far away around the camp-fire, still at their meal, and there was no one to witness her degradation. She flung herself on her cot in a storm of despair and rage. I shall never crawl to him, she vowed to herself, *never!* I hate you, Damien Granville, do you hear me? I *detest* you and the very ground you tread on!

She suffocated her sobs with her pillow. Oh, if only that were true, if only that were true!

CHAPTER NINE

CRYSTAL HAD been back at Shalimar a week—a week of undiluted wretchedness. Indeed now, even the wretchedness had gone, leaving in its stead just a numbness that pervaded every part of her mind and body. Fortunately Damien had remained in Srinagar for a further day and she had grabbed his offer of sending her back to Shalimar immediately on their return from Martanda. The thought of having to share the houseboat with him, in such close proximity, was agonising. At Shalimar she could at least lose herself sometimes to be alone with her misery.

The journey back from Martanda had been excruciating, all the more so because of Damien's brazenly high spirits. That he had humiliated her beyond forgiveness, decimated her so totally with his sadistic trick, seemed not to have affected him at all. Crystal cringed when she thought of how easily she had let herself be gulled into a sense of security and how quickly he had demolished the pathetic little house of cards she had built for herself upon her idiotic fantasies. She had actually believed that he had begun to care for her—how foolish a notion that was! Damien Granville was a man made of iron and in place of his heart the divine hand had placed a stone. How remiss she had been in allowing all her bitter memories of Delhi to sweeten in the dreamlike surroundings of Kashmir! Damien had not changed—nor would he. Only she had changed by stupidly, blindly, letting herself fall in love with him. Nothing that she did or said could touch his heart. Even after the horrible rout of her self-respect, he had continued to mock her by his very lightheartedness, pretending to be unaware of her shattered pride.

He had arrived at Shalimar the day after her return, and the odd charade they were playing with each other continued. He was unfailingly polite, even cheerful, again oblivious of her torment. She had retaliated by retiring again behind a curtain of frost, maintaining a cold distance, determined never again to let him pierce her defences so brutally. Theirs was indeed a marriage of some uniqueness, she thought with bitter amusement, a strange masquerade being played to what end she knew not. But Crystal's composure did not crack. Nobody watching her could be aware of the anguish that tore her apart every moment of her waking day. Certainly, Damien appeared to be blissfully ignorant of it. Or pretended to be.

There was now some talk of a celebration feast being held at Shalimar for the staff and tenants to commemorate so significant and joyous an event as the Sarkar's marriage.

'Yes, I have been thinking of it myself,' said Damien blandly when Gulab Singh made the suggestion to him. 'What do you think, Crystal? Is it not a splendid idea?'

'Certainly,' she replied sweetly. 'After all, we do want everyone to participate in our happiness, do we not?'

Damien nodded pleasantly and Gulab Singh beamed. 'Shall I make the arrangements for the banquet, then?' he asked.

'Yes, do. Draw up a complete list of people to be asked and get the cooks to make calculations of the provisions required. My wife will supervise the planning of the menu, guided by you, of course. And spare no expense.' He smiled at Crystal with cold, sardonic amusement.

Abruptly she left the room. He will never stop punishing me, she cried unhappily. He will never forgive me for my earlier rejection of him. Oh you fool,

Damien, her heart mourned, if only you could forget the past and know what is in my heart now! But that was exactly what he was not prepared to do.

It was the same night that, pleading a headache, Crystal retired early. Damien had been out all day somewhere on the estate discussing a new consignment with some carpet-weavers in a far village. As was her practice every night, Crystal sat on her balcony before going to bed, drinking in the pure, fresh air of the mountains and observing how much the moon had waxed since they were at Martanda. Her thoughts flitted about like grasshoppers, unable to settle on any one subject. Her mother had written that Robie was doing well in the Army and there was talk of a posting to Peshawar on the North-West frontier. He had not, to her mother's relief, been near a gaming-table since she had left. Her own health was improving vastly and Norah Hawthorne was busy preparing for Sally's forthcoming marriage. They both hoped that Sally would be as happy with her John as Crystal appeared to be with Damien . . .

Immersed in her flickering thoughts, Crystal lost count of time. It was close upon midnight when she rose, stretched lazily and made to go indoors to bed. Suddenly, out of the clear night air, she heard the sound of voices coming from Damien's balcony further along. She listened for a moment, wondering who his callers might be at such a late hour. The voices were low but carried through the night air with sharp clarity. She pricked up her ears and discovered, with some surprise, that although she could hear almost every word, she could not understand a single one. Then, with a shock she realised the reason. The conversation was taking place in a foreign language!

She strained her eyes through the dark, but Damien's balcony was cloaked in half-gloom. How odd! Why should he be sitting with his visitors in the near dark? Her own lights were extinguished and, as the moon came floating out from behind a cloud, she saw faint outlines of figures on the balcony separated from hers by the length of her sitting-room. Instinctively, she knew not why, she ducked, unwilling for them to see her. Peering cautiously, she could distinguish three figures. One was Damien, this she could see quite clearly—but the other two? A man and a woman! She could hear their strange voices with absolute clarity, talking low, but excitedly. It was with a chill sense of shock that Crystal suddenly knew, instinctively, what the foreign language was. It was Russian—and Damien was speaking it with commendable fluency!

Crystal stayed riveted to the spot, mind stilled in horror, unaware that the voices had now ceased and the figures were no longer on the balcony. For a while she could neither move nor think. Who were these people with whom Damien, by the tone of his voice, seemed so familiar? She was sure now that he obviously had some connection with Russians. But what? Henry Saunders's seemingly ludicrous charge against him appeared far from ludicrous now, well substantiated by the evidence of her own ears. Her heart filled with dread. Damien Granville was, possibly, a traitor to his country!

There could be no sleep for Crystal that night. She spent it pacing up and down her bedroom, her mind a maelstrom of question and conjecture. That Damien loved and lived by challenge and adventure she already knew. His lust for gambling, the dangerously high stakes he did not balk from, and his iron nerves—all this she was already only too aware of. Could it be that now, in his insatiable thirst for further adventure and daredevilry, he had decided to gamble his life away on espionage, the most deadly game of all?

Just as the pastel pink dawn was struggling up the mountainsides, Crystal fell into an exhausted sleep and did not open her eyes again until the sun was well on its way up. As the chilling revelations of the night came to her sleep-dulled mind again, she hastily tumbled out of bed, although she knew not why. What was she to do? Confront Damien and demand an explanation? But surely that was not the next step. He would only laugh at her, deny everything and carry on his nefarious activities even more secretly. She could not help it, but her heart filled with fear for him. What if he were caught? *Killed*? She went white and weak at the mere thought that his life might be in danger. She knew it was a perilous game that spies played, when each day could be their last and death stalked at every corner.

Deeply agitated, unable to eat even a morsel of the breakfast Sharifa had laid on the table, Crystal felt sick with worry and fear. For Damien. She could not bear the thought of losing him, facing life without him. That he did not care for her in any way, she did not worry at the moment. It was only important that, loving him as she did, even without hope of reciprocation, she should do everything in her power to help him. If this made her too a traitor to her country, well, she did not care. Her life was to be lived only for him—England could look after itself!

While still wondering what she should do, Crystal learned—with undiluted relief—that Damien had already left early for Gulmarg. Confirming his absence from Gulab Singh, she locked the doors to her room, sending Sharifa and Rehana off on an errand of some length. Then, cautiously, she opened the connecting door which led into Damien's apartment and, making certain that his *khidmatgar* was down in the laundry pressing his clothes, she locked all the doors in his suite as well. Then, very systematically, she set about making a thorough search of all the papers in his escritoire. She riffled through them frantically in case the *khidmatgar* should return and wonder about the locked doors. In the top shelves there was nothing of interest, but in a bottom drawer she chanced upon a packet of envelopes pushed in at the back. She looked at one, and froze. The script on the envelopes was Russian! Quickly she withdrew the book of poems she had discovered in the bookshelf earlier. She compared the two scripts. Yes, there was no doubt about it. All the sheets of paper in the carefully secreted packet were written in Russian! Some letters seemed to have dates, others not. The most recent she came across was the date of receipt scribbled in pencil on a short note written on white paper. It was only two days earlier!

There was a discreet knock, and Crystal jumped in alarm. Hastily replacing all the papers as she had found them, she closed the escritoire and opened the door for the bearer. Making some hurried excuse, she returned to her own suite, pale and trembling. There appeared to be no more room left for doubt. Damien was a Russian agent or, at least, had connections with Russian agents that were of necessity covert. She remembered the grim set of his face when the Maharaja had asked him about infiltrators. He had then denied knowledge of any, but he had undoubtedly lied. The two people he had been conversing with last night, hushed and under cloak of darkness, were without question infiltrators whom he was helping. She did not yet know why. But about one thing Crystal was determined. She was going to find out!

She had no idea how to start her investigations. Perhaps a more thorough search of Damien's room would reveal further information. In a perhaps futile attempt to familiarise herself with the Russian script, she again took the book of poems from Damien's bookcase and sat down to study it in her sitting-room. She pored over it through the morning, not making much headway, and wondering again and again about the identity of the mysterious Natasha, whose name was on the first page. Then, more confused than ever, she lunched briefly and retired for a much-needed siesta.

She was roused an hour or two later by a soft knock. It was Sharifa, bearing a card on a tray. 'There is a gentleman to see *memsahib*,' she announced. Crystal irritatedly picked up the card to see who it was—and the blood congealed in her veins. The neatly printed name confronting her was that of—Captain Henry Saunders!

Her first panic-stricken reaction was to return the card and refuse to see him. But then she realised how foolish and incriminating such an action would be for Damien's welfare. Reluctantly, hating the thought of seeing this odious, despicable man again, she asked for him to wait in the formal drawing-room. Grimly, but with heart palpitating with nervousness, she set about preparing herself for the interview.

To her surprise, a few moments later Sharifa arrived with another note from her unwelcome visitor. *I would prefer to see you in greater privacy in your own sitting-room*, it read impudently. Once again she was sorely tempted to send this insolent wretch packing, but better sense prevailed. She knew she dared not. She had to find out why he had taken the extreme step of calling on her in spite of knowing well how much Damien disliked him. Very grudgingly, she sent for him to come upstairs, refraining from ordering a tray of tea in case he misunderstood the quality of the reception that awaited him.

He sauntered through the door with supreme confidence, a sarcastic grin on his face. She had a wild desire to slap it off his mouth, but restrained herself with effort. Instead, she looked at him icily and inquired abruptly. 'Well, what is the purpose of this visit that requires the privacy of my sitting-room?'

His smile widened and, although she herself was standing, he seated himself comfortably on the sofa without being asked to. She did not comment on his rude behaviour but merely made her stare more glacial. 'Well?'

He examined his fingernails before replying. 'I wonder if you by any chance recall our little conversation in the Shalimar Gardens the other day?'

She knew that he was only too well aware that she did, and said nothing. He waited an instant; then, with a shrug, continued. 'Your valiant defence of your husband that day was, I regret to say, all to no avail.'

Crystal felt her hands go cold but she did not bat an eyelid. 'I'm afraid I do not quite understand your meaning.'

'Oh yes, you do,' he said smugly. 'But if you insist that you do not, nothing will give me greater pleasure than to make it even clearer.' He narrowed his eyes. 'Damien Granville has been harbouring two Russian infiltrators. We have indisputable proof of that through our own totally reliable sources. In addition, we also know that your valued husband has had dealings with the Russians for many years.' He laughed and looked round the room, spreading his arms to encompass it. 'How do you think he manages to retain so elaborate an establishment? Not only through farming—and gambling—I can assure you!'

Slowly Crystal sank down in the chair, her knees unable to take her weight any more. But, clenching her fists, she clung on to her icy composure. 'I'm afraid I have . . . no idea what you are talking about. It is utter rubbish . . .' Even to herself her words sounded false and hollow.

He laughed. 'It is hardly necessary for you to waste words,' he said softly. 'Your face, I regret to say, tells me everything that I wish to know.' He stood up abruptly and leaned his elbow on the mantelpiece. 'But I have not come here for confirmation of my suspicions. Indeed, I have all the confirmation I want without reference to you. What I have come here for is to—offer you a chance of salvation.'

She stared at him in dumb horror, bewildered as to what his next outrageous statement might be.

He continued, pacing up and down the room. 'I see no reason why you yourself should be penalised for the sins of your husband. I am reasonably convinced that you know little about his activities. When he is arrested, which should be soon now, he will not see the light of freedom for many years, indeed, if at all! Execution is the usual method of dealing with those who betray their country. However, in view of your own lack of complicity in his work as a Russian agent, I shall see that no harm comes to you.' He paused as Crystal listened in utter silence. 'In exchange for . . . certain favours, naturally.'

Henry Saunders would have been surprised to know how little of what he said had permeated into Crystal's consciousness. Just one phrase seemed to block her mind to all other thoughts. *When he is arrested . . .*

With an effort she roused herself to ask dully, 'You are going to arrest my husband?'

He smiled in satisfaction. 'I know that he is in Gulmarg—with the infiltrators. He has been concealing them there for some time. But we have our own little ways of getting information,' he rubbed his hands in anticipation, 'and they will not be there for long. In fact, I am expecting to perform the delightful act of arrest myself no later than tomorrow morning.'

Crystal sat absolutely still, the turmoil behind the stony façade of her face remaining unrevealed. 'Tell me, Captain Saunders,' she asked suddenly, 'why do you hate my husband so much?'

He seemed taken aback at the unexpected question. Then his face darkened. But, collecting himself quickly, he smiled and the sight was not pleasant. 'His Highness is concerned very seriously about infiltrations into his kingdom—and so is the British government. After I have delivered Damien to the appropriate authorities, I intend to ask His Highness for a suitable reward.' He stopped abruptly. Crystal looked at him blankly. 'The reward,' he breathed softly, 'will be Shalimar.' She gaped at him thunderstruck. 'Granville has no heirs,' he said thoughtfully, almost talking to himself as he built his ambitious castle in the air, 'and the only claimant might be you. Which is why,' he paused and smiled beguilingly, '. . . I would like you on my side.'

Abruptly, unable to tolerate this despicable, repulsive man in her vicinity any more, Crystal stumbled to her feet. 'Get out of my sight,' she ground out vehemently, pointing to the door. 'Get out this instant or I will have you thrown out forcibly . . .' She choked in sheer fury.

Henry Saunders stared at her for a moment, then shrugged. 'I came here to offer you refuge from the law, but since you choose not to consider my offer . . .' he stopped suddenly, stared, then leaned forward and picked up something from the table. His eyes widened. 'Ah!' he exclaimed, 'Better and better! What could be more incriminating for you than a book in Russian! I see that I was mistaken about your own complicity in this sordid affair!' He flicked through it with growing interest as Crystal watched horror-struck, sick with remorse. She had forgotten all about the book!

'Natasha,' Saunders mused, 'Natasha! A Russian name, undoubtedly. I see that your husband's tastes in mistresses transcends all international barriers! How very cosy—a collaborator *and* a mistress.'

Crystal's hand flew out before she could stop it and caught him a stinging slap across the mouth. The book dropped from his hold like a hot brick and his palm went up to cover his cheek. He swore vilely. Quick as lightning, Crystal retrieved the book and ran into her bedroom, to emerge in an instant holding her pistol. She pointed it straight at him.

'Now get out of this house or, I promise you, I shall put a bullet through your heart.' She laughed hysterically, no longer aware of anything except her need to get rid of this vermin. 'I am a crack shot, I assure you. I shall not miss.'

Eyes wide with alarm, he backed away. 'You will regret this as . . . as nothing you have ever regretted in your life,' he gasped furiously, his eyes spitting venom. 'I will have you both behind bars by tomorrow!' He pulled a handkerchief from his pocket and held it to his mouth. Crystal noted with vicious satisfaction that it soon became stained with blood. He turned and almost ran towards the door. 'I shall leave my guards here to see that you do not leave the house,' he gave an ugly laugh. 'With both of you out of my way, Shalimar will be mine all the sooner.' With another oath, he turned and fled.

Slowly Crystal sank into the chair just as Sharifa came running in to see what the shouting had been about. '*Memsahib, memsahib*,' she cried in consternation. 'What has happened? Are you all right?'

Crystal nodded, swallowed hard, and forced a laugh. 'Nothing has happened and of course I am all right! I was just . . . showing Captain Saunders my pistol.' She suppressed a sob that rose to her throat. 'Please . . . please send Gulab Singh to me.'

'But he is not here, *memsahib*, he went to Gulmarg not half an hour ago. Shall I send for any of the others?'

Crystal shook her head despondently. She knew that only Gulab Singh could be trusted to perform the task she had in mind. Damien had to be warned! She had to get a message to Gulmarg—but she had no idea which of the servants she could trust, which of the innumerable staff at Shalimar could be sent to Gulmarg in safety. If the two Russians were indeed at the Gulmarg house, it might mean further disaster for someone untrustworthy to see them. She wrung her hands in despair. What was she to do?

Shalimar soon became agog with the news that Saunders *sahib* had asked his guards to remain at the house. For what reason? It was an unheard-of procedure and the Sarkar would not tolerate it! There would undoubtedly be hell to pay when he returned. In the meantime, they turned to Crystal for information. Once again in complete control of herself, she faced Gulab Singh's assistants coolly. 'The guards have been placed here at the Sarkar's own orders,' she lied glibly. 'I do not know why, but I assure you it is undoubtedly trivial.'

She hoped fervently that they would believe her, and

they did, with touching faith in the Sarkar's orders and in his wife's explanation.

'Er . . . how many guards are there?' she asked Sharifa with forced casualness.

'Four. They are walking up and down the corridor outside the room.' Sharifa's disapproval of the entire procedure was very evident.

Crystal laughed lightly. 'Well, please see that some tea is offered to them and the evening meal also.' But, privately, she felt anything but light-hearted. There was no one among the staff whom she knew for a certainty could be trusted. There was no alternative but to go herself to Gulmarg! But how? She first had to get out of her rooms, then saddle a horse in the stables and then make her way past everyone who happened to be around! It was not going to be possible—but she had to try, she *had* to! She could not let Damien down and allow him to be arrested without even a word of warning, whatever the facts about the situation.

Over a frugal supper which she forced herself to eat with a show of appetite, Crystal devised a plan. It might not work at all, but it had to be tried. It was the only way she could at least make an effort to reach Damien. Her heart bled for him, tucked away in his mountain-top retreat, unaware of the hideous danger that awaited him in the morning. It was an unbearably painful prospect and she felt close to tears of frustration and hopelessness as she saw her world collapse around her ears. But, if the plan were to succeed at all, she knew she had to keep a cool mind, to restrain her emotions and her racking anguish.

She bid Sharifa a pleasant goodnight, adding nonchalantly, 'I did not sleep too well last night. I would like not to be disturbed, no matter what, until the morning, when I shall ring for you.' Then she locked her doors securely and set to work. Leaving the room would not present an unsurmountable problem. The apartment was on the first floor and her balcony overlooked a part of the gardens that did not lie in the usual path of the servants. Carefully she knotted all her bedsheets together, securing them several times. Then she waited until the clock chimed ten. At this hour, she knew, the servants liked to gather in the far compound around a bonfire and take their ease over idle chit-chat, their day's duties concluded. Only the night guards patrolled the grounds but, since there was very little petty crime in Kashmir, they did not take their duties too seriously, often wandering off their allotted paths.

She tied one end of the long chain of bedsheets firmly to the balcony rails, hoping they would not give way under her weight. She had changed into a pair of riding-breeches that she had used occasionally in Delhi only to horrify gossipy old dowagers and to enjoy the sight of them reaching for their smelling-salts at so shameless a garb on a woman. But now they would stand her in good stead. Her jacket and hood helped to conceal her build and face completely. For added anonymity, she covered her face with a silk scarf, leaving room only for the eyes. She also put on heavy fleece-lined gloves and sturdy boots.

The journey down from her balcony was frightening but successfully completed. The gardens below were deserted. From the direction of the servants' compound she could hear sounds of singing and laughter. There was little danger that anyone there would leave the enticing warmth of the fire and wander out into the cold. There was, unfortunately, a moon, but the present disadvantage of the moonlight would be a definite advantage once she was on her way, helping to illuminate sufficiently the road to Gulmarg.

Silently she made her way across the gardens to a corner away from the stables, where she had noticed a disused barn piled with discarded oddments. She took the precaution of keeping as close to the walls of the outhouses as possible, but there was no one to detect her presence. She reached the deserted barn with ease and looked round for a moment. She could see the servants' compound, but it was unlikely that anyone would notice her at that distance even if they happened to be looking in her direction.

Taking a small bottle from her pocket, she sprinkled its contents liberally over some of the dried, rotten planks in the barn wall. Then, satisfied, she set a match to them. Instantly, the paraffin burst into flames, soon enveloping the entire wooden wall. As the timbers roared and crackled she sought the safety of a clump of trees, wondering how long it would be before the blaze was noticed. It was not long.

Within a few moments she heard a shout of 'Fire, fire!', which was taken up rapidly by everyone. She could see a crowd of servants run towards the barn and all confusion was let loose. There was much shouting and swearing, with everyone yelling out instructions at the same time. Crystal watched in silence, pleased at the success of her little diversion. Soon the area containing the stables appeared to be reasonably clear of people. Carefully, keeping to the belt of trees, she crept towards it. She need not have bothered. No one cast a single glance in her direction; they were all too busy watching the fire.

The stables were completely deserted, not a single groom remaining behind at his post. Comfortably, without undue haste, she saddled Sundari, feeding her with lumps of molasses. In less than ten minutes she was done. In her tour of Shalimar with Gulab Singh he had pointed out a path across the saffron-crocus field that, he said, joined up with the Gulmarg road ahead. She mounted her horse quickly and headed now for the field, knowing that the lands were deserted at night. She met no one as she waded through the sea of waving flowers and in less than fifteen minutes she was on the road to Gulmarg.

In spite of the ease with which she had managed to make her escape, Crystal felt limp with relief. There would be pandemonium, of course, when the absence of the horse was discovered, but she could not be bothered with that now. Gulmarg, she knew, was about twenty miles away. The moonlight was not strong, but it was sufficient to show her the way ahead and help her to avoid potholes and dangerous ruts. It was a reasonably straight road, but she did not know the way and at this time of night there was not a soul from whom she could seek directions.

The silent valley stretched black and sleeping at her feet for miles around. The snow peaks shimmered like silvery caps and the stars seemed close enough to reach up and pluck. A dark bank of clouds appeared to be building up in the north and a chill wind whistled round her ears and knifed through even her thick jacket and hood. A moving veil of black obscured the moon and the going became even slower. The night was now as thick as pitch, and she could hardly see her hand before her face. Before long, a fine drizzle started, making visibility hopeless. She gritted her teeth and plodded on, getting colder and wetter by the minute. There were leopards and tigers in these parts, she remembered Damien saying. Determined not to give in to fear, she quelled her sense of growing panic and forced her mind on to other matters.

But no thoughts seemed to arise except those of the repugnant Henry Saunders—and Damien. She was broken and bitter at what he was doing—and for the sake of what? Excitement? Adventure? More money? It was reprehensible that he should be involved in something as sordid as this. Much as she tried to invoke her love and loyalty, she could find no excuse in her heart to dismiss this excess.

And . . . Natasha? Who was she? Was she also one of Damien's many mistresses serving the dual purpose of collaborator in his nefarious activities? Her heart was wrung with pain at yet another of his infidelities. What an incorrigible fool she was to waste her love on him!

And how little he deserved the benefit of this horrible, frightening journey she was undertaking for him now. Oh, if only love could be made to listen to logic!

The rain was now pouring down in buckets, drenching her through to the skin. Cold and shivering, she listened miserably to the growling clouds above and knew there was still more to come. She had no idea how long she had been on the road or how far she had travelled. She had not even reached Tanmarg yet—and heaven knew how far that might be still. Huddling as close to Sundari as she could manage, she crawled along at a snail's pace, eyes closed with fatigue and against the driving rain. She did not notice the clustered huts of Tanmarg until she was upon them. She looked around fearfully, but all was silent and dark. The village slept uncaring.

The road soon began to rise and wind round the mountain. The air bit into her with viciously icy teeth. Gulmarg was more than seven and a half thousand feet high, much higher than either Shalimar or Srinagar. Closing her mind to everything except Damien, Damien, Damien, she struggled on uncaring.

The rain-clouds were beginning to disperse and the deluge petered out, but her clothes were icy and sodden. Violent shivers shook her through and through but she knew that if she stopped and rested—not that there was any place to rest!—she would never start up again. Her body became numb with cold and her mind went blank. The road was getting steeper by the minute but where the top of the mountain was she no longer saw nor cared. It was as though she sat upon the horse only by the grace of some divine power. She herself was long past being in control of her fate.

Crystal had no idea she had reached Gulmarg until the looming shape of a house appeared not twenty feet ahead. She reined her horse and halted, trying to regain the focus of her eyes. A stray thought flashed through the fog of her mind. She had no idea where Damien's house might be!

The rain had subsided into a steady drizzle and she peered around for some sign of human presence. There was none. She could give no instructions to Sundari, for she had no idea which way to turn. But, miraculously, Sundari appeared to know her way and turned right or left without indication. Fatigued as she was, Crystal remembered that Gulmarg was where Sundari had been reared and trained and, miracle of miracles, she knew where home was. At the end of a curving tree-lined track she suddenly saw a flickering light. Almost sobbing with relief, she made her way towards it. A pair of large iron gates barred her path. She dismounted and touched them. They were open. Gasping and panting to rustle up enough strength to push them open, she stumbled through, and walked heavily through the slush towards the blessed light. Without warning, she almost walked into an outhouse, and heard an angry snort and a shuffle of hooves. She peered in and almost fainted with joy. Standing inside the stables contained in the outhouse was Damien's black horse, Shaitan!

Sobbing, barely able to drag her body towards the house that loomed ahead, she walked towards the entrance. The flickering light came from a downstairs window. She paused and peered in. The curtains were drawn on the inside but, suddenly, through a chink, she saw the most miraculous sight in the world—the back of Damien's tousled black head. On the eastern horizon, the sky was just beginning to be touched with pink.

Lifting her hands up with a final effort, she banged them against the door, again and again and again, until the din resounded through the dawn countryside with alarming echoes. The door was flung open, and she saw in her blurred vision a human shape that might have been Gulab Singh. Without pausing, with a superhuman burst of energy, she stumbled past him heavily. An enormous, crackling log fire burned in a grate in the room on her right. There were people in it of whom she was only vaguely aware. She had eyes only for Damien sitting transfixed in his chair, mouth agape, staring at her in utter disbelief. She managed to reach a chair just as her knees began to buckle, and her head swam in dizzying circles. She felt a strong pair of arms enclose her and a hand steadied her neck.

'Henry Saunders,' she gasped weakly, '. . . coming to arrest you . . . morning . . . knows . . . the Russians. Run, Damien, you have to run . . .'

The voice died in her throat as blackness finally descended. She laid her uncontrollable head on his chest and, with a long-drawn-out sigh, slipped into unconsciousness.

CHAPTER TEN

THE SKY was filled with molten colour and, in its depths, ever-changing strange shapes melted and re-formed and melted again. Sometimes it was dark and sometimes it filled with brilliant light that pierced the eyes and made the head throb. There were voices, soft and hushed, and hands that stroked her hair and soothed the fevered brow with feathery fingertips. Sometimes she was awake but mostly she slept, hovering on the edges of misty chasms in her consciousness, whirling through meaningless hallucinations and hot, incomprehensible dreams . . .

For three days and nights Crystal lay racked with pain and fever, slipping in and out of reality. She had no memory of where she was or who was with her, but she knew she was somehow surrounded by love. The hands that never strayed far from her hair and face were gentle, but she had no idea to whom they belonged. Sometimes she heard her name whispered in her ear, and she smiled, but without knowing why.

On the morning of the fourth day, the fever broke. Crystal opened her eyes to reality in a veil of darkness which gradually dissolved as a light flickered into focus. It was a low fire, warm and comforting. She was bathed in sweat and her body felt light and lifeless. Weakly, she struggled to raise her head. A hand on her forehead pressed it down again and she fell back into the pillows.

'Don't try to sit up,' a voice whispered against her ear. 'Lie still.'

Her eyes groped the gloom for a face. 'Damien . . . ?'

A finger rested against her lips. 'Hush . . . go back to sleep. I'm here.' His voice wafted languidly through her mind and lingered there. She smiled. Lying cradled against warm flesh, encircled in the safety and comfort of his arms, she sighed with deep contentment, and slept.

Now the room was filled with sunshine. Her eyes opened wide and confident and she was suddenly awake. She was in a large room, cosy and secure and bright with colour. Over her head were thick, heavy wooden beams supporting a roof that slanted downwards over her bed. She turned her head. On a couch by the fire, gazing into it with his back to her, sat Damien.

She whispered his name and, in a flash, he was by her side. His dark face loomed over hers and his eyes were clouded with anxiety. 'How do you feel?'

'I don't know . . . very strange . . .' She looked round the lovely room again and frowned. 'Where . . . is this place?'

'Gulmarg,' he said gently. 'Don't you remember?'

She started to shake her head, then stopped. Gulmarg! In a blinding flash the memory came thundering back. She had to warn Damien to get away from here! She tried to struggle up against the pillows as her eyes dilated with fear. 'Saunders,' she gasped, 'he will be here this morning . . . to arrest you and the Russians.' With horrible lucidity she recalled the sequence of events that had brought her here.

He did not move. 'I know.' For a man faced with ignominy and disgrace, he looked remarkably unworried.

She was suddenly gripped with panic. 'He knows everything, Damien.'

'So he told me.'

'He's already *been*?' she whispered in despair. 'I was too late . . .'

He stretched his hand and gently removed a vagrant lock of hair from her forehead. Instinctively she recoiled. He paused, then withdrew his hand with the ghost of a smile. 'No, you were not too late. You arrived in very good time indeed.'

'But what happened? What did you do?' Her eyes were frantic with worry.

'Well, thanks to your warning, I had time to put on my thickest boots. I did what any man worth his salt would do—I kicked him all the way down the hill right to the bottom!' He was very matter-of-fact.

'What!' she sat up, appalled. 'Oh, Damien, was that wise? He knows *everything*! How could you *do* such a thing?'

His face lit up with a smile of satisfaction. 'With the greatest of pleasure, I assure you, with the greatest of pleasure.'

She was shocked. 'But he knows about the Russians— he will come back to get you.'

He rose and stretched lazily. 'He will not come back. He came and went three days ago.'

'*Three* days ago . . . b-but I came only last night . . .'

'You came three days ago, my beautiful, brave Crystal.' He sat down again and took her hand. 'You have been very, very sick.' The inky blackness of his eyes was intense with worry. 'How could you undertake such a terrible journey alone?'

'I had to warn you,' she said in a small voice. Then, without looking at him, she asked, 'Is it true, Damien? Have you been harbouring Russian infiltrators?' She disengaged her hand from his.

'Yes, it is true.'

She slumped back into the pillows. So, Henry Saunders was right after all. Damien denied nothing. Her face went ashen as the last vestige of hope disappeared. She averted her face. To make matters worse, he had assaulted an officer of the British Army. Henry Saunders would take his revenge! She was shocked, all at once, to hear him chuckle. She stared at him aghast. On his face there was not a single sign of repentence. On the contrary, he seemed vastly amused. 'I am glad you can find something to laugh about!' she said crossly.

'I understand you relieved him of one of his canine teeth!'

Crystal's face became scarlet as she recalled, with a guilty start, her own reception of Captain Saunders. She bit her lip. 'I could not restrain myself. He made . . . s-suggestions . . .', she said, wanting to defend her own behaviour. 'I should not have done it!'

'No,' he said severely, 'Of course you should not have! You should have relieved him of *both* his canines!' He threw back his head and guffawed. She watched him in silence, bewildered and appalled at his continuing flippancy. Did he not realise the seriousness of his crime?

'Considering the consequences of espionage,' she lashed out sarcastically, 'you appear to be in excellent good humour!'

'Oh, indeed I am,' he agreed, his face serious but his eyes continuing to dance irritatingly. 'I cannot seem to comprehend how a hand as soft and delicate as this,' he held it in his own enormous palm and stared at it wonderingly, 'could possibly cause so much damage! It is rather difficult to take an arresting officer seriously when he has a disgusting gap in his teeth and whistles air through it every time he speaks!'

Without intention, Crystal's own lips twitched in an impending smile which she nipped in the bud. She removed her hand from his with some force. 'The Russians,' she said anxiously. 'Have they gone?'

'No,' he was still very cheerful. 'They are very much here. And waiting very impatiently to meet you.'

The infiltrators were still on the premises! Surely even in his present, totally incomprehensible, mood Damien knew the penalty for that?

'Did Saunders see them?'

'Oh yes,' his face was very bland. 'They even helped me to kick him down the hill.'

With an angry flourish, Crystal turned her back on

him and buried her face in the pillow. 'I don't understand anything any more,' she said in a voice muffled and dismal. 'You are talking in riddles and I am not at all amused.'

'All right,' he conceded. 'Explanations, I grant you, are due. To you more than to anyone else, after . . . after what you risked to come here.' For a few bare seconds he seemed overcome with some strange emotion, then he cleared his throat and the bantering tone returned. 'But first things first.' He flung open the door and yelled at the top of his lungs. 'Gulab Singh? *Gulab Singh!* Luncheon, please!'

Luncheon! Crystal could quite clearly identify the gnawing pains in her stomach as hunger. She felt ravenous, as though she had not eaten for weeks. He stood by the window, gazing out at the mountains.

'Is Natasha here too?' she asked, trying to make her voice cold, but succeeding only in making it tremulous and pathetic.

'Natasha?' He seemed surprised at her knowledge. Then he nodded. 'Oh, yes. It is especially Natasha who wants to meet you.'

Her eyes became dangerously moist. 'I don't want to meet her . . .' The quaver in her voice was more pronounced.

'Oh? Why ever not?' Now he not only sounded surprised, he even sounded . . . hurt!

She sat up angrily. 'I've already met two of your misbegotten mistresses,' she stormed, 'how many more do you plan to introduce me to?'

His eyebrows shot up in startled astonishment, but the infuriating twinkle in his eyes stayed exactly where it was. 'You said every wife should get to know her husband's mistresses well.' He actually had the nerve to sound injured! 'But if you are jealous . . .'

Her head jerked up high and she subjected him to a look of superb hauteur. 'Jealous? *I* of *you*? *Hah!* You preen yourself quite unnecessarily!' She was furious at the fact that her eyes had become unusually bright with threatened dampness.

'Oh well, in that case you will surely not mind meeting just one more. You see, Natasha is . . . ,' he paused, but her blurred vision failed to see his twitching lips, 'very special to me.'

She looked away, sick with misery. Did he have no shame at all? Not a single bone of compassion in his body, or a scruple of decorum? But before she could send her scathing retort flying into his face, the door opened and into the room stepped two strangers. The man, she noticed, was very old and, astonishingly, so was the woman. She was small and petite with hair like spun silver coiffed high on top of her head. Her face was lovely and unlined and there was something strangely familiar about her eyes.

Crystal stared at them in silence, trying to recapture a vague memory of the night she had seen them in the downstairs room beside the fire. The woman came towards the bed, observing her closely. Crystal was surprised to see that her eyes brimmed with tears. She stretched out her arms as the tears spilled over. 'Crystal, my dearest child . . . how I have longed to meet you.' Her arms closed around Crystal.

In the background she heard Damien's quiet voice. 'This is Natasha,' he said. 'My mother.'

It was a long and fascinating story. Wrapped snugly in blankets, dumbstruck and with wide, staring eyes, Crystal sat on the couch in front of the fire and listened. The hearty luncheon had done its duty and infused strength into her limp body, and, with the fever well past, she felt alert and anxious to learn the truth behind all the jigsaw of events that had so marred her life in Kashmir. Beside her sat Damien's mother—how extraordinary that sounded!—holding her hand with gentle affection. Crystal could hardly bear to take her eyes off the beautiful face, striking even in advanced years. Her voice was soft and lilting, and she spoke English with a delicate accent. Opposite sat her brother Ivan, not understanding English but nodding happily as though he did comprehend every word. Damien gazed into the fire, sucking lightly on his pipe, his face more placid than Crystal had ever seen it before.

His mother, said Damien, had first come to India through the Khyber Pass, the unwilling companion of an uncle who was, indeed, a Russian agent sent out to chart the topography of the area secretly. Her uncle's intentions in bringing her with him were as clear as they were sordid. While he remained in hiding in the mountains of Afghanistan, Natasha, a young and exquisite nineteen-year-old, was to extract information from susceptible British Army officers through the generous use of her charms. She was to pose as a Viennese countess, set up home in Peshawar on the North-West frontier, and entice officers into her net by getting to know the best people in town. Money, her uncle promised, was to be no consideration, for there was plenty available from Russian government funds.

While pretending to agree, but secretly detesting the idea, Natasha decided to escape from her uncle's clutches at the first possible opportunity. At this time, Damien's father happened to be stationed in Peshawar and, quite by chance, the two met and fell madly in love. When he heard of Natasha's tragic plight, Edward Granville immediately offered a solution. They would run away to Lahore, get married there and eventually make their way to Srinagar, where he would offer his services to the progressive new Maharaja of Kashmir, Gulab Singh. Of course it meant resigning from the Army, but Edward Granville did so willingly and happily, delirious in his new-found love.

A year after they married, Damien was born in Amritsar and soon the couple made their way up to Srinagar together with their infant son. Life in Kashmir was idyllic. Edward Granville served the Maharaja well and, although money did not flow, what they lacked in finances they more than made up with their deep happiness in each other and their abiding love. When peace returned to Kashmir and signs of prosperity appeared, Edward Granville decided to retire and raise special shawl goats. The Maharaja's generous gift of Shalimar seemed to be the answer to their prayers and, for a few years, life was idyllic. Because of the growing suspicion of Russians in India, it was decided that Natasha would continue to pretend to be Viennese and the lie was accepted easily by everyone.

But there were unexpected storm-clouds on the horizon. One day, out of the blue, Natasha's uncle appeared at Shalimar. It had not been difficult to discover the whereabouts of his absconding niece. Unless she agreed to return with him to Russia, he threatened to expose her to the authorities and ruin Edward Granville for ever. The fact that she was innocent of wrong-doing did not matter any more. With the current fear of Russian infiltrators, a few words of fabrication in the right quarters would be enough to see her expelled from the country.

Rather than destroy her husband as well, although Edward Granville stood solidly behind his wife and not at all afraid of possible consequences, Natasha decided to leave. Without a word to her husband, knowing that he would not let her go, she kissed her son goodbye and silently slipped away one night into the mountains. Edward Granville was shattered when he learned of her disappearance. He knew it would be useless to try to find her. At the time, Damien was only ten.

Somehow, over the years, she managed to retain contact with her beloved son but Edward Granville, bitterly hurt and unforgiving at her desertion, refused to respond. The only memento of her that he allowed at Shalimar was the oil portrait hanging next to his own in the formal drawing-room. When his father died, nine years earlier, Damien inherited the vast and now prosperous estates of Shalimar and decided to spare no effort in getting his mother back to her rightful home in Kashmir. Letters, of necessity, were infrequent and had to be sent via friends in London. Or Damien had secretly to seek out Russian agents—at great peril to himself— and persuade them—at an exorbitant price—to act as couriers. Furthermore, they were unreliable and often cheats as well. Many letters were lost, and the years passed without any concrete plans being made for Natasha's return until the year before, when matters were finalised.

But the journey had to wait until the warmer winds of spring prevailed and the snows in the passes melted. It had nevertheless been a horrendous experience for them both, Natasha and Ivan, and by the time they had arrived at Shalimar, broken, sick and desperately exhausted, Damien had left for Delhi. Receiving news of their arrival on the morning after his wedding, he had immediately sought out his friends in high places for permission for them to stay on in India under his care. The permission had not been easy to obtain in view of Natasha's earlier background, and, while waiting, they were forced to remain discreetly hidden from the prying eyes of suspicious officers such as Henry Saunders, assigned specially to smoke out suspected political agents in the area.

The permission had finally arrived four days before. Damien had immediately come to Gulmarg, where they were living, to take them back in triumph to Shalimar— and to his wife. Henry Saunders's unusually rapid, and undoubtedly painful, descent down the hill at the end of Damien's boot had therefore been not only pleasurable, but also long overdue.

By the time the story had been told and all Crystal's excited questions answered, the fire burnt low and dusk was beginning to settle on the spectacular mountain scenery around Gulmarg. There were tears pouring down her face and her heart was wrung with compassion for the gentle and beautiful woman by her side. She leaned forward and kissed Natasha impulsively on the cheek. 'It is over now,' she whispered comfortingly. 'You are home again.'

Natasha nodded, her black eyes so like Damien's, dimmed with tears, but no longer of sorrow. She smiled, and in her beaming face Crystal saw that of the man she loved beyond all the bounds of reason. How could she not love as well this warm, radiant woman who had given him to her?

Very soon they were left alone, Damien and Crystal. The room was filled with a glowing stillness. Damien leaned forward to stoke the fire and pile on some more logs of wood.

'Why did you not . . . take me into your confidence?' she asked him sadly, her voice small and tremulous.

'Would you have believed a word of what I said? Besides, you seemed . . . unduly impressed by Saunders.' His voice was abrasive. 'There was no knowing what you might blurt out to him.'

She was deeply wounded. 'Is that all the faith you place in me?' She laid her head back against the couch and closed her eyes, sighing. Instantly, he was by her side.

'Are you tired?'

Without waiting for an answer, he lifted her as easily as a bundle of washing and placed her gently back on the bed. One arm remained beneath her as he reclined alongside. He cleared the tendrils of hair off her face and his eyes were, suddenly, bruised with pain. 'I couldn't bear to lose you now, Crystal,' it was the merest whisper. 'Keep well, my darling, for me . . .'

She did not open her eyes for fear that this too was a fevered dream that might vanish in daylight. In her mind unfolded the delirious fantasies that she had suffered these past few days and nights. She recalled the feel of someone's flesh, warm and yielding, no more than a heartbeat away from her own; the touch of lips buried deep in her hair; and the unmistakable fragrance of a masculine chest pressed against her face, shielding her, infusing her with comfort and strength. She remembered now the overpowering sensation of being surrounded by love. Had it been Damien who had lain next to her and cradled her in his arms through her tormented ravings—or some figment of a diseased imagination?

Her heart suddenly overflowed with a cascading emotion which she no longer had the strength to fight. She raised a feeble hand and stroked the rough stubble on his cheek so close to hers.

'I love you, Damien,' she whispered weakly, her amber eyes abject in defeat. 'You have well and truly won your wager.'

He did not reply at once. For an interminable moment he was still, looking at her with unblinking, imponderable eyes. Then he smiled and ran his finger along her nose. 'I know, my beloved, I know . . .'

She frowned at his inscrutability. 'How can you know, when I have never said so?'

He laughed and gently buried his face in the hollow of her neck, kissing her delicately. 'I know because, my bad-tempered little goose, you have done little else but repeat it to me incessantly over these past days and nights. In fact,' a riot of mischief played havoc with his face, 'I was beginning to despair of ever hearing anything else!'

'You mean—I said so in my fever?'

'Constantly.'

'Oh!' How annoying that he should know already what she had striven to conceal for so long! She turned to kiss his shoulder. Without looking up at him, she murmured inaudibly against his shirt, 'And . . . do you find any place at all in your heart for me?'

'What do you think?'

Still not looking at him, she shook her head. 'I don't know . . . I can't seem to think. But if it is so, then, for pity's sake, tell me, *tell* me, Damien . . .'

The beseeching, pathetic little voice was lost in the fierceness of his sudden embrace. 'Did you not feel it,' he demanded stormily, his fingers biting into her flesh, 'when I made love to you—the only time that you would let me?' His eyes clouded with anger and he shook her almost impatiently.

'But you have made love to so many!' she cried out in despair.

Tongues of flames from the fire reflected ominously in his cavernous eyes. 'I have made love to many,' he muttered gruffly, 'but I have loved only *you*! Were you so blinded by your own thoughts of revenge that you could not see it in my every gesture, in my eyes each time I looked at you, in every breath that I drew?'

'Then why have you been tormenting me like this?' she whispered in anguish.

There was no remorse in his face. 'Because I had to know that you loved me too—no, not through mere physical arousal! I can get that at any time for the price of a kiss! But with your mind and your heart and soul, and with every fibre of your body, do you understand? I cannot accept less, because I do not give less. It has to be everything or . . .' his voice became flat, 'nothing.' He spoke with such intensity that she shuddered, ravaged by the same passion that consumed him.

'You have my everything,' she murmured brokenly. 'There is nothing within me with which I do not love you.' She reached up her hand and kissed with a finger the scar upon his cheek.

A massive shudder, almost of relief, seemed to surge through the length of his frame. He bent his head and brushed her lips with his as tenderly as the touch of a feather. 'I have loved you, you silly little girl, from the moment I set eyes on you.' His murmur against her ear was the sweetest music she had ever heard. 'In that miserable village by the Jamuna when you so magnificently pulled a whip on that drunken lout. My God . . . ' his voice broke, 'how I loved you then! I knew in that fleeting moment that no other women would ever satisfy me.' His stroking fingers insinuated themselves and caressed the moulded curves of her breasts. 'Within the mere blink of an eye, you had ruined me for every other damned woman in the world. By heaven, you owe me compensation for that!'

She closed her eyes and trembled at the unbearably exquisite spell his fingers wove against her skin.

'The very contempt in your eyes whipped me into a frenzy of desire and I knew I would not rest until I had you as my own—not for a night or a week or a month, but for every day of my life, for ever.' His lips, burning and sensuous, branded her with a hundred kisses, claiming her eyes, her hair, her neck and her face, and the straining, aching mounds of her breasts. Every vestige of breath deserted her as the blood in her veins throbbed and thundered. 'You were born for *me*, Crystal.'

She whimpered and dissolved into his body, raking her fingers through his tangled hair, returning his kisses with an ardency she had not known herself capable of. Against the tender cushion of her breast, his tongue felt like tiny licks of fire, searing her flesh until it seemed singed and scarred. 'Don't hold back anything from me, my darling,' he gasped huskily. Then he laughed, and it was like the soughing of the wind through the pines. 'There is a wanton in you, my fiery Crystal, begging to be released . . .'

She stilled momentarily, alarmed. 'You find me wanton?'

'I find you delicious! Perfect in every way . . . ice mixed with fire. The ice, God knows, needs no help,' his eyes above her danced. 'But the fire . . .' His tongue ran nimbly over her lips as sensual as a kitten's fur, 'the fire needs to be coaxed.'

She catapulted into space like a fireball. 'Then coax it,' she pleaded against his mouth, 'Oh, Damien, coax it as you will, my dearest. *Teach* me how to love you . . .'

With a groan, he captured her mouth, probing without pity every little crevice within. With his hands, silken and strong at the same time, he tantalised her body until the very ends of her nerves screamed out in agonised, exultant protest. She arched against him, frantic to be tortured with such exquisite ecstasy, and he explored and caressed and extracted from her responses that seemed never to end. It was as if she was being transported, heaven only knew where, by a raging, ravaging flood that could not, would not, be stemmed.

Higher and higher she soared as if destined to touch the skies and tug at the stars in the furthest recesses of the universe. There were no more words, no sounds except for the tumultuous crescendo building up within her own body. And yet he would not rest, determined to explore every last vestige of her consciousness. The waves rose higher, frothing and lashing, until she felt fragmented to an agonising pulp and she could tolerate it no more. She knew not whether she screamed, but his mouth devouring hers strangled all sound and, without warning, the world exploded into a million lights and a thousand colours, blinding her, blotting out everything. Slowly, oh so very slowly, the lights began to dim and the colours faded as she wafted down again on the shoulders of a wisp of breeze, and slipped languorously into an ocean of exquisite mindlessness.

The tempestuous fury of his love-making, the shattering release of her own storm within, left her drained and deprived of all strength. His arms around her did not loosen for a moment as he lingered still for endless kisses. His breath on her skin was hot and his voice a mere wisp of a whisper. 'To be loved by a woman such as you, my beloved, my very own, is to taste the nectar of the gods . . .'

She smiled in her half-sleep and curled her fingers round the thick tangles on his chest. 'It engages the senses,' she sighed dreamily, 'but does it disturb the heart?'

He laughed softly against her cheek. 'It *devastates* the heart!'

He held her all night next to his heartbeat, his hands tender and silken against her honey-brown skin, his lips never far from hers, even in sleep. 'I want you to be happy, my precious,' he murmured anxiously a dozen times through the night. 'I want you to have everything you want . . .'

And a dozen times she murmured back, deep in contentment, 'I have everything I want within my arms.'

It was a fulfilment such as she had never dreamed possible.

They did not return to Shalimar until Crystal was once again strong and well, nor was there any urgency to do so. The feast that was planned, and postponed because of her illness, would now take place at the next full moon. It would now be an occasion not only for true rejoicing, but also for twofold joy. The news that Natasha had returned to Kashmir spread far and wide. She was the subject of much happy comment throughout the Vale. Revived and rejuvenated by the reunion with her beloved son, Natasha flowered again into a woman of beauty, all savage souvenirs of her tragic life now a part of the forgotten past. Her radiating happiness was a joy to behold, enlivening everyone around.

Crystal had loved Natasha from the moment they met and each day she loved her more. It was a bond that Damien watched grow stronger with deep contentment and pleasure, for it was between the two women in the world he loved best. Uncle Ivan, benign and beaming, was already making persistent assaults on the intricacies of English grammar, producing much affectionate hilarity with his unabashed attempts at speaking the language, and they gave him lessons enthusiastically.

The crisp, fresh air of the high mountains, the brilliantly sunlit cerulean skies and the healthy perfumes of pine forests soon brought back the damask blushes into her golden cheeks. Not that the healthy climate of

Gulmarg was the only reason for the persistent sparkle in Crystal's eyes or the heightened colour in her face! She blossomed under Damien's untiring care, basking in his love like a sunflower under the summer sun. She had no idea that so much happiness could be had in the world, and each day seemed to bring more.

It was a time of fulfilment and laughter. But what Crystal loved most were the hours she could spend with Damien, alone and unhurried. Gulab Singh had been despatched back to Shalimar to take care of matters there, and it was the first time Crystal had known Damien to be so much at ease and unworried about problems of business. The untamed wildernesses of Gulmarg, high above the valley, never ceased to delight her and they walked for miles each day, hand in hand, marvelling anew at the beauty surrounding them. The snowline was much closer up here, but was held in abeyance by the warm spring. The hill slopes were covered with a profusion of cascading wild flowers carpeting every foot of space on the meadows as far as the eye could see.

'Which is how Gulmarg got its name in the first place,' said Damien, as he watched her stunned amazement the first time she could venture out of doors.

'Of course!' she exclaimed. 'Gul means flower. It had not struck me before.'

They strolled along the circular walks that ran round the mountain-top, hands entwined, unmindful of curious eyes. But everyone for miles around knew Damien well, and people nodded and beamed and laughed as they passed by, happy that the Sarkar had at last found a woman he truly loved. One day, as they sat in a field of riotous rhodedendrons, he told her about the legend of the great Kashmiri poetess of love, Habba Khatoon, who loved and was loved by the king Yusuf Shah. It was here in this magical valley of flowers that she had composed her joyous, lilting verse to her beloved prince.

'It is indeed a place where it is easy to love,' said Crystal dreamily, slipping her hand in Damien's.

'You mean, had we not been in Gulmarg,' he asked, squinting his eyes against the blinding sun and assuming an expression of severity, 'you would not have loved me?'

'I would have loved you anywhere,' she said simply. 'Even in the desolation of a desert.'

One morning, while inhaling the intoxicating scents of a sage-green, marvellously serene, pine forest, a long-forgotten question tugged at Crystal's memory.

'Tell me, Damien,' she asked thoughtfully. 'Had you lost that game with my brother—would you have really given up Shalimar?'

He halted in his tracks, taken aback. 'What made you think of that all of a sudden?'

'It is a question that has never really left my mind. Well, would you?'

His sable-soft eyes twinkled. 'I would not have lost,' he said quite complacently.

'But if you had?' she persisted.

'I made sure that I didn't.'

She stared at him. 'What do you mean?'

He stared back without flinching, his expression bland. 'The dice I played with were loaded.' He smiled disarmingly.

She stood rooted to the spot. 'You mean you . . . *cheated*?'

'Naturally!' He was outrageously cool. 'You don't think I would have risked Shalimar on dice that *weren't* loaded, do you?' He sounded actually surprised.

She felt herself chill. 'Do you often . . . cheat when you are gambling?' She was bitterly disappointed in his seeming lack of scruples.

'No,' he said, rubbing his chin thoughtfully.

'Then *why*, did you with poor Robie?'

'Because,' he remained brazenly cheerful, 'it was the only way I could think of to get *you*.'

His audacity took her breath away. 'And if I had *not* agreed to marry you?' she asked, aghast.

'The thought,' he said with disgraceful immodesty, 'had never even crossed my mind.' His hand curved round her neck and he drew her to him. 'I knew you would love me, the first time you looked at me—only you were too stubborn to see it then.' His kiss threatened to linger for ever, but she pulled away, frowning.

'Robie might have killed himself . . .'

He shook his head, untroubled. 'I came to know Robie very well during those games at the Chowk. I studied him for days. He would never have had the courage to pull that trigger. Ask him honestly the next time you see him. You will find that my assessment was correct. And,' he reminded her grimly, 'the young scamp needed to be taught a lesson that would cure him of gambling for ever. It has, hasn't it?'

She nodded slowly, then subjected him to a long, stern stare. 'Who are you to talk,' she exclaimed tartly, 'considering your own propensity for it?'

'I have never gambled in my life, before or since.'

Her eyes widened in surprise. 'But you went to the gaming-house every night, Robie said.'

'Only to get to know him well—and to develop a reputation that would terrify the trousers off him! I knew it would be you who came to bargain with me—Robie would not have had the pluck.'

Her throat tightened. 'You took all these dreadful risks—just to marry me?'

He laughed and gathered her into his arms. He nuzzled her neck lovingly. 'Why? Don't you think you are worth it?'

She sighed and capitulated against his chest. 'But supposing, just supposing, I had *not* agreed—would you have claimed Khyber Kothi for yourself?'

'No. But I should have had to do something even less attractive.'

'What?'

He landed an affectionate pat on her behind. 'Blow my brains out,' he said cheerfully. 'That's what!'

The mellow colours of autumn lay over the valley like a coverlet woven in a hundred shades of gold. Leaves of vermilion and yellow and all the colours in between strewed the meadows and the lovely lawns of Shalimar. Crisp winds from the gathering snows of the Himalayas heralded the coming winter with incisive warning. The clustered leaves of ochre hung on the trees valiantly, knowing that they had but a few more days to live. Yet it was a September of breath-catching beauty, indeed, a season of joy.

Natasha had settled back into Shalimar as though she had never left it, as though the threads had never been broken. She brought with her an atmosphere of such serenity, such pervasive happiness, that the house seemed to come alive again under her tender ministrations. Crystal was content to hand over the reins of the house to her, far preferring to spend time with Damien or working on her father's papers, still not completely ordered. Uncle Ivan, unwilling to sit back and waste his days, had taken charge of the grounds, driving the gardeners to frenzy in his now reasonably fluent English and his still fractured Urdu. But under his ceaseless labours the gardens of Shalimar fruited and flowered as never before, surrounding the house with the russet and gold splendours of an extraordinary autumn.

Sitting in the garden beside a steaming samovar of *qahwa*, Crystal looked up from her letter as Damien galloped up the driveway. Alighting from Shaitan, he tossed the reins carelessly to a groom, strode across the grass and, with a kiss upon her forehead, flung himself down on the lawn at her feet, looking exhausted.

She handed him a cup of tea. 'Don't sit on the grass, darling, it's damp,' she said absently, returning to the reading of her letter. He did not move, sipping the tea and ruminating. With an exclamation of sudden delight, she looked up.

'Robie will bring Mama and Norah Hawthorne up before the passes close for winter. We shall not be going to Delhi this winter, shall we?'

He shook his head and smiled drily. 'I think not. I would hardly want my son to be born in the middle of the Banihal Pass! Besides,' he added mischievously, 'it would shock the coolies!'

'Your son,' Crystal said softly, 'will not be born for at least four months yet, and your *son*,' this with an air of tolerant amusement, 'may well turn out to be a *daughter*!'

'He would not dare,' said Damien smugly, 'to show his father such utter disrespect.'

Crystal laughed. 'If you have a daughter, you will love her just as much.'

He dropped a kiss on her hand resting in her lap. 'Only if you can guarantee that she will be like her mother in every single way.'

Her lovely amber eyes filled with melting love. 'And if it is a son,' she began, but stopped abruptly with a gasp as her stomach heaved.

Instantly, face white with anxiety, he was on his feet with his arm round her shoulder. 'What is it?' he asked in panic, 'Are you ill? Shall I call Natasha?'

Crystal clutched his hand until the spasm passed, then laughed breathlessly and kissed the tip of his nose as his stricken face hovered above hers. She shook her head. 'He only wants to make his presence felt, that's all. There's no cause for alarm.'

Damien groaned and threw his hands up in the air. 'I cannot bear the thought of you in pain . . .'

Her eyes softened further. 'I am young and strong and healthy,' she assured him for the hundredth time, 'and I shall deliver your son to you with no more discomfort than a wild animal delivers its young.'

His raven-black eyes were suddenly filled with anguish. His hand reached out and stroked her cheek. 'I struck you once,' he muttered in a voice shaking with emotion.

'And threatened to do so again,' she teased impishly, not noticing the pain in his face. He did not reply and she turned to look up at him. His expression was one of deep unhappiness. 'I would cheerfully give my right hand to undo that. You will never know with how much torture I have paid for that one moment of uncontrolled anger.'

She sprang to her feet, distressed at the misery in his tones. She put her arms about his neck. 'Why Damien, darling, you have given me enough to eradicate for ever that moment from my memory. I have not thought of it in months!' She kissed him on the chin, desperate to divert his brooding thoughts elsewhere. Quickly she ran a finger along the scar across his cheek, then stood on her toes and kissed it. 'Tell me, darling, how did you get this scar? I have always wanted to know but could never remember to ask.'

He took a deep breath, and slowly his brow unfurrowed and the ebony of his eyes burst into dancing lights. 'Are you sure you really want to know?'

Her heart sank and the pit of her stomach felt strangely hollow. What bizarre dare-devilry was he going to reveal to her now? A duel over a lady-love's honour? The lancing fury of a cuckolded husband's sword? A wound received in an inglorious brawl?

She nodded. 'Yes.' She spoke bravely, swallowing hard. 'I do.'

'Well, as a matter of fact,' he said, his face turning a deep red, 'I slipped on a cake of soap in the bathroom!'

Mills & Boon

Your chance to step into the past Take 2 Books FREE

Discover a world long vanished. An age of chivalry and intrigue, powerful desires and exotic locations. Read about true love found by soldiers and statesmen, princesses and serving girls. All written as only Mills & Boon's top-selling authors know how. Become a regular reader of Mills & Boon Masquerade Historical Romances and enjoy 4 superb, new titles every two months, plus a whole range of special benefits: your very own personal membership card entitles you to a regular free newsletter packed with recipes, competitions, exclusive book offers plus other bargain offers and big cash savings.

AND an Introductory FREE GIFT for YOU. Turn over the page for details.

Fill in and send this coupon back today and we will send you
2 Introductory Historical Romances FREE

At the same time we will reserve a subscription to Mills & Boon Masquerade Historical Romances for you. Every two months you will receive Four new, superb titles delivered direct to your door. You don't pay extra for delivery. Postage and packing is always completely free. There is no obligation or commitment – you only receive books for as long as you want to.

Just fill in and post the coupon today to MILLS & BOON READER SERVICE, FREEPOST, P.O. BOX 236, CROYDON, SURREY CR9 9EL.

Please Note:- READERS iN SOUTH AFRICA write to Mills & Boon, Postbag X3010, Randburg 2125, S. Africa.

FREE BOOKS CERTIFICATE

To: Mills & Boon Reader Service, FREEPOST, P.O. Box 236, Croydon, Surrey CR9 9EL.

Please send me, free and without obligation, two Masquerade Historical Romances, and reserve a Reader Service Subscription for me. If I decide to subscribe I shall receive, following my free parcel of books, four new Masquerade Historical Romances every two months for £5.00, post and packing free. If I decide not to subscribe, I shall write to you within 10 days. The free books are mine to keep in any case. I understand that I may cancel my subscription at any time simply by writing to you. I am over 18 years of age.

Please write in BLOCK CAPITALS.

Signature _____

Name _____

Address _____

_____ Post code _____

SEND NO MONEY — TAKE NO RISKS.
Please don't forget to include your Postcode.
Remember, postcodes speed delivery. Offer applies in UK only and is not valid to present subscribers. Mills & Boon reserve the right to exercise discretion in granting membership. If price changes are necessary you will be notified.
4M Offer expires December 24th 1984.

EP9M